The Rogue Scorpion

The Rogue Scorpion

a novel

Lynda Faye Schmidt

OC
Publishing

First published in 2023 by

Halifax, NS, Canada
www.ocpublishing.ca

Illustrations and cover art by Ria Cornall
Cover and interior book design by David W. Edelstein

ISBN 978-1-989833-33-9 (Paperback edition)
ISBN 978-1-989833-35-3 (eBook edition)

DISCLAIMER
This novel is a work of fiction, inspired by experiences of the
author. While some scenes describe real places and events, the
story and characters and are from the author's imagination.

The Rogue Scorpion is dedicated to the Isabellas in our world, who see negative life experiences as opportunities for growth. Isabella's healing journey is a reminder to us all, to live our authentic purpose and to love and accept ourselves unconditionally. It doesn't mean we don't have work to do. It doesn't mean we accept disrespectful or aggressive behaviour. It means we let go that which doesn't serve us without judgment and allow our fellow human beings to live their own unique journey. It means trusting in the process of life, and in a higher power.

Praise for the work of
Lynda Faye Schmidt

The Rogue Scorpion

The Rogue Scorpion had me captivated from the first page to the last page. Lynda Faye Schmidt weaves so much emotion and adventure in her storytelling that you can't help but wonder what will happen next in the story. This is a book that is hard to put down once you start reading. Very well done!

– Karen Dean, Canadian bestselling author of *We Are Unbreakable*

The novel touched my heart. (Lynda Faye Schmidt) captured the souls of each character and the compilation of unconditional love and acceptance. Isabella shares her inner strength time and time again, always believing in the process of life.

– Ramona Coulombe, advanced reader in Mill Bay, Canada

A captivating tale of a young woman's journey into life and how she guides herself through the many unexpected, at times harrowing, twists and turns tossed her way. A refreshing tale of resilience, adaptability and trust in how life unfolds. In my view, the main character Isabella shows us how practicing mindful choice can create authenticity, joy and strength within.

– Carol Kujala, S.W., yoga instructor

The Healing

Lynda Faye Schmidt has expertly written a story about inner freedom, self-love, and the quest for meaning amidst the vicissitudes of life... A rare literary gift for fans of deeply moving and emotionally captivating tales.

— Jane Riley, reviewer for *The Book Commentary*

Plot-wise, *The Healing* is an immensely entertaining, feel-good novel...the storyline truly waxes in emotions... If you are charmed by stories like *Eat, Pray, Love*, *The Healing* is the book for you.

— Vincent Dublado, reviewer for *Readers' Favorite*

The Holding

I don't want to give too much away, but by the time I finished the book, I was emotionally spent as I had gotten to know Cate and her family so personally, having been fully invested in what was happening to them. It's not often that I cry when reading a book, but I needed a Kleenex by my side by the time I turned the last page of this novel, and the poem that Cate writes at the end of the book wrecked me ... but in a good way. *The Holding* is an emotional and intimate read.

— Barbara Wilcov, reviewer @ BookTrib

I still have tears streaming down my face and my throat is closed up. This AMAZINGLY written book, is going to be one that stays with me for the rest of my life... I loved this book of love, joy, and heartbreak and I am honestly lost for words trying to describe how much this novel has touched me. Outstanding!!! My Rating ***** 10/5

— Leanne, reviewer @ Leanne Read's & Review's

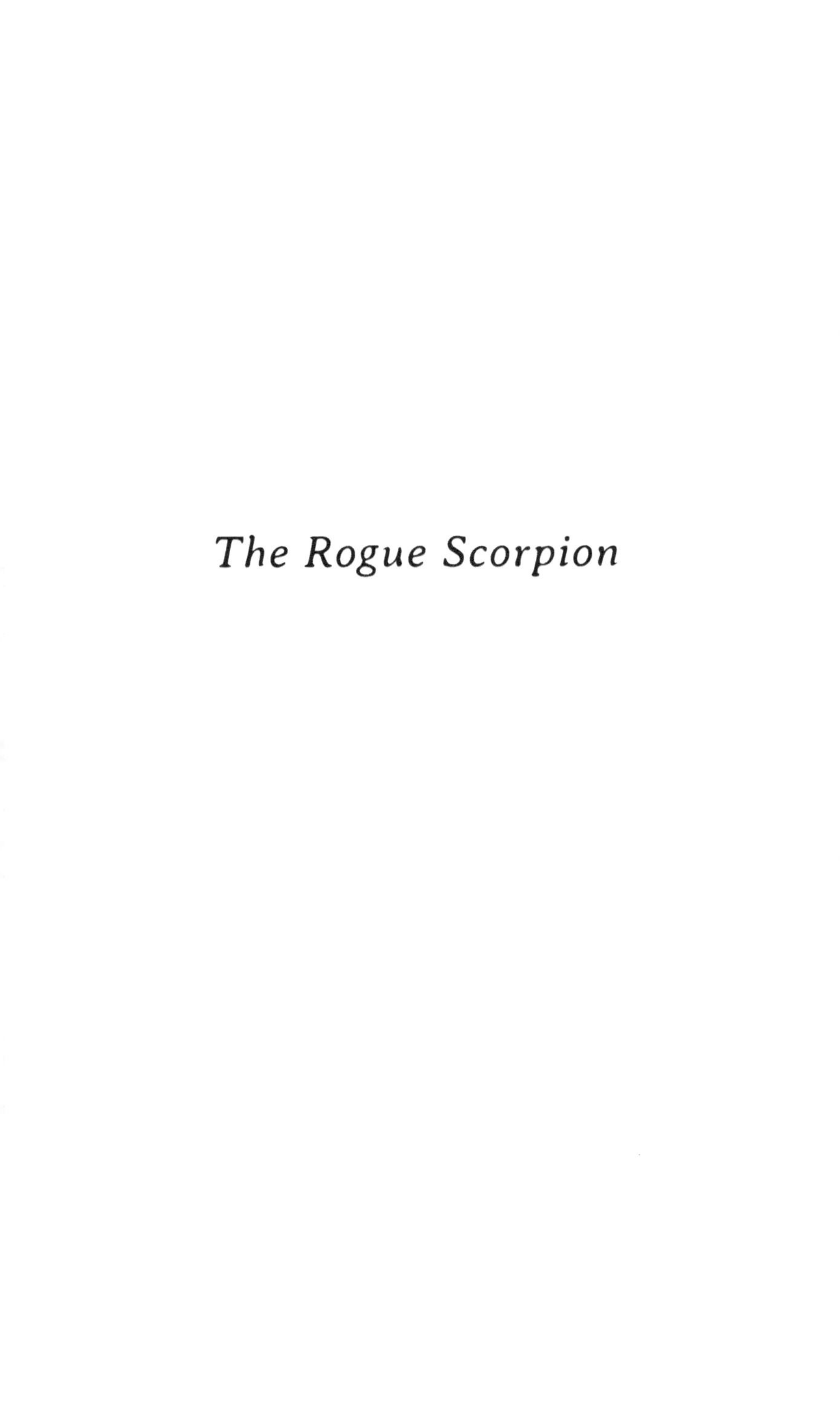

The Rogue Scorpion

Chapter One

The tavern in the heart of downtown Winnipeg isn't remarkable at first glance. A grey cement exterior featuring two large square windows. A simple black sign over the door with the logo in golden font. Yet for locals in the know, it's an iconic meeting place, a home away from home.

When you venture inside, it's like you've entered a whole new world, like Alice when she falls down the rabbit hole, into Wonderland. The original, hand-carved mahogany bar extends along the entire back wall, with mirrors that reach from the counter to the ceiling, making the space seem larger than it is. Slim, sleek shelving showcases liquor bottles from low-end local to high-end imports.

Polished glasses gleam in the soft light from the overhead pot lights, while the brick walls and well-worn maple floors create a welcoming atmosphere. People from all walks of life are packed in groups, gathered for the live music, craft beer, and Canadian comfort food. Smells of sweat, fermentation, and a cocktail of conflicting colognes permeate the air. Laughter mingled with animated conversation fills the room.

Isabella has fifteen tables to manage, but in the three years she's been serving since she finished high school, she's become proficient at organizing her priorities. Her slight build affords her ease in navigating the small spaces between tables, and her Scorpio resourcefulness is an asset in juggling the demands of her often fast-paced, high-intensity job.

"Can I get you anything else to drink?" Isabella asks the crowded table of university students nearest to the bar. She tucks the slip of paper with her last order in the pocket of the stained cotton apron tied loosely around her waist, then slides the strand of chestnut-brown hair that has escaped her ponytail behind her ear. "It's last call."

"Last call?" Greg says, a look of disbelief on his face. He's a regular customer that Isabella knows well. "Well, Izzy, I guess you better bring us another round."

"Do you want your usual, tequila shooters?" Isabella asks.

"Yeah, sure, and you can put them on my bill, Izzy," pipes in the glassy-eyed, platinum-dyed blonde beside him, the latest in Greg's parade of girlfriends.

Isabella places her final orders with the bartender, then makes her way to the rest of her tables, collecting payment and saying good night. Within half an hour, the last few stragglers are weaving their way out.

"I hope you called a taxi," Isabella says, following

Greg's group to the door to lock up behind them. "There's no bus service at this hour."

"Yeah, yeah, we're all good, thanks Izzy, see you next weekend," Greg slurs, giving Isabella a sloppy fist bump.

Isabella closes the door and locks it, then sets to cleaning up and cashing out. She grabs her tin tip bucket and dumps the stash. The bills are as thin as onion skin, each with its own unique smell, captured and released. She counts the stack. Over three hundred dollars. She smiles. *A few more nights like this and I'll have enough money saved to travel to Thailand, no problem.*

Outside the tavern, the streets are deserted. Isabella strolls along at a relaxed pace, lost in thought. It's less than a fifteen-minute walk to her tiny studio apartment in an old building, not far from the impressive six-columned Bank of Montreal edifice on the corner of Portage and Main.

She keys in her access code to the building, then takes the stairs two at a time to her studio apartment on the third floor and unlocks the door. She doesn't bother to remove her makeup; she just gives her teeth a quick brush and falls onto her bed, a thin IKEA mattress, no box spring, covered in cheap polyester sheets she bought on sale at Walmart. It isn't long before she's in a deep slumber, dreaming of travel adventures abroad, someplace sunny and warm.

The next day is Sunday, and after a lazy morning, Isabella catches the bus to her parents' home on Ritchot, a quiet street in St. Boniface. When she arrives at her bus stop, Isabella picks up her pace, excited to be reunited with the two people she loves most on the planet, even though it's only been a week since she last saw them. She walks up the cement sidewalk, a grassy boulevard separating the path from the asphalt road, through the back alley, then one block over. Two tall poplar trees flank either side of the front door of a narrow two-storey home with aluminum siding and a tidy wooden veranda. Isabella sprints up the three creaky stairs and opens the front door, unlocked as usual.

Tantalizing aromas of her mother's gourmet home cooking greet Isabella as soon as she enters. She walks through the living room and into the kitchen. Her mother is at the stove, stirring a wooden spoon in circular motions over a four-litre cast iron pot, a threadbare, washed-too-many-times apron tied around her trim waist. Her father, already into the wine, is seated at the solid Canadian maple table he carved himself, the crossword puzzle from the newspaper spread out in front of him.

"Izzy! *Cara figlia!*" Toni says, reverting to his customary Italian greeting, his thick, bushy black eyebrows like arched caterpillars. He takes off his reading glasses and stands up, then comes around the table to embrace his daughter in a huge bear hug, his six-foot-one frame towering over her. "*Como va?*"

"I'm good, Papa," Isabella says. She hugs him back, her thin arms stretching to accommodate his thick torso. "It smells amazing in here. Maman, what's on the menu tonight?"

"Baked onion soup, scalloped potatoes, and a rack of ribs your father already has slow cooking on the barbeque," Sylvie says, wiping her petite hands on a dishcloth that is hanging from the fridge door handle.

"Yum, one of my favourite meals," Isabella says. She moves over to where her mother is standing and hugs her briefly. "Anything I can do to help?"

"You could grate some fresh Parmesan for the soup," Sylvie says, fishing the silver grater out of a drawer.

"Now, Sylvie, she just got in the door. Let me pour her a glass of wine first," Toni says.

"Fine, fine, but there's no reason she can't contribute and drink some wine at the same time," Sylvie says. "Pour me a glass too, if you don't mind."

It goes on like this, with the three of them changing subjects, interrupting one another, and talking about everything under the sun. When the meal is prepared, they sit in their usual places and hold hands while Sylvie leads them in prayer.

"Bless us, O Lord and these thy gifts, which we are about to receive from thy bounty, through Christ our Lord, Amen."

Isabella and Toni add their amens in chorus, and they all bless themselves with the sign of the cross before filling up their plates.

"So, Isabella, have you applied to university yet?" Sylvie asks not long into the meal, her strongly defined, pencilled-in eyebrows drawn into a scowl. "The deadline to register for fall classes is probably approaching soon."

"Maman, we've been over this a thousand times," Isabella says with a sigh. "I'm not going to university. I know how disappointed you are after you and Papa saved so diligently so I could have the education you never had the opportunity for. But institutionalized learning just doesn't suit me. Even high school was nothing but a drain on my creativity. You remember how my teachers tried to fit me into their boxy ideas, to become a computer engineer or something boring like that, just because I'm good at math, and you know perfectly well all I've ever wanted to be is an artist."

"Yes, well, that's all well and good, but there are bills to pay, your future to think of," Sylvie says, her full lips pouting like a closed flower.

"I've always paid my own way," Isabella says, softening. She knows her mother's question is coming from a place of love, that her mother only wants the best for her. "Try not to worry so much. And I know it's not university, but I did register for an online TESL course."

"TESL? What's that?" Toni interjects, his dark brown, almost black eyes animated with curiosity.

"It's an international standard for teaching English as a second language," Isabella explains.

"That sounds interesting, and practical too," Toni says, always the go-between with his opinionated wife and feisty daughter. "With globalization and English being the international language of business, I think there are great opportunities."

"Thanks, Papa," Isabella says, smiling over at him. "I agree. I'm hoping it will come in handy. In fact, I'm planning to travel abroad, to Thailand, hopefully before the end of the year, if I can save enough money by then. I read they are desperate for English teachers over there, and it sounds so different from here. And let's face it, a break from our frigid winter weather would be nice too."

"Thailand?" Sylvie says. She stops cutting the chocolate torte, knife poised in mid-air, and turns around. "Isn't that where there was a massive tsunami? It sounds dangerous. And besides, don't you want to create a life and settle down here? Why, I was already married to your father by your age."

"That's right, you were, *il mio amore*," Toni says. "But we used to be adventurous too. Both our parents were horrified when we eloped to Canada. I still remember back when we were young and thought we had all the time in the world, don't you?"

Toni gets up from the table and grabs a bottle of Vin Santo from the side cupboard, imported from his family vineyard in Tuscany, as Sylvie finishes plating dessert.

"I suppose you're right," Sylvie concedes. "But I do hope you'll wait until after Christmas to travel, Isabella. It will be so lonely for us here without you."

"I am right," Toni says, with a laugh and a sparkle in his eye. He comes up behind Sylvie and wraps his big, strong arms around her tiny frame. He kisses the top of her head, her thick hair dyed auburn and worn in a sleek bob. "And if Izzy decides to go before Christmas, I will just spoil you all the more, and make it a romantic holiday. All will be well, you'll see."

The next morning, as Isabella waits for her toast to pop, a breeze comes through an open window and flutters the pages of her sketchbook that is open on her nightstand, catching her eye. She sets the butter knife on the counter and walks over to close her journal, seeing that it is open to a drawing she did from a selfie she took with Mark in front of the bridge on Jubilee Avenue on Canada Day. She smiles to herself, recalling how much fun they had clowning around in their red-and-white costumes, complete with face paintings of miniature flags and maple leaves, and treating themselves to decadent ice cream sundaes at the Bridge Drive-In. She doesn't know what she'd do, or where'd she be now, if it weren't for Mark. Isabella closes her book and tucks her memory away. She returns to the table and shovels down her breakfast, then tosses her dishes in the sink. She's feeling confident after a night of being showered with her father's praise and is determined to approach the art galleries again, on a quest to be a part of an exhibition.

Isabella chooses a soft grey cashmere sweater that brings out the amber flecks in her eyes, which have the same colour and shape as almonds. She picks out a pair of black trousers, then slicks her thick hair into a low ponytail. She applies a little makeup: black mascara and eyebrow pencil, a stroke of blush, and pink lip gloss. For the final touch, she puts on her gold hoop earrings, a graduation gift from her parents. When she's ready, Isabella grabs her black leather art portfolio from the corner of the room and heads out the door.

The bus ride to the University of Winnipeg doesn't take long, and soon Isabella is walking the manicured grounds of the campus. She knows the way to the art building by rote, and is soon heading down the hall toward the reception desk.

"Hello, how can I help you?" a secretary she doesn't recognize behind the department desk asks, looking up from her computer screen.

"Hi, I'm Isabella. Is the director in?"

"Oh, do you have an appointment?" the receptionist says, squinting her eyes behind her silver glasses, her mouth moving into a frown.

"No, I don't, but Ms. Flannigan knows me. I've been here before, many times actually . . ." Isabella stumbles on her words, her confidence feeling like a burst balloon. "I was hoping there might be space to show some of my work at the next exhibition."

"Ms. Flannigan has a very busy schedule, and she doesn't see anyone without an appointment. I can book you in now, if you like?"

"Yeah, sure, okay," Isabella says. "When is her first opening?"

"Let's see now," the secretary says as she clicks on a

new window on her computer to pull up a day planner. "There is an opening next week, at nine in the morning. Does that suit you?"

"Yes, please, go ahead and book me in, and thank you very much for your time," Isabella says.

The next stop on Isabella's list is a gallery set amongst rows of boutiques and restaurants on Academy Road. It isn't as prestigious as the university, and Isabella hopes her spontaneity will be better received. As it is, the curator gives her portfolio a quick look-over, but then tells her that although her collection is quite impressive, their small space is fully booked for the next eight months. Isabella has two more disappointing visits where, after cursory glances at her work and CV, she is told that her artwork shows a lack of awareness of basic techniques.

"If you're serious about becoming an artist, you should consider enrolling in a bachelor of fine arts program," the curator at the last gallery advises.

"I respect your opinion, and thank you, but I don't have the kind of determination and study ethic you need to take on four years of theory and exams," Isabella says.

A long day of bus rides and rejections has Isabella feeling heavy. She resents being told that the only way to become an artist is through an academic route. She knows she still has a lot to learn, but at the same time, she believes wholeheartedly that painting every day and experimenting with new techniques better suits her learning style.

The last thing she feels like doing is putting on her happy face and going to work, but she's never missed a day and she isn't about to start. By the time she gets back to her apartment, she is still feeling drained but is determined not to let the negativity undo her. She changes into a pair of skinny jeans with tears in the knees and a white T-shirt, then pulls on her worn sneakers and heads to the tavern for the evening shift.

It's quiet, even for a weeknight, and when Isabella counts her tips at the end of her shift, she's disappointed to find the grand total is a mere fifty-six dollars. She sighs. A day of disappointments. She walks home, devoid of the characteristic skip in her step.

Back at home, Isabella rummages around in the scant cupboards, looking for something to munch on. She finds a bag of stale cashews that she pours into a wooden bowl. After putting on the kettle for a cup of tea, she retrieves her sketchbook from her bedside nightstand. When the tea has steeped, Isabella sets the steaming cup of tea on a coaster, then gets comfortable on her bed and opens her journal to a fresh page.

Her feelings of rejection, hurt, and disappointment are brought to the surface as Isabella draws a caricature of herself sitting on a street corner, her knees pulled up to her chest. She almost tears the page as she presses her pencil into the paper with so much force. She adds in dark shadows, as though somehow her depiction on paper can release her pain.

When she's finished, she feels a little better, a bit lighter. She flips back to the image of her and Mark on the bridge, then back further, to a portrait she made of her father. Her fatigue from the heaviness of her emotions catches up to her. Her eyelids flutter closed. Her last thought before she drifts off to sleep is how some days are just difficult; it is the natural ebb and flow of life. Her half-full cup of tea remains on her nightstand, cold and forgotten, as Isabella falls asleep, still in her work clothes.

On the first Sunday in November, just after her twenty-second birthday, Isabella's mother treats her to her favourite dinner: fettuccine alfredo and steamed asparagus smothered in butter and garlic. When dessert is ready, her mother's homemade chocolate soufflé replaces a traditional birthday cake. Isabella takes her seat at the table where her mother has set a shiny Cellophane gift bag by her place setting.

"What's this?" Isabella asks. She reaches into the colourful tissue-packed bag and plucks out a manila envelope.

"Open it and see," Toni says, barely able to suppress his excitement.

"Maman, Papa, this is so sweet and supportive," Isabella says and opens the envelope to pull out a huge stack of baht, the official currency of Thailand. She tucks the small faded bills back into the envelope, then gets up from her seat to give them both big hugs. "*Grazie.*"

"You're welcome," Toni beams. "We wanted you to know you have our support to follow your dreams. How close are you now with your savings?"

"Actually, since you asked, I checked my balance last night and I've done it. I've saved four thousand dollars, which was my goal," Isabella says. "And I was looking at flights. There is a super cheap Air Canada itinerary for just under five hundred dollars that leaves from Winnipeg to Vancouver, then on to Japan and Bangkok. All I have to do now is give my notice at the tavern and book my flights."

"That's such exciting news," Toni says. "When are you thinking of leaving?"

"I'll have to check flights for availability, but I figure, now that the decision has been made, why wait?"

"Once you've researched and made your plan, let us know and we'll drive you to the airport," Toni says.

"I hope you find whatever it is you're searching for," Sylvie says, hands on her hips.

"Thank you, Maman," Isabella says. "And thank you for your blessing, despite your misgivings. It means so much to me."

At work the next day, the sixty-inch wall-mounted television blares, the game between the Winnipeg Blue Bombers and the Saskatchewan Roughriders attracting a large crowd. Isabella barely has time to worry about her conversation with her manager.

When the Bombers win by a landslide, pandemonium breaks out and everyone is in a mood for celebration. Isabella can hardly keep up with the demand for more rounds of drinks. A couple of guys drink a little too much and get out of hand, but the burly bouncer, Eddie, keeps everything under control.

At the end of her shift, Isabella finishes drying the last glass to a sparkling shine before going over to Frank's office. She's fond of him and has strong relationships with all the staff at the tavern. She knows saying goodbye won't be easy, but she's ready for the difficult conversation.

"Do you have a minute?" Isabella asks, opening the door and peeking her head around the corner.

"Yeah, sure, c'mon in," Frank says, looking up from a stack of paperwork on his desk. He looks tired, the lines around his eyes tight, and he's sprouted a few more grey hairs at his temples. He sets down his pen and leans back in his swivel chair, the wooden arms worn smooth and faded. "What's on your mind?"

"Well, actually, I have some really big news," Isabella begins. "I'm leaving Winnipeg, travelling to Thailand. I hope to book my ticket as soon as possible."

"Thailand, eh?" Frank says, scratching his stubbled chin. "I can't say I'm surprised. I knew we couldn't hold on to someone like you forever, even though I hoped as much. What do you mean by 'as soon as possible'?"

"Do you think you can find a replacement if I give my two weeks' notice right now?" Isabella asks.

"It will be impossible to replace you," Frank says with a genuine smile. "But I'm sure we can find someone to fill your position by then. What do you say to us having a farewell party for you here next weekend?"

"That's so sweet of you," Isabella says. "Thank you for being so supportive. I really appreciate it. I've loved this job, and working with you over the years has taught me so much. A party would be awesome."

"All right, let's have it on Saturday. If it's quiet, we can close down the bar a bit early."

The work party turns into an emotional event, with most of the staff having one drink too many and everyone toasting and lamenting Isabella's decision to leave.

"To Izzy, the best damn server in the business!" Frank says, sloshing his beer as he clanks his glass mug enthusiastically with Isabella's best friend, Mark.

"Forget about the best server," Mark slurs, his silver-blue eyes tearing up. "She's the best friend I've ever had. I don't know how I'll manage without her."

"Now, Mark," Isabella says. "Don't be a drama queen. It's not like I'm falling off the planet. There's this little thing called the internet."

"It's not the same," Mark says, his voice cracking. "And besides, I'm determined to give you at least a little guilt trip, it's no use denying me that."

"Okay, if you must," Isabella says, letting out a joyful laugh.

Isabella exudes a contagious energy as she tells her friends about her plans for Thailand. When the party is over, Mark and Isabella are the last people to leave. They are standing on the sidewalk outside the tavern, huddled against the frigid winter air, ready to go their separate ways, when Mark pulls Isabella to him and holds her tight. She wraps her arms around his wiry but solid frame.

"I am going to miss you, my dear, sweet Izzy," Mark says. He swipes at his mop of thick hair, forever dangling into his eyes, and tugs the hood of his parka closer. "But I know your heart is calling you. I get that you need to switch things up, and despite my teasing, you know I wish the best for you."

"I know," Isabella says. She releases from his embrace and steps back, then gives his scruffy, thick beard a scratch, a habit she's had since he decided to grow it the year before. "Our friendship isn't the kind that falls apart so easily. We've been through so much since we met. Remember that day? We were working together to put on the annual Holy Cross High School art charity fundraiser."

"How could I forget?" Mark laughs. "You were totally pushing boundaries with that portrait you entered, of the half-naked woman."

"I know, right?" Isabella laughs, then turns sombre. "You'll always be with me in spirit," she says, choking on her words as the reality of what she is about to do hits home. "And I'm committing to stay in touch and reach out regularly."

"I hope so," Mark says, a puff of condensation cloaking his words.

"I know so," Isabella reiterates. "I suppose it's time we both went home and tried to get at least a little sleep. Morning will come sooner than either one of us will welcome."

Isabella books her plane ticket for the last day of November. It departs early and she won't arrive in Bangkok until a day later, her total travel time almost twenty-eight hours.

It's still dark outside when Isabella hears the distinctive sound of her father's rap on the door.

"Papa, you're here—right on time, as usual," Isabella says, opening the door wide to let her father into her apartment. "I'm ready."

"Is this it?" Toni says, eyeing the single overstuffed traveller's backpack leaning against the wall.

"Yep, that bag holds the contents of my life, along with my carry-on and this massive purse," Isabella says, lifting the bag slung over her shoulder with exaggeration. She looks around the empty apartment one final time. "Thank you again, to you and Maman, for agreeing to store my most precious belongings, especially my art portfolio, at your place."

"It's our insurance," Toni says with a wink. "This way, we know you'll be back."

"I suppose none of us really knows what the future holds," Isabella says. "All we have for sure is today. But I do feel so grateful to always have you and Maman to come home to."

Isabella turns out the light and hands the key to Toni, who has agreed to pass it off to the landlord later that morning and pick up Isabella's security deposit refund for her.

———

Toni hoists the deceivingly heavy pack into the trunk, and Isabella climbs into the back seat of her parents' rusted-out 1995 Toyota Corolla, almost as old as her.

"Do you have your passport and boarding pass?" Sylvie asks from the front. "And your phone is fully charged?"

"Yes, Maman, everything is sorted. Try not to worry. When I arrive in the Vancouver airport, I'll message you and Papa with an update, and then again at each stop along the way."

Isabella leans forward and pats her mother on the shoulder. Soon, Toni is pulling into the departures drop-off area of the Winnipeg airport. Sylvie gets out and locates a trolley for Isabella's things while Toni opens the trunk to retrieve his daughter's pack.

"I'll be right here," Isabella says, holding her hands against her mother's and father's hearts.

"Be safe," Sylvie says, trying unsuccessfully to blink back her tears.

"Have an amazing adventure, *cara figlia*," Toni says. He takes Isabella's hand from his chest and lifts it to his face, then kisses her knuckles. "*Arrivederci.*"

Isabella takes the trolley by the handles and pushes it towards the sliding doors. She turns and waves one last time before her parents climb back into the car. Isabella waits under the building's overhang until the car pulls out of sight, then heads inside. She glances right, then left, spotting the Air Canada check-in, and marches up to the counter, ready to embrace her destiny.

Chapter Two

Twenty-eight hours and twelve time zones would leave most people off balance, exhausted, and overcome with jet lag, but Isabella arrives in Bangkok at midnight the next day feeling bright-eyed, running on sheer adrenaline.

She managed to sleep for more than seven hours on the longest leg from Vancouver to Narita International Airport in Japan, then grabbed another few winks on the short flight from Narita to Bangkok. In between, she became totally engrossed in the paperback she bought before leaving home, *Siddhartha* by Hermann Hesse. She read the slim volume cover to cover twice, entranced by the story of the Brahmin prince who, discontent with his destiny, embarked on a quest to find his innermost Self. The themes of self-discovery and empty spirituality resonate with Isabella, who feels a lack of fulfillment from the Bible teachings of her youth. She yearns for something deeper and hopes to learn more about Buddhism while in Thailand, inspired by the words from *Siddhartha*, "Your soul is the whole world."

Upon disembarking from the plane, Isabella looks around for a food kiosk, starving after the objectionable airline fare and having run out of her own stash of snacks hours earlier. The one bite she'd had of her airline meal of tofu in a green curry sauce over thin rice noodles was so spicy it had taken two full bottles of water to douse the flames. At breakfast service, the three ridiculously tiny cups of coffee left her caffeine craving unsatisfied.

On her way to the luggage carousel, Isabella spies what appears to be a coffee shop, but soon it's clear there isn't a lineup because it's closed. Grumbling under her breath, Isabella notices a lone vending machine. She counts out a few hundred baht and inserts them into the slot, grateful for her parents' gift, then presses the button for a cold Starbucks drink. She takes a long sip before continuing on to baggage claim and through customs, the lineups small with few people about at the early hour.

Outside the terminal, the thick, humid air, rank with the smell of pollution, accosts her nostrils and suffocates her skin, like an invisible blanket. There are rows of taxis and tuk-tuks in the queue, and Isabella makes her way into the line.

"Where you go?" the taxi driver asks, eyeing her suspiciously. Isabella thinks he looks a hundred years old, with his wrinkled skin and snow-white hair.

"Bode-San hostel, on Khaosan Road, *kap khun ka*," Isabella says, hoping she is pronouncing "thank you" in Thai correctly.

"*Dai, dai krup*," the taxi driver replies and merges onto the highway, then into the crowded streets of the city, thick with traffic even at this hour. Isabella doesn't bother to attempt a conversation, her knowledge of Thai limited to a few short phrases. The driver makes his way slowly, cars bumper to bumper. At one point, the taxi grazes along so closely to the car approaching in the other direction, his side-view mirror gets knocked to the ground. He stops the car and steps out to retrieve it, then throws it in the back seat with seeming nonchalance, no irate exchange for insurance and phone numbers, like there would have been in Canada. Soon the driver is pulling over at the end of the busy pedestrian-only road.

Isabella glances at her phone. It is just past four in the morning, but the parties seem to be in full swing. She pays the driver the fare illuminated on his screen on the dash, including a generous tip, then steps out of the car, hoisting her heavy pack onto her shoulders.

The noise, the glaring lights, the smell of sewage and urine are her first sensations as she walks up the steep incline. She pulls her carry-on up the cobbled road, past bars with neon signs advertising bucket drinks, no ID required, shisha, and massage. She passes food carts offering everything from fried grasshoppers and crickets to pad Thai and mango rice. An aggressive middle-aged man jumps out from an alley and flashes her a business card. "You like Ping-Pong show?" he says, showing his crooked yellow teeth and leering at her while making popping noises, sucking in his cheeks. Isabella keeps her eyes downcast and hurries past without responding.

Eventually, Isabella spots the sign for the hostel above a wooden stairwell tucked into a cramped entranceway.

She climbs two flights, then spots the check-in desk and fishes out her Visa card in exchange for the key to the four-bed shared room she booked online. The jet lag has finally caught up with her. She literally stumbles across the threshold, then falls, fully dressed, onto the thin, narrow cot.

Hours later, Isabella opens her eyes and squints into the bright morning sun that peeks in through a high window across the room. She pulls herself up into a sitting position and looks around. The three other beds are empty, the duvet covers tucked snugly under the mattresses. She hears the swishing sound of a broom and looks over to see a petite woman or girl—she can't be sure—sweeping the floors vigorously.

"*Sawadi ka*," Isabella says, using one of the three expressions she's managed to remember from her notes.

The stranger looks up and over with a shy smile and returns the greeting, then goes back to her task.

"My name is Isabella," Isabella says, speaking in stilted English and patting her chest like a cavewoman. "And you?"

The woman, who Isabella now guesses to be close in age to herself, perhaps a bit younger, continues to sweep but answers softly, "I am Chuanna." She bends over to pick up a dustpan in the corner and collects the dirt, then disappears into thin air, as if by magic.

"Chuanna," Isabella repeats, enjoying the sound of the

syllables as they roll off her tongue. Her stomach rumbles. *You'll have to wait a little longer*, Isabella thinks to herself. *We're not doing anything until we take a long, hot shower.*

The shower turns out to be an electric set-up that is neither long nor hot, but rather brief and ice-cold. Isabella isn't certain all the soap and grime have been washed away as she takes the towel off the hook marked with a number three, the same as her bed. She dries herself off the best she can, the towel threadbare and well-used judging by the stains. *I guess you get what you pay for*, Isabella thinks to herself. She remembers a sign she saw beside a nail salon on the walk up Khaosan Road in the wee hours of the morning: "Cheap nails ain't nice and nice nails ain't cheap." She lets out a sharp, nervous laugh, totally out of her comfort zone, but loving the thrill of it all just the same.

Wrapped in her scant towel, Isabella checks the weather app on her phone. It is already twenty-six degrees, with a projected high of thirty-two. She fishes out a pair of loose-fitting linen shorts and a tank top, relegating her travel sweatshirt to the bottom of her pack. She slips into the practical walking sandals she bought just before she left, grabs her purse, and tucks her room key securely into an inside pouch.

———

On the sidewalk outside the hostel, the street looks nothing like it did when she arrived. It is deathly quiet, almost deserted. Isabella walks a few blocks before she stumbles onto an internet café. She orders an Americano and a bowl of pad Thai before taking a seat at an empty table in the corner. She plugs her phone into one of the charging stations along the wall and sips the watery, weak coffee between mouthfuls of spicy food, already beginning to develop a taste for the thick, flat rice noodles mixed with bean sprouts and fried egg. She writes a long email to her parents, followed by a brief note to Mark on Messenger.

Hi Mark, I hope you are well. I've just arrived, and honestly, I hardly know where to begin. My head is spinning and the jet lag is intense. The road that my hostel is on is like some kind of crazy party street that was going full swing into the early hours of the morning. I hope it's not like this every night. There was this geezer who I'm sure was a pervert, waving a card and trying to convince me to come see a Ping-Pong show. I don't what the heck that is, but I have a feeling it isn't for the faint-hearted. The pollution here is unbelievable. Some of the locals even wear medical masks. It makes me appreciate the clean, crisp air of home. I'm not complaining, though. I know this is an opportunity of a lifetime that not everyone gets a chance at, and I plan to make the most of it. I miss you, so much, already. xxoo

After breakfast, the first thing on Isabella's to-do list is to find the train station. She ends up catching a tuk-tuk to the station, which turns out to be closer to her lodgings than it appeared on Google Maps. She purchases a round-trip ticket to the end of the line and sits back to enjoy the ride.

Isabella had known that Bangkok was a huge city, with a population of over 5.5 million, but somehow, she wasn't prepared for all the skyscrapers and tall buildings that seem to stretch in every direction, for as far as she can see. Everything seems coated in a film, the humidity and pollution staining the whitewashed stucco black. The sky train hums along at top speed over the intricate system of bridges and tunnels, and Isabella's head bobs as she dozes in intervals. During lucid moments, she glances out the window as the sights whiz by in a blur. She attempts to take a few photos on her phone, but at the high speed of the train, the images are nothing but indistinguishable blurs. As people enter her car, they gawk openly at her. At one point, a little girl sitting across from her reaches out to touch her, as if to determine if she is indeed a human being or a figment of the girl's imagination. Isabella doesn't mind. She smiles and waves and says, "*Sawadi ka*," but the girl pulls her hand away and moves in closer to her mother.

Isabella likes the inflective tones of the Thai language and listens attentively to the conversations around her, hoping to get at least a cursory auditory education. She smiles to herself, feeling the massive contrasts from her own country at every turn, but delighted to be immersed in the fullness of the experience.

It's early afternoon when Isabella returns to the hostel from her exploration of the city, and the energy of Khaosan Road is already shifting. She checks out some of the clothing shops that line the street and buys a few sundresses for super cheap, then stops at one of the fresh market stalls to purchase a papaya, a bag of roasted cashews, and a large bottled water.

Back in her room, there is no sign of her roommates or the mysterious Chuanna; the only sound is the rattle of the floor fan in the corner. Isabella curls up on her cot and opens her book, rereading a few pages that describe Siddhartha's decision to become a wandering ascetic, called a *Samana*, with the single goal to become empty. She can't imagine what that must feel like, but then her eyes are suddenly heavy, her brain a fog. Her hand goes limp. Her book falls to the floor.

In the middle of the night, Isabella wakes up in a sweat, confused and disoriented, having had a terrifying dream about a boa constrictor coiling itself around her body. She hears the commotion from the street below and remembers where she is. In the dim light, she can make out two figures asleep on the beds across from her. She picks up her book, but it's too dark to read, so she dog-ears her page, then pops in her earbuds and presses play on a podcast she's following. After an hour or so, she drifts off again and sleeps until sunrise. She gets dressed, then slips quietly down the stairs, almost bumping into Chuanna on her way out.

"*Sawadi ka*," Isabella says. She holds out her hand, then remembers the traditional Thai Buddhist greeting and puts her palms together and bows her head. "*Namaste*," she says.

"Welcome," Chuanna says in a thick accent, the *l* sounding more like an *r*. She looks pleased with Isabella's gesture. "Everything okay? You like your room?"

"Yes, thank you, all is well," Isabella says. "Thank you for taking such good care of the space. Have you been a housekeeper here long?"

"Two years," Chuanna says, holding up two fingers. "You like Khaosan?"

"Err, well, it is a bit on the noisy side," Isabella admits. "But the price is right. I wonder, can you direct me to somewhere a little quieter nearby, where I might get something to eat?"

"Yes, I show you," Chuanna says with a smile. She leads Isabella out onto the street and down several alleys to emerge onto Soi Rambuttri. The street is tree-lined and, although also packed full of shops and restaurants, the vibe is less intense and more to Isabella's liking.

"Have you eaten at that restaurant?" Isabella asks, pointing to a terrace with small tables covered with black-and-white-checkered tablecloths, and red paper lanterns dangling from lines strung overhead.

"Oh, yes, many time, it very good." Chuanna swipes her silky black, shoulder-length hair from her eyes. "But be careful, water in Bangkok not good. Ice in drink must have holes, then it from factory."

"Thanks for the good information," Isabella says. "Would you like to join me? My treat?"

"Treat?" Chuanna says.

"I mean, I would be happy to pay for you, to join me for breakfast," Isabella says, suddenly feeling awkward, wondering if she's just made a major cultural blunder. "It's so nice to be able to have a conversation with someone who speaks such excellent English."

"No can, *kap-khun-ka*, I must get back to work," Chuanna says. She shuffles off back down the alley toward the hostel before Isabella can thank her.

Isabella walks over to the terrace restaurant, and the hostess leads her to a table.

Over the next few days, Isabella scopes out Chuanna whenever possible to seek her advice. When she finds out Chuanna has Sunday off, she asks if she would accompany her on an adventure to one of the many famous markets, or perhaps to a Buddhist temple, and Chuanna is only too happy to show her around Bangkok.

Chuanna picks up Isabella at the hostel early in the morning. Isabella is dressed appropriately in long sleeves and loose pants that cover her ankles, knowing that the temples require modest dress. They grab mango sticky rice sticks and hot coffees to go from a street vendor, then make their way first to the reclining

Buddha temple, Wat Pho, a short twenty-minute walk and one bus ride away.

Isabella is awestruck by the twenty acres of land devoted to the temple and makes her way, wide-eyed, to the entrance.

"How much is the fee to enter?" Isabella asks Chuanna, her voice a whisper.

"Fifty baht," Chuanna says, reaching into the silk purse she has criss-crossed over one shoulder.

Chuanna leads Isabella through the souvenir shops to the main attraction, the gold-plated reclining Buddha that measures forty-six metres long and fifteen metres high.

"This is absolutely incredible," Isabella says. She stares at the statue, roped off for security, and notices a sign: "Careful of non-Thai pickpocketing gangs."

"Pickpocket gangs?" Isabella says with a laugh. "Surely there's something lost in translation?"

"It not funny, it true," Chuanna says, wagging her finger at Isabella. "Tourists are best choice to rip off, only the non-Thai part not always true."

"Is that why you wear your money purse draped across your shoulder and in front like that?" Isabella asks.

"Yes, and you should be careful, Izzy, you too much trusting."

"You're probably right," Isabella agrees. "At least, that's what my mother always tells me. Oh, look at all of the mother-of-pearl engravings on the Buddha's toes!"

"Yes, they show one hundred of Buddha, um, no say, how you say in English?"

"I have no idea, but this placard gives the English

translation," Isabella says, stopping to read the sign. "The reclining Buddha depicts the 108 auspicious characteristics."

"Aw spice tics?" Chuanna asks.

"Close enough," Isabella laughs. "If my Thai was even half as good as your English, I would be so happy."

"It okay, I teach you," Chuanna says.

"Thank you," Isabella says. "I would love to learn more about Buddhism as well as the Thai language. Are you Buddhist?"

"Yes, I am and happy to teach you everything," Chuanna says.

"This is all so precious. I must take a photo to send back home," Isabella says. "Chuanna, will you pose for a selfie with me?"

"Okay," Chuanna says, somewhat reluctantly, then stands beside Isabella as she stretches her arm out in front and takes several pictures.

***

The temple is located directly south of the Grand Palace, so Chuanna takes Isabella on a second tour after they enjoy a street lunch of fresh papaya salad and guava juice.

"This is so massive," Isabella says as she and her friend approach the entrance to the palace from the sidewalk that runs along a high white fence and sculptured green gardens. "How large of an area does the Grand Palace cover, do you know?"

"It 200,000 square metre, I think," Chuanna says,

squinting her eyes as she looks up to the heavens in thought. "It built in 1782, very old."

"Wow, Canada wasn't even a country yet," Isabella marvels. "You have such a fascinating history."

Inside the palace, Isabella is even more blown away by the opulence as well as the historical and religious significance. They tour the Temple of the Emerald Buddha, which Chuanna informs her is the most important image in Thailand. There is a vendor selling flowers and incense as offerings, and Isabella purchases a packet and bouquet for each of them. They continue their tour of the chapel, the six pairs of demon guardians, and the royal throne and halls.

"I think you could solve world poverty if you could convince the king to sell all of this and give the money away," Isabella says, feeling a little overwhelmed by it all. "It seems crazy to have all of this wealth, just on display, while there are beggars crouched out in the streets."

"You no have rich king in Canada?" Chuanna asks innocently.

"No, no royalty," Isabella says. "Although Canada does have close ties with the UK. Some of my mom's friends go ape for any media coverage of the British royal family."

"Go ape?" Chuanna asks, clearly confused.

"Oh, sorry, there I go again," Isabella giggles. "It is only an expression, and not a very modern one at that."

By the time they've seen everything the palace has to offer, it is already getting late and Isabella's feet are aching, despite her sensible shoes.

"I think I have to pass on the market tour for another day," Isabella says. "I'm ready for some downtime."

"Okay, no problem," Chuanna says. "We go back. We go to market next Sunday?"

"Yes, I would like that, very much," Isabella says, giving Chuanna a hug.

Isabella pulls away, feeling an unfamiliar energy that surprises her. She can't identify if it is her intuition warning her about something, or something else. It feels almost sensual. As she walks up the stairs to her room, she decides it was nothing but fatigue, and by the time she drifts off to sleep, she is certain it was only a figment of her imagination.

Isabella and Chuanna become inseparable. Isabella leaves the hostel and moves in with Chuanna when her roommate marries her high school sweetheart and moves out. Falling into a comfortable routine, Chuanna teaches Isabella some Thai vocabulary and customs, as well as more about Buddhist traditions. Isabella is surprised to discover it isn't the loosey-goosey religion her father described, that it has at least as many rules, doctrines, prayers, and dogma as Catholicism.

Isabella's savings are already beginning to dwindle, so she takes a crash course in esthetics and finds work painting intricate designs on acrylic nails at one of the bustling open-air markets.

One day, a regular client, who happens to be a teacher at a public school, gives Isabella the inside scoop that her principal is looking to hire an English-speaking person to teach English as a second language to the children in years one to six, and that she is more than happy to give Isabella a recommendation. Soon after applying, she has an interview and is hired, the position set to begin the first week of March.

"Looks like I'll be staying in Thailand longer than I thought," Isabella says. She is hanging clothes on the line that runs diagonally across the room, including the freshly washed navy uniform that she received when she was hired.

"That make me so happy," Chuanna says. "I think you always stay here in Bangkok and never go back to Canada."

"Never is a long time, but at least now I have a secure work visa." Isabella says. "Let's just take things one day at a time."

"One day?" Chuanna asks. "But you signed three-month contract!"

"Okay, you're right," Isabella laughs. "We will take it three months at a time."

At the school, Isabella is surprised to discover the children are subjected to even more religious protocol than she endured as part of her Catholic school education. Each day begins with a long prayer, followed by an even longer meditation after lunch. On Friday, the children gather for an assembly where they repeat prayers for the entire afternoon.

Even so, she feels so fortunate, and to celebrate,

Isabella asks Chuanna to request the weekend off so they can enjoy the famous Ko Samet Beach together. They get up early Saturday morning to catch a taxi to the Victory Monument bus station, where they board a bus that will take them to the ferry. Along the way the bus makes a pit stop for gas.

"I have to pee like crazy," Isabella says, descending the stairs of the bus. She stretches. "Do you know where the bathrooms are?"

"Follow your nose," Chuanna laughs. "Out here in country, only squat toilet."

"Ew, that's just plain nasty," Isabella says with a sniff and frown.

"You need these," Chuanna says, passing Isabella a packet of tissue and a bottle of hand sanitizer she pulls out from her seemingly bottomless purse.

Isabella approaches the outbuildings, a row of toilets with no door, only a cement wall to separate them. She lowers her pants to her ankles and crouches down, wondering, not for the first time, what on earth she's gotten herself into.

During the long bus ride, Isabella is absorbed by Chuanna's stories about her childhood, growing up in Bangkok.

"My mother, very strict," Chuanna says. "She wake me up before sunrise, every day, even weekend, with long list of chores to do before breakfast. It my job to sweep floor and put on daily pot of rice to cook. I use day-old rice from cold box with water to make Khao Tom."

"Khao Tom?" Isabella says. "What's that?"

"It traditional Thai breakfast, I prepare for family every day," Chuanna says. "It like porridge. I add egg, mustard greens, and chopped chilies. So yummy."

"It doesn't sound very appetizing to me," Isabella laughs. "But it does sound vaguely similar to a breakfast we have in Canada quite often: oatmeal with brown sugar and cream"

"Ew, sugar and cream?" Chuanna says, a look of disbelief and horror on her face. "I no like dairy; it smell like dirty cow."

The two friends continue the conversation, bridging the gap between their cultures, until the bus pulls up to the pier. They pay the ticket collector for the ferry ride to the island where they have booked a cheap room a short walk from the beach. The ferry speeds along, bumping against the waves, a party atmosphere on board where the bar is open and drinks are flowing. Chuanna treats Isabella to a coconut water, served fresh in the brown, leathery coconut shell.

"We need a picture of us, with this stunning view," Isabella yells above the din. She marvels at the scene in the distance, of turquoise waters lapping against pristine white-sand shores, craggy ochre rocks looming above, like nature's stone sculptures.

After checking in at the front desk and being shown to their room, Isabella and Chuanna unpack the few items they brought, then throw on their bathing suits to enjoy the last few late afternoon hours of sunshine by the beach. Chuanna has a speedo-style one-piece, very modest, while Isabella dons a skimpy bikini that barely covers her, exposing the sides and cleavage of her small breasts.

"You driving boys crazy," Chuanna says, wagging her finger. "You be careful."

"Don't worry so much. I'm sure I'm fine here at the resort," Isabella says, thinking her friend a little old-fashioned. "This is what everyone in Canada wears to the beach."

"I know, I see tourists," Chuanna says. "But you are special, Izzy. You save nice body for husband to look at."

Isabella brushes off Chuanna's advice and takes her by the hand, in a mood for fun. It is only a few minutes down a winding stone-paved pathway that weaves through tropical trees and vegetation to the beach. They lay out their towels on the silky white sand and have barely begun enjoying the sun before an enterprising young man approaches them waving a plastic menu in front of them.

"You want margarita? Diet Coke?" the boy, who looks barely fourteen, asks them.

"Naam bplau song na kha," Chuanna says in Thai. She turns to Isabella and says, "I order us two water, my treat,"

"Okay," Isabella says. "But I'm ordering us both pina coladas the next round."

Isabella gets a little carried away with the party atmosphere and consumes two cocktails on an empty stomach, followed by two glasses of white wine over dinner. By the time the disco starts up, she's got a good buzz on.

"We go back to room, get some sleep?" Chuanna says, taking Isabella by the elbow.

"It's way too early for that," Isabella says, swiping Chuanna's hand away. "Oh, and look, there are flame-throwers putting on a show on the beach! C'mon, let's go watch!"

Chuanna follows, Isabella running ahead.

"I told you," Chuanna whispers to Isabella. She points at a group of men who are ogling Isabella openly. "You drive men crazy. I no-like how they stare." Chuanna glares at the men with eyes like daggers.

"Whatever," Isabella laughs. "They're just embarrassing themselves, behaving like entitled oafs. What I wear is my business, and I'm not about to change how I choose to dress because of a bunch of drunk men trying to impress one another."

"Okay," Chuanna says, shrugging her shoulders.

While Isabella and Chuanna are watching the adrenalin-pumping fire performance, a man approaches carrying three cans of cold beer.

"Can I interest you lovely ladies in one of these?" he asks.

"Thank you, I was just thinking of making my way to

the bar," Isabella says, accepting the offer while noting his fit, tanned torso, naked to his low-riding beach shorts.

"No thank you," Chuanna says. "I so tired. We go Izzy?"

"Izzy? Now that's an interesting name," the man says, ignoring Chuanna's protest. "I'm Darius. Where are you from, Izzy?"

"I'm from Canada, and you?" Isabella says. She takes a long drink of Heineken.

"No shit!" Darius says. "I'm from Canada too! What part of the country do you call home?"

"What a small world," Isabella says. "I grew up in Winnipeg. And you?"

"I was born and raised in Toronto, have lived there all my life. Have you been in Thailand long?" Darius asks.

"Just over two months now, actually," Isabella says. "I love it here. And the weather sure beats the snow and cold they're getting back home right now."

"I know, right?" Darius says, laughing along. "Although Toronto doesn't get dumped on as seriously as Winnipeg. I'm pretty sure I read Winnipeg tops Nunavut and Alaska for worst weather."

Isabella sips at her beer and Chuanna takes the opportunity to try and convince Isabella to leave with her, but Isabella brushes her hand away again. With a sigh, Chuanna says good night and heads back to their room.

When Chuanna wakes up in the morning, Isabella's cot is still made. Her stomach lurches, and an uneasy feeling comes over her. She sends Isabella a text, but when there's no reply, she hurriedly gets dressed and goes off to look for her.

Evidence from the party litters the beach: beer bottles, half-empty plastic cups, and cigarette butts. Chuanna notices a used condom lying discarded on the ground next to one of the plastic recliners, and goosebumps appear on her forearms despite the heat already emanating from the early morning sun.

A clump of palm trees marks the end of the resort's perimeter, and Chuanna feels propelled forward. There, lying almost hidden by the grove of trees, is Isabella. Her half-naked body is encrusted in sand. Chuanna lets out a strangled sob and falls to her knees. She shakes her friend by her shoulders.

"Chuanna?" Isabella says, waking and squinting up at her while raising her hand to cover her eyes. "What, where . . . ?"

"Shh, it okay," Chuanna says.

Chuanna takes Isabella by the hand and helps lift her up. Isabella attempts to cover herself with her hands once she sees her bathing suit bottoms are lying in a wet clump beside her, in the indents her body made in the sand. She picks them up and shakes off as much sand as she can before putting them back on, all the while stifling her tears.

"I, I, I don't remember . . ." Isabella trails off. She looks around and up and down the beach, as though in a dream.

"No need, no explain," Chuanna says, hurrying her along.

"No, I do, you don't understand," Isabella says. By this time, they have arrived at their room and Chuanna has unlocked the door. Isabella turns around just inside the doorway. "Not long after you left, Darius and I were dancing, and I got really dizzy. Everything started to spin. The fire, Darius, all the other people; everything looked like cut glass. I stumbled, but Darius was holding me around the waist. It's all fuzzy after that, but I must have passed out. I remember waking up at one point, and he was on top of me. I think he raped me, Chuanna." Isabella slumps forward and lowers her head onto Chuanna's slight shoulders. She lets out a strangled cry, deep, from the gut. Her chest heaves with each breath, and tears pour down her cheeks in rivers, soaking Chuanna's blouse.

"I sorry," Chuanna says. She holds Isabella tighter, completely heartbroken for her friend. "You were too much drinking, but . . ."

"No, Chuanna, it doesn't make sense," Isabella interrupts. She lifts her head and looks Chuanna in the eye. "I only had four drinks before that beer, over the course of the whole afternoon and evening, and I had dinner too. I've never felt like that before. Back home, I worked at a bar. I know how to handle myself." Isabella stops for a moment before she continues, the words thick with emotion as awareness comes over her. "I, I think Darius drugged me, that he put something in that beer he gave me."

"What you do?" Chuanna asks, a worried expression on her rounded face. "Report to police?"

"No, Chuanna," Isabella says, her voice suddenly calm and certain. She straightens her shoulders. "We're both foreigners from the same country. I don't want any trouble with the police or my work visa. I just want to forget the whole thing." She shrugs and shakes her head. "I guess it's lucky for me, that I don't remember much." She tries to laugh it off, but it comes out more like a kitten's mew and gets caught in her throat.

"You right," Chuanna says as she pulls Isabella in closer and pats her back. "It make me so mad, he get away with this."

"I know, me too, but it's for the best," Isabella says. She takes a deep breath and swallows back the last of her tears. "I'm going to go take a shower. I just hope I don't have to look at his face, that I don't see him again before we leave."

"Me too," Chuanna says. "We change plans? Exchange ferry ticket for early?"

"That's a good idea. Thank you for thinking of it," Isabella says. "Would you ask the front desk if they can do that for us, while I shower?"

"Yes, I go now," Chuanna says, already turning toward the door.

———

Inside the cramped shower stall, Isabella scrubs her body vigorously from head to toe, rubbing the soap into her skin with a vengeance. She digs her nails into her flesh, tearing her tender breasts and the folds of her vagina, as though somehow, she might wash away all traces of what happened to her down the drain.

The smell of salt. The ocean. His skin. A cramp forms in her abdomen. She bends over in pain. It feels like a steel ball-bearing is lodged in her left ovary. An image comes to her, of the tiger amidst the tattoo sleeve collage on Darius's right arm. Isabella cringes. The pain expands and moves upward toward her throat, and a low growl escapes from her lips. She tries to swallow, to quieten the primal sound, now a full-on howl, but she can't. Isabella's entire body shakes and convulses. She collapses to the floor of the shower and pulls her knees to her chin. Each howl seems to scrape the sides of her throat raw. She hears the sound of Darius's laughter and repeats a prayer of hope in her mind, that the sound of the running water will drown it out. The water, turned ice-cold, pelts against the back of her neck. Her skin numbs to match the hollowness she feels in her soul. She hears the sound of Chuanna entering the room and forces herself to be silent. She pulls herself up and steps from the shower. Still trembling, she stands on the bathmat, naked in front of the mirror over the vanity. She looks herself in the eye and makes a conscious decision. She isn't going to allow this to define her.

The nine o'clock ferry isn't full, and Chuanna is able to exchange their tickets. They pack their belongings and grab a light breakfast at the hotel restaurant, thankfully with no sign of Darius. They catch the ferry back to the mainland. It is a long drive back to the city on the hot bus.

Isabella closes her eyes and tries, unsuccessfully, to sleep her wounds away.

That night, Isabella has her regular weekly FaceTime with her parents. She dials them up from her laptop, propped up on the small desk in the corner of the room, with only a curtain draped across to separate her space from Chuanna's, but Chuanna is at her parents' house for a family visit too.

"*Ciao* Izzy, how was your weekend at the beach with Chuanna?" Toni asks. "Was it as gorgeous as you'd hoped?"

"Toni, you have the camera pointed at my wrinkled old neck, for goodness' sake," Sylvie says, leaning forward on the kitchen chair to adjust the screen. "There, that's better. Hello, Isabella, how are you?"

"Hi, Maman. The beach was beautiful," Isabella says. "The sand here is just like in the postcards, the shade of linen. And the ocean is a gorgeous shade of turquoise, the water clear and sparkling."

"Hmm, if it was so wonderful, why does my Izzy look so sad?" Toni asks. "And don't try to tell me everything is okay. I know when my daughter is unhappy."

"You're so perceptive, Papa," Isabella says. "But it's nothing to be worried about. I'm just exhausted from the long ferry and bus ride. I'm sure I will be back to my usual bubbly self by tomorrow, after a good sleep."

"Are you sure that's all?" Toni asks, his brow furrowed.

"Yes, Papa, you both worry too much," Isabella says. "Now, let's change the subject. I want to hear all about the snowstorm that blew in on Thursday. And don't bother denying it; I saw it with my own eyes on my weather app."

"Ha, ha you're right, it was a doozy," Sylvie says. "It took your father all morning on Friday to clear the sidewalk. The snow was at least six inches high."

It carries on like this for an hour, then Isabella blows kisses across the miles to her parents and says goodnight.

I hope this horrible feeling I have in the pit of my stomach will go away as easily as the snow, Isabella thinks to herself as she turns off her bedside lamp and tucks into the sheets, careful to pull the mosquito netting around her.

—————

Isabella immerses herself in work, trying to put the trauma behind her, but the light of her soul feels dimmed to near extinction.

The one-hour bus ride to the school and back each day, plus six hours of teaching, along with her weekend job giving manicures and pedicures at the market, keep her occupied most of the time. Too often, her mind wanders back to that night in Ko Samet.

Isabella brings her sketchbook and pencils along in her day pack, her drawing a kind of therapy during the long bus ride to work. Her abstract drawings betray her hidden feelings. They depict strong, jagged lines, heavy clouds, lightning, and fires raging. She draws herself as an anime-inspired character, a female warrior dressed like Lara Croft, wielding a dagger and sword.

When she isn't drawing, Isabella rereads the part in *Siddhartha* when the seeker is bereft with grief, so overwhelmed with the emptiness in his soul that he wishes he were dead. She feels the same, and prays to God for healing, for a sign of some sort, to help her find her way.

***

Isabella's three-month contract at the school is extended and she stays in Thailand. She feels like she is just drifting along, like a robotic drone, unsatisfied yet somehow complacent. She's been in Thailand for just over two years when she receives a message from Mark.

Hi Izzy, I hope you are well. I have some good news and some bad. The good news is that I met a guy at The Forks on the weekend and, well, I think it might be something special. It's too early to tell, but we just hit it off so quickly, talking into the late hours of the night on our first date, never seeming to run out of things to say. The bad news is that I saw your mother and father at the hospital, on the cancer ward. Remember I just got transferred over there last month? Anyway, they looked embarrassed to see me. They probably didn't expect to run into me there, and your father didn't look well. I think he might be sick. I hope I'm not out of line, spilling the beans like this, but I feel sure you would have mentioned it if you knew, and you deserve to know. I'm thinking of you, sending love and prayers. Xxoo

Isabella swipes the message closed. She sits on her bed, in a state of shock. Her mind takes off in a million directions. She remembers how sad Siddhartha felt when his son left him. How he thought about how he left his own father to go on his quest, never to see him again. She knows with absolute certainty that isn't her path, that her love for her father means everything to her. Isabella packs her things and books the first available flight home. She writes a quick email to the principal of her school to explain the situation.

"I will miss you, so much," Isabella says. She wraps her arms around her dear friend.

"Me too," Chuanna says, her own eyes welling up with tears. "Maybe someday, when your father is better, you will come back?"

"Who knows what the future will bring?" Isabella says. "But I promise, I will stay in touch, always."

Chapter Three

Isabella's return to Canada after almost two years away feels surreal. Facing her father's illness is devastating enough, but to make it worse, she had become so accustomed to the noise and chaos of Bangkok; she finds herself feeling culture shock on arrival in her own country. As she waits for her luggage at the carousel, she notices how clean the floors are compared to the scuffed up, sticky ones her feet stuck to in the smaller Thai airports. The calm patience of the crowd is even a bit unsettling. It smells different, with no undercurrents of the unpleasant scents of mould, perspiration, seafood, and chilies frying.

Isabella turns to see her father bounding toward her from the pick-up zone. She steps back as he reaches for her.

"Papa, how could you keep something so important from me, week after week, during our FaceTime chats, never once letting on that anything was wrong?" Isabella says, a quiver in her voice. "I felt almost betrayed, having to hear the news from Mark. Can you imagine what it would feel like if the shoe were on the other foot?"

Toni stops dead in his tracks as he reaches to take Isabella's backpack from her.

"I'm sorry," he says. "That never occurred to me." He shakes his head, a deep crease in his brow. "When I first found out, I was in a state of shock, and I didn't know how to tell you. But then, when Dr. Cohen said he'd caught it early, only in stage 2, I thought it would be better not to worry you. Just the word 'cancer' sounds so scary, but as you can see for yourself, I'm doing just fine."

Isabella doesn't think her father looks fine, but she follows him to the car in silence. She climbs into the front passenger seat beside her father. She's glad her mother chose to stay at home.

"What kind of treatment are you on?" Isabella asks. She reaches her hand over to pat Toni's, firmly placed on the steering wheel.

"I'm getting radiation therapy," Toni says. "But it's nothing to worry about, *mi bella.*"

"Radiation?" Isabella's hand goes to her heart. "How often?"

"Every day, but only for a few hours," Toni says. He averts his eyes and shoulder checks, then pulls into the road.

"Well, starting tomorrow, I'm driving you to the hospital," Isabella says. "And don't even bother trying to argue with me."

Isabella unpacks and gets settled back into her old room, still exactly as it was before. True to her word, she drives Toni to his daily treatments at St. Boniface Hospital. She and her mother dote on him night and day. Isabella signs out every book in the library with advice on how to treat cancer. She convinces Toni to try alternative treatments in conjunction with the radiation, including a modified diet, which he grumbles about at every opportunity but follows through with to please her. She finds a book by Gabor Maté in the self-help section, *When the Body Says No: The Cost of Hidden Stress*. After reading it cover to cover in two days, Isabella urges her father to give counselling a try, with the goal of uncovering any past traumas that may be at the root of his disease.

Over breakfast, Isabella sets the book beside his placemat and hands him a kale and blueberry antioxidant smoothie, sits across from him, and takes a sip from her own.

"What do you think, Papa?"

"This is just complete and utter nonsense," Toni says, taking one look at the back cover. He slides it back across the table to her.

"Well, Papa, that may be your opinion," Isabella says. "But what if Dr. Maté is right, and physical illnesses like cancer are manifestations of some unresolved emotional trauma from the past? Wouldn't it be worth the effort to give counselling a try?"

"It would be, if that were possible," Toni says. "But I had the happiest of childhoods, growing up in the beautiful hillsides of Tuscany. What could be traumatic about that?"

"I don't know, but if it was so picture-perfect, how come you were so anxious to leave? All the way to Canada, no less?" Isabella asks.

"Now, Izzy, you are cut from the same cloth. Why don't you answer that yourself?" Toni says, gesturing emphatically with his hands. "Did you not just return from two and a half years in Thailand? And were you running from something, or toward adventure?"

"That's different, Papa," Isabella says. "I didn't pick up and move away forever. But maybe you're right. I might be grasping at straws. I just so want you to be back to your old self, to be well again."

"I know, you only have my well-being at heart," Toni says. He gets up from his chair and comes over to Isabella's side of the table, and reaches for her. Isabella rises and her father wraps his arms around her. "It touches me deeply, that you care so much," he continues, whispering softly in her ear. "*Grazie, mi bella*, I appreciate you. But truthfully, your willingness to come with us to church every Sunday and our daily prayers at dinner have felt the most supportive to me of anything. I know you've kind of lost your faith, so it means even more to me that you're willing to join your mother and I."

By this time, Toni's eyes are watering. Isabella is overcome with feelings of love and protectiveness for her father.

"Oh, Papa, I'm just so afraid for you and of losing you."

She sighs and holds him closer. In this moment, she's

never felt closer to her father, and even her connection to God seems to shift to another level.

"Pray with me?" Toni says as he takes both of her hands in his, looks into her eyes, and begins.

"The Lord is my rock, my fortress and deliverer . . ."

Isabella joins her father in saying aloud the rest of the familiar verse.

". . . in whom I take refuge, my shield and horn of my salvation, my stronghold. Give me relief from my distress, have mercy and hear my prayer. Heal me, Lord, in your infinite power, amen."

Six weeks later, Isabella and Sylvie accompany Toni to his follow-up appointment with his physician at St. Boniface. The three of them are gathered in the specialist's office, awaiting the latest results, Toni looking stoic, his legs crossed. Sylvie is so beside herself she's pacing the floors. Isabella sits tight, but feels as if she is on pins and needles.

"Toni, it's so good to see you," the doctor says as he comes into the room. "And Sylvie and Isabella, how wonderful you two are here to support our outstanding patient." He shakes everyone's hand, pumping each up and down in turn, then takes a seat behind his desk. He takes his reading glasses out of the case, sets them on his prominent nose, then thumbs through a stack of paperwork on his desk. "Ah, here we are then, let's see . . ." He runs his finger down a column and then stops to look over at the ensemble. "I'm delighted to be the bearer of good news. Toni, all of your tests came back negative. There's absolutely no sign of cancer. By all accounts, you are cured, or at the very least, in a full remission."

"Papa, this is a miracle!" Isabella says, rising from her chair to take her father by the hand. She pulls him to her for a huge embrace, then releases her hold and dances a little jig.

"Now, now, we are in public," Sylvie tut-tuts, although her matching smile of joy gives her own feelings away.

"The first thing I'm going to do is request that my lovely wife prepares me a proper, high-fat, high-calorie meal," Toni says, rubbing his ten-pound-smaller tummy for emphasis. "If I have to consume one more spinach and God-knows-what-else smoothie, I might die from an overdose of healthy food, forget about cancer."

"Oh, Papa, always the drama queen," Isabella laughs. "You look so handsome, at least five years younger with the weight you've lost. I think you should consider keeping with some of the changes you've made, even if it isn't every day. I read somewhere that following an eighty-twenty rule can help you stick to a healthy lifestyle."

"Humph," Toni grunts. "We'll see about that, *la mia bella ragazza,* who always seems to have her nose buried in a book, just like her mother. What do you say, Sylvie, will you prepare us something delicious for dinner tonight, to celebrate?"

"I already defrosted the veal this morning to make your favourite, parmigiana," Sylvie says with a smile. "I just knew you were going to get good news."

"I'm so happy for all of you," the doctor beams. "These are the kind of days that make my job worthwhile."

———

By the end of May, Toni is back to his old self, tinkering around in his woodworking shop out back, having retired from his wine importing business the year before at the age of sixty-five. Sylvie is always busy too, doing community work through their church and still taking on a few shifts at the Clinique beauty counter at The Bay.

Isabella starts to feel restless, her childhood home suffocating. She's ready to move out, but the apartment scene in Winnipeg is uninspiring and she doesn't feel like serving again. She's given up on her dreams of being an artist, no longer creating larger-than-life paintings on canvas, her portfolio gathering dust in the cellar. Even her friendship with Mark feels unsatisfying, with him back in school to get his master's in nursing, working night shifts at the hospital, and being in a committed relationship with his partner, Filipe, whom she hasn't even met yet.

Not long after, Isabella makes a decision. She's ready for a change.

———

"Maman, Papa, you both know it's high time for me to find my own place," Isabella says one night after dinner. She is drying the dishes from the rack in the sink and putting them away in the cupboard.

"Now, Izzy, there's no rush for you to leave, but I agree. You do need to get your own life back on track, now that your old man is cancer-free," Toni says. "Why don't you drop by the tavern? I'm sure Frank would hire you back in an instant—if he is still the manager there, that is."

"I'm sure you're right," Isabella says, tucking away the last plate and closing the cupboard door. "But I'm ready for something different and more rewarding than serving alcohol in a pub. One of my Facebook friends posted something about living on Vancouver Island. It looks amazing, so I've decided to move there, and I signed up for an intensive 200-hour yoga certification program."

"Yoga?" Sylvie says, wrinkling her nose. She drops the tablecloth she'd been gathering for the wash on the floor. "Isn't that some kind of New Age, pagan-worship thing?"

"Maman, I swear, I don't know where you pick up such ideas," Isabella laughs. "You've clearly watched way too many episodes of your daytime soap operas and gossip panels that pretend to be news programs. Yoga is an age-old practice that originated in India. It doesn't have anything to do with religion, although I've heard it can be a very spiritual experience. The course I've enrolled in includes instruction in yoga philosophy and the principles of living with a focused mind, as well as the Mysore postures associated with Ashtanga flow. I'm so excited."

Her mother clucks her tongue. "I've heard stories about the bohemian lifestyle there."

"That's exactly what I'm looking for," Isabella says and laughs again.

"Sounds like you've already made up your mind," Toni

says, getting up from the table to pick up the tablecloth from the floor. "When are you planning to leave, *mi bella?*"

"The course starts in three weeks," Isabella says. "But I still need to find a place to live and make arrangements. I'm hoping to hitch a ride with one of Mark's friends from the hospital, who is moving out there to start a new position at an alternative, integrative medical clinic in Nanaimo, next week, I think."

"Well, I suppose it's as good as any other job you might consider. I only wish you would try to find something satisfying for you here," Sylvie says. She sighs, then takes the tablecloth from Toni and disappears downstairs to put it in the washing machine.

Isabella finds a studio apartment to rent in Duncan that is available the first of July, just two days before Mark's friend, Anita, is planning the long road trip and one week before Isabella's yoga course starts.

Sylvie, who has been watering and adding compost to the soil in the window boxes out front, is the first to spot Anita when she drives up and parks her Ford station wagon a block down the street. Sylvie waves her over as she gets out of the car and approaches. Anita's dark eyes light up as she waves back, her dark hair falling in long waves to her waist.

"Hello, you must be Anita," Sylvie says. She removes her gardening gloves before offering a handshake. "Isabella is all packed and ready to go. I'll let her know you're here."

"Thank you, Mrs. Ricci," Anita says, following Sylvie into the house. "I can help Izzy load up her things."

"Yes, she tried to go 'minimalist' as she calls it, but as it is, she's got two oversized suitcases, her travel backpack, and two cardboard boxes. It's good you have a station wagon."

"Yes, but even still, with all that, plus my things, we'll be packed to the rafters," Anita says.

When the last box is stowed in the back seat, Toni and Sylvie take turns hugging Isabella close and bringing up last-minute concerns, both of them uncomfortable with goodbyes. They are still waving when Anita turns left at the end of their street to pull onto Provencher Boulevard and then onto Highway 1 heading west.

"This is so kind of you," Isabella says. "I've never set foot in Western Canada before, and I'm so excited for this adventure."

"You're actually doing me a favour, especially if you don't mind taking turns with the driving," Anita says. "I've driven this route twice before, and it's gruelling, even with a stop halfway in Medicine Hat."

"What a crazy name for a city," Isabella laughs. "But yeah, sure, I'm happy to share the driving." She opens her oversized purse and pulls her license out of her wallet, giggling at how young she looks. "I have my driver's license, although I never got around to updating the photo. I haven't driven much, since I don't own a car and I took public transportation for the two years I was in Thailand, so I might be a little rusty."

"You can take the easy parts then, through the Prairies,"

Anita says, her eyes on the road. "They are beautiful in their own way, so vast and seemingly endless, like you've arrived at the end of the world. Nothing like the mountains and beaches of Brazil, where I grew up. But I want to hear more about your adventures in Thailand."

"Brazil?" Isabella says, instantly intrigued. "Clearly we're not going to run out of stories to share. Tell me all about Brazil. What's it like there?"

———

Isabella and Anita fall into an easy rhythm, and the first day disappears in a series of deep conversations. They catch a few winks at a super cheap roadside motel in Medicine Hat and are back on the road as soon as the sun is up. By late afternoon the second day, they are at the Tsawwassen Ferry Terminal, ready to travel from the mainland to the island. It takes an hour and a half to cross the channel over to Victoria, but Isabella is enraptured by the views of the ocean, she and Anita choosing to stand near the railing for most of the crossing.

The final leg of the drive, up the Malahat Highway, is as scenic as anything Isabella has laid eyes on before, including the islands of Thailand. Isabella is thrilled she's made the decision to move, intoxicated by the abundance of nature all around her. She stares out the window of the car at the massive, old-growth trees as they make their way through Cowichan Valley. When Anita drops her off at the apartment building where she's signed a month-to-month lease, a worn-down establishment within walking distance of Duncan's city centre, she is tired from the twenty-six-hour drive, but excited to be starting a new adventure.

"Thank you so much, Anita," Isabella says as she climbs out of the passenger seat. She ducks her head down to peer in the car window. "Look me up if you're ever out this way, and good luck to you in your new job."

"It's no problem, it was fun to have some company, and you're so easygoing and comfortable to talk with," Anita says. "Let's stay in touch."

———

The next day, Isabella goes on a tour of the quaint downtown area of Duncan. She finds the hodgepodge of businesses interesting, and especially loves the First Nations totems, hewn from red cedar, that are interspersed throughout the area. She stops to read each placard that explains their historical relevance. Each story is compelling, but her favourite is the imposing *Thunderbird with Dzunuk'wa* by Moopin'kim. After everything she's been through, she feels drawn to the totem's energy of strength.

After an hour, Isabella crosses the train tracks and locates the funky locally owned café and organic market-bakery combo she read about online.

"I'll have a chai tea with almond milk and a vegan energy ball, please," Isabella says to the smiling young man behind the counter, a hoop earring in his nose, and his hair, longer than hers, held back off his face by a colourful bandana.

"To stay or to go?" he asks.

"To stay," Isabella says. "I wonder, do you have any openings for a server? I have quite a bit of experience."

"Ah, sorry, we don't use servers here," the guy says, taking a pair of tongs from the counter and choosing an energy ball from the stack in the cooler before setting it on a plate. "It's self-serve, cafeteria style. It's possible we need someone to clear tables, but it doesn't pay much. Can you cook?"

"Uh, no, I'm afraid my cooking skills are limited," Isabella says. "But if you do have an opening, maybe for a dishwasher or something? I'd be happy to try just about anything."

"What did you say your name was?" he asks, taking the ten-dollar bill Isabella has set on the counter and passing her change.

"I'm Isabella, but friends call me Izzy," Isabella says, scooping the coins.

"Okay, Izzy, why don't you send me your contact details?" He fishes out a business card from under the counter. "I'll reach out if anything comes up."

***

Isabella gets a call from the manager the next day, offering her a position to do various odd jobs, including clearing tables, washing dishes, and restocking the cooler. She starts her yoga certification program the day after.

Only a few days into the intensive, four-hour-a-day schedule, Isabella finds herself unlocking a deep spiritual awakening like nothing she's ever experienced before. When she's sitting on her mat in stillness, meditating on the foundational states of mind—non-violence, truthfulness, contentment, and surrender—she notices sensations arising that aren't thoughts or feelings. When she discovers *pratyahara*, or "sensory transcendence," it's like being on the outside looking in. Her relationship with God, or maybe just a higher being, transforms too, to something more personal. When in the stillness of *savasana*, or "corpse pose," she hears and sees visions in her mind, of ocean waters, exotic trees, and landscapes that feel from a long-ago past of her ancestors.

Over the duration of her classes, Isabella discovers that the postures in the first series feel natural. Others, like triangle, lotus intense stretch, and shoulder stand, challenge her to the core. She pushes through the discomfort at her own pace, and, with the gentle support of her instructors, she recognizes how each part is necessary to the whole.

When she finishes the course near the end of September, Isabella is offered a part-time job at the studio, her gift for teaching and easy grasp of yoga theory having been noticed by her instructors. She teaches yoga classes in between her shifts at the café. She makes low wages at both jobs, but between the two gigs, she gets by, and her life feels full.

***

"Hey, Izzy, that was an awesome class," Sunrise says while rolling up her mat. A short, heavy young woman with a string of eight silver studs lining each earlobe, Sunrise is a regular at the studio. "You've got a natural gift for this, my favourite teacher here yet."

"Thank you," Isabella says, a huge smile on her face. "I love it so much. I can't believe I walked the planet for so long with no concept of the benefit of a regular yoga practice. I never imagined I could become so strong and flexible in only a few months, with a daily commitment, not to mention so grounded and able to be in the present moment."

"I know, right?" Sunrise says. "I think my idea of a yogi was some old man, like Gandhi or something, sitting around in a loosely gathered sheet-toga thing." She laughs, a sweet, high-pitched cross between a giggle and a guffaw. "Hey, there's a group of us meeting up later for sushi at a bomb restaurant a few streets over. Want to come?"

"Sushi?" Isabella says, lighting up. "I haven't had sushi since I was in Thailand."

"That's trippy," Sunrise says. "When were you in Thailand?"

"Actually, I only came back to Canada in the spring, when I found out my father had prostate cancer."

"Cancer, ooh, that's a rough thing to go through," Sunrise says, her heart-shaped face melting into an expression of compassion. "How is he doing?"

"We were so lucky. He caught it early on, and after radiation and a few lifestyle changes, he's totally recovered. Thank you for asking."

"Sweet," Sunrise says. "I love stories with happy endings." She packs her water bottle into her burlap sack and slings it over her shoulder. "The restaurant is on Kenneth; we're meeting up at seven thirty, if you decide to come along."

———

Isabella closes up the yoga studio, her class the last one for the day, and locks the door. She goes back to her dreary, dark apartment and takes a hot shower, then changes into a cozy sweater and loose jeans. She puts on a coat of mascara and brushes her long hair, then grabs her purse and heads out the door.

Kenneth Street is only a few blocks from her place, but an autumn wind has picked up. The first newly fallen leaves dance along the pavement as Isabella makes her way, head down.

A bell rings when Isabella opens the door of the restaurant. A sushi station is straight ahead, the dining room to the right. She sees two sushi chefs wearing starch-white aprons and chef hats behind the counter, one slicing paper-thin fresh tuna and the other deftly rolling nori sheets filled with sticky jasmine rice. The loud hum of group conversation drifts toward her, and Isabella follows her ears to a group of people sitting at the back, where several tables have been pushed together.

"Izzy!" Sunrise calls out as she gets up from her chair and comes around to give her a hug. "I'm so glad you decided to come. Once you try the sushi here, you're going to become addicted."

Sunrise introduces Isabella to all her friends, including Alex, a handsome, blonde-haired man with compelling turquoise eyes that remind her of the ocean waters in Thailand. A memory of the night on Ko Samet flashes into her mind. Isabella has to fight back the urge to leave, determined to push through the fear that has kept her from dating in the years since. She pulls up a chair with a shaky hand and sits across from him.

"I love the name Izzy," Alex says. "I think I might steal it for a character in my next book."

"You're a writer?" Isabella says. "I'm addicted to books! Reading is one of my most treasured pastimes. What is your genre? How many books have you written? Are you published?"

"Wow, aren't you the curious one?" Alex says with a laugh. "I've written and published two science fiction novels and I'm working on my third."

"Oh my God, that is beyond cool," Isabella gushes. "I read a lot of different genres, but I can't say I've read much science fiction. Right now, I'm totally into non-fiction books about spirituality."

"Well, hopefully I can convert you," Alex says. "I'd be happy to give you a free copy if you're interested."

Over the course of their conversation, Isabella finds herself attracted, not only to Alex's sexy smile, white teeth framed by a full mouth, and deeply tanned skin, but also to his intelligence. He is funny, yet serious at the same time. By the end of the night, when Alex asks Isabella for her number, she has almost forgotten Darius and feels ready to get back into the dating ring.

A few days later, Isabella is feeling aglow with the first intoxicating blush of meeting someone new, but she is still battling the ever-present fear of allowing herself to trust again.

She is browsing through a small independent bookstore when her eye is drawn by the scarlet wax seal on the cover of a compact little book called *The Secret*. She picks it up and turns it over to read the synopsis: "You'll begin to understand the hidden, untapped power that's within you, and this revelation can bring joy to every aspect of your life." It is just the nudge she needs to support her desire to get to know Alex better. She chooses to spend some of her limited entertainment budget to purchase a copy.

That night after her yoga class, Isabella reads the book front to back in a single sitting. Inspired by the notion that by identifying the things that light up her soul and setting an intention, she can manifest them into being, she writes a list of everything she is grateful for. Then she compiles another list, of the things she'll need to create her own vision board—a collection of images, quotes, and affirmations that represent her goals and dreams.

Isabella finds an art store downtown on her day off and loads up on art supplies, including poster paper and acrylic paints. At a thrift store, she purchases a stack of old magazines for super cheap, then swings by Staples to print off some photos. When she gets back to her apartment, she sets everything out on the kitchen table. Hours fly by as she pastes and cuts, draws and paints. She chooses one of her favourite photos of her mother and father, taken on an outing to Assiniboine Park just before she left Winnipeg, and places it in the centre. Scenic shots from her time in Thailand and some other destinations on her bucket list, including Italy, where her father grew up, fill in spaces. She finds a spot for photos of Chuanna and Mark. Her attempts to reach out to Chuanna have fizzled out, as long-distance relationships often do, but she and Mark message each other several times each week and she still considers him her best friend in the world.

When Isabella finishes her vision board, she hangs the poster-visual of her life goals, and everything she is grateful for, on the wall over her bed. Then she gets out her sketchbook journal from her nightstand drawer and starts sketching a portrait of Alex as she daydreams about how their first date will go. When her arm is too tired to continue, she tucks her half-finished caricature away, yearning for something more fulfilling. She falls asleep, to dream of passionate but gentle embraces with Alex and visions of herself walking on a tropical beach she doesn't recognize, but which feels like home.

The evening of their first date, Alex pulls up outside Isabella's building in his sporty black Corvette and honks the horn. Isabella is so nervous, fussing with her hair and changing her mind about what to wear, that she is running a little late. Alex looks impatient when she walks up to the passenger side and hops in.

"I've been waiting five minutes," Alex says, the first thing out of his mouth, before even a hello.

"Sorry, I lost track of time," Isabella fibs, not wanting to admit she has the jitters.

"Yeah, well, I hope that isn't a habit of yours," Alex says. "I don't like to be left waiting."

"I'm sorry, I'm usually very punctual," Isabella says. "But I hope it isn't going to set things off on the wrong foot." She giggles, hoping to ease the tension.

"Naw, it's no big deal to be late now and again," Alex laughs along. "I'm glad to know you aren't one of those people who shrugs off tardiness, but I'm happy to let this one go."

"Great, let's move on," Isabella says. "Where are we going for dinner?"

"I've made reservations at this amazing local restaurant on an apple orchard just a half hour or so from here. They make their own ciders and have amazing wood-fired pizza, and now that it's autumn, the colours of the leaves will be gorgeous."

"That sounds lovely," Isabella says. "To be honest, I've never tasted cider before, despite working at a pub for several years."

"What?" Alex says. "You don't know what you're missing. We'll have to do the cider flight-tasting for sure."

"What's that?" Isabella asks.

"Oh, it's a great concept," Alex says. "The bar serves up

four different ciders for you to sample and explains a little about each one."

"That does sound fun," Isabella says.

Alex makes a right turn to head south on the highway. The drive is scenic, with farms and forests dotted with small villages along the way and giant leaves of the maple trees red and golden along the edges. He is a skilled driver and navigates the turns and curves expertly. Soon he is turning onto a back road and up a steep incline. He parks his car in a gravel clearing and Isabella gets out and stretches, then looks around the property.

"Wow, this is gorgeous," Isabella says.

Alex smiles, clearly pleased with himself, and leads Isabella across the gravel, down a stone path, and through a tranquil garden to the restaurant.

"Hello, do you have a reservation?" the hostess greets them.

"As a matter of fact, I do," Alex says. "But my friend here is new to the area and has never tried cider. Is it possible to book a tasting first?"

The hostess scans an open reservation book in front of her.

"It looks like there is an opening in half an hour. If you want to start with a drink and appetizer, I can seat you at your table and then call you when it's your turn."

"What do you think?" Alex asks.

"That sounds perfect," Isabella says.

Alex takes it upon himself to order them each a glass of white wine from a nearby winery and chooses a cheese plate for them to share. Isabella thinks it's a bit forward of him, not knowing her preferences, or if she has allergies. With her recent decision to try going vegan, she isn't thrilled with his choice, but she stays quiet and picks at the brie.

When it's their turn to go to the tasting section, the hostess leads them to the bar, and they each take a seat on a stool at the gnarled wood counter, polished to a high sheen. The server greets them, his lips almost invisible under his long, scruffy, ginger moustache and beard.

"This one is a local favourite," the bartender says, pouring a generous serving in a glass for each of them and placing them on napkins set on the bar. "Our first of the four you'll be tasting is called Scrumpy. It's a strong blend with sharp crab apple undertones."

"Scrumpy?" Isabella chuckles. "What the heck does that mean?"

"Glad you asked," the bartender laughs along with her. "In medieval England, farm workers used to steal apples—or scrump as they called it back then—from the rich land barons."

"Oh, I love stories of underdogs and outliers," Isabella says. She takes a sip, then puckers her cheeks and purses her lips together. "Ooh, that is a strong one, not to my taste."

"I bet you're gonna love the next one," Alex says. "The Cyser combines local wildflower honey with the apples for a sweet, smooth flavour."

As the tasting goes on Isabella feels relaxed and is enjoying Alex's company. After it's done, they return to their table for a two-hour meal. The conversation is animated and interesting, not the usual first date fluff.

"Wow," Isabella says as Alex reaches for the bottle of red wine they've been sipping on over dinner, only to discover it's empty. "We went through that entire bottle . . . and four ciders. Are you ready to call a taxi?"

"Naw, don't worry, I can drive," Alex says. "Besides, it's almost impossible to get a taxi out here."

"Uh, I'm sorry, but that's not okay with me," Isabella says. "You're probably over the limit, and it would ruin a beautiful evening to get into a fender-bender, or worse."

"Really, I'm fine to drive," Alex says. "I never would have guessed you were such a stickler."

"Yeah, well, I never would have guessed you were such an oaf," Isabella retorts. "I'm a stickler, as you call it, for good reason, but if you're hell-bent on driving, I'll happily make my own way home."

Isabella rises from the table and leaves hastily. She forgets they are out in the middle of nowhere. The sun has set, and she gets lost in an apple orchard in her attempt to find her way down the hill to the sort-of-main road. Tired and frustrated, Isabella plops down in the thick field of dry grass and cries. She doesn't have the number for a taxi service. There's no internet and she doesn't have data on her phone. She gets up and dusts off her dress, then starts fumbling along in the dark once again when she hears the honk of a car horn.

"Come on then, get in," Alex calls out.

Isabella peers into the pitch-black night and sees the

bright headlights of a blue taxicab. Alex is in the back seat with the window down. She hesitates.

"Don't be so damn stubborn," Alex grumbles. "I'm here, in a taxi, like you wanted, so let's just get on with it."

Isabella climbs into the seat beside Alex, crosses her arms over her chest and turns to face the window. After Alex gives the taxi driver Isabella's address, neither one of them says a word until they are outside her building, and Isabella departs with a curt "thank you."

Isabella sulks for days after, refusing to answer Alex's texts.

I'm sorry, Izzy, please forgive me? I feel sick thinking of my cloddish behaviour. I don't know what came over me. Please, will you give me another chance?

Isabella doesn't think there is anything Alex can say to justify his actions. She opens her sketchbook to the portrait of Alex she started the night she met him. She erases one side of his face and draws a two-faced depiction: one smiling and charismatic, the other scowling and sinister.

Just when she's certain he's given up and moved on, Alex shows up at her yoga class, dressed in full yoga gear, toting a mat and water bottle.

"I heard this is an amazing class," Alex says. "And that the instructor is pretty kick-ass too."

"Thank you," Isabella says, as curtly as she can muster, finding it hard not to feel at least a little impressed with his effort. "Please find a spot to roll out your mat."

When the class is over ninety minutes later, Alex gets up from his mat and approaches Isabella.

"I'm sorry, Izzy, please, it's making me sick that you won't even talk to me," Alex says. He reaches out to put his hand on her arm. A shock of electricity shoots through her.

"Alex, I'm sorry, I do like you, and I totally enjoyed our conversations, but the drinking and driving is a non-negotiable for me," Isabella says. "A cousin of mine was killed by a drunk driver, and my aunt and uncle have never gotten over such a senseless loss. I don't understand why someone would make that decision when there are so many options to avoid it."

"Geez, that's heavy," Alex says. "And I totally agree. I wasn't thinking straight. I should have had a plan before I started drinking, but I got carried away. I haven't dated or met anyone in a long time that I feel as strongly for as I do for you."

"Really?" Isabella says. Her heart softens a little more. "Well, I suppose we all make mistakes now and again. If you're willing to agree to always take a taxi or plan for one of us to be the designated driver in the future, I'm willing to forgive you and wipe the slate clean."

"Wipe the slate clean?" Alex says. "I never realized you were starting a slate of grievances. I guess I have a lot of making up to do."

He bends down and takes Isabella's chin in his hand. He tilts her face upward and leans in for a long, gentle kiss. Time seems to pass as if suspended, their lips locked, when a voice at the doorway interrupts them.

"Hey, lovers." Melanie, the motherly owner of the studio, is standing in the doorway with her arms crossed. She smiles at them. "It's time to close up."

"Oh, sorry about that, I just, well . . ." Isabella stammers.

"Never mind, it's all good," Melanie laughs.

Isabella finishes tidying up the space and turns out the light. She doesn't bother to change out of her yoga clothes. Outside the studio, Alex is waiting for her, his car parked on the sidewalk across the street.

"Can I take you home with me?" Alex asks.

Isabella hesitates a beat, then draws in a deep breath. "Yes, you can," she says, then walks around to the passenger side, and hops in.

Two hours later, completely exhausted and satiated, Isabella kisses the middle of Alex's well-developed pecs. She feels the reverberations of tingling sensations up and down her arm as she trails her fingers over his waxed, tanned skin.

"Umm, that was the best sex I've ever had in my life," Isabella says, moving her mouth down toward his belly button.

"Was?" Alex says, almost purring. He takes Isabella's hand and leads it to his crotch. "Or did you mean to say, is?"

"Looks like you have quite the stamina," Isabella giggles, feeling him harden. She moves her head down, kisses the dimple just below his waist, and keeps going.

It isn't long before Isabella is spending most nights sleeping over at Alex's apartment, which is brighter and larger than hers. He has a dishwasher in the galley kitchen, which makes cooking together at home more enjoyable. And the mattress on his bed is way, way better than hers.

They've only been seeing one another a month when he asks her to move in with him. Despite a voice that whispers inside her, *It's too soon, you don't really know him*, she agrees. She gives her landlord notice, and the next weekend, Alex comes over to pick her up, along with all her belongings. She writes a long email to her mother and father and jots a quick note to Mark to update them on her situation.

Hi Mark, just wanted to let you know things are going great out here. I love my new job teaching yoga and work at the café is super chill. It's getting serious with the guy I told you about a while back. In fact, I moved in with him today. I know, it's a bit impulsive, and to be honest, I have a few misgivings, but I somehow convinced myself that I shouldn't worry so much. Any advice? Anyway, I hope everything is well with you, that you're enjoying your courses and work, and that you and Filipe are still an item. I miss you, my friend. Take care. Love, Izzy.

"What do you say to me inviting a couple of my buddies over for a pizza and beer night?" Alex says, not long after she's tucked her clothes into the two drawers he cleared out for her and hung up a few things in the closet. "They're both dying to meet the girl who has me over the moon, smitten and . . ." He stops.

"Smitten and falling in love?" Isabella teases, finishing his sentence for him. She comes up behind him, seated at his desk by the window in the living room, and kisses the back of his neck.

"Yeah, Izzy," Alex says, turning his face to kiss her full on the lips. "I haven't said as much, it feels too early, but that's how I feel."

"I love you too," Isabella says. "And it would be fun to meet your friends. I'm planning on going to a yoga class tonight, so I'll come back and join you after."

When Isabella walks into the apartment later that evening, the party is already in full swing. Fahad and Cory are seated at the kitchen table with Alex. Fahad has a slight build, with thick, dark hair. In contrast, Cory is a bulky man who Isabella imagines must be a weightlifter, with his barrel-chest and biceps that bulge like two bowling balls underneath his T-shirt. Poker chips, playing cards, and empty beer bottles litter the table.

"Hello," Isabella says. She sets down her gym bag at the door and comes over to join them.

"Hey, babe," Alex says, bumping his knee on the table as he gets up, almost knocking over a beer. He stabilizes the bottle and comes over to kiss her. "Fahad, Cory, this is Izzy."

"Nice to meet you," they both say, not bothering to get up. "We're in the middle of a tight game here, but we can deal you in the next one."

"Oh, thanks, but I don't know much about poker," Isabella says. "I'll go take a quick shower and just watch."

"No way, you're not getting off that easy," Fahad jokes. "We're happy to teach you our tricks, right guys?"

"Okay, well, maybe," Isabella says.

Fahad wins the game by a landslide, his collection of poker chips almost spilling onto the floor.

"Looks like Fahad should be your poker guru," Alex says with a laugh, turning to Isabella who has returned, her hair still wet and wearing a tank top with sweats. "What do you say, Izzy, shall we deal you in?"

"Yeah, sure, why not," Isabella says, taking the last seat at the table. "How do you play?"

"With Texas Hold'em, it's easiest to just learn as we go," Cory says. "I'll be the dealer. We each get two cards called hole cards that stay face down. Then there are several betting rounds after the dealer lays down five community cards."

"The goal is to make the best five-card hand possible," Fahad continues, Cory already having laid out the hole cards in front of each of them.

"What is the best hand?" Isabella asks, taking a peek at her cards.

"A royal flush, but those are rare and hard to come by," Cory says. "The most common are a full house or straight."

"Oh, now that I think of it, there are similar terms in

Yahtzee," Isabella says. "I used to play that game with my mom and dad all the time, when I was a kid."

"Yeah, Yahtzee is a similar concept, but with dice instead of cards," Fahad says.

"But poker is a way more challenging game," Cory adds.

After a few hands, Isabella discovers she is a natural. She wins a few, loses a few, but in the end, Cory wins more games.

"That was fun," Isabella says, rising from the table. "Thank you for teaching me. It was so good to meet you both, but I'm afraid I'm an early riser and I need to call it quits."

"So soon?" Alex says, sounding disappointed. He glances down at his phone. "It's not even midnight yet. We're just warming up, right guys?"

"Yeah, we three stooges are total night owls," Fahad agrees with a laugh. "And I'm ready for another beer."

"Well, have fun," Isabella says. "I hope to see you both again soon." She stoops over to kiss Alex on the top of the head. "Good night, babe."

Isabella is in a deep sleep, dreaming about being lost in a maze at one of the large markets in Thailand, naked with her sand-filled bathing suit bottoms in her hand, when Alex crawls into bed.

"Hey you," Alex says, shaking her shoulder gently. He reaches his hand down, cupping her breast, and she can't resist. Soon she is wide awake, her body fully aroused,

Alex's naked body beckoning. He starts off strong, as she has become accustomed, but with the excess alcohol, he doesn't have his usual stamina. He's barely inside her when she feels his release.

"Sorry, Izzy," Alex says as he rolls off her and onto his side. "I'll make it up to you next time, I promise."

Chapter Four

"I would do almost anything for a second cup of this delicious latte," the lanky man with dreadlocks and a serious forearm tattoo says. He slurps back the last sip and runs his tongue along his top lip. "I haven't had coffee this good since I was in Panama. They harvest amazing coffee beans, but I couldn't find coconut or almond milk down there. They'd never even heard of it."

"Panama?" Isabella says, her curiosity piqued. "Where's that?"

"Seriously?" Isabella's customer says, leaning forward on his chair. "It's in Central America. It borders Costa Rica."

"Oh yeah, now that you say it, I think I read something about some scandal. The Panama Papers or something like that?" says Isabella.

"That's the place," her customer says with a chuckle. "But don't let that exaggerated story deter you from visiting Panama. I fell in love with it before I even landed at the airport, the view from the plane was so spectacular."

"That's saying a lot," Isabella says. "Hey, I'm on my break in fifteen minutes. I'd love to hear more if you don't mind sticking around. Second cup of kick-ass coffee on the house."

Over her break, Isabella and her customer, who tells her his name is Brian, become so engaged exchanging travel stories, Isabella loses track of time. He's as enthralled with her adventures in Thailand as she is with his in Panama.

"Wow, it's four o'clock already," Isabella says, glancing down while pressing the button on her phone. "I have to get back to work, but I really enjoyed our conversation. Maybe I'll see you around sometime?"

"Yeah, sure, I'd like that," Brian says. He slides a loonie under his plate and gets up to leave. "*Hasta luego*, as they say in Panama."

On her way home from work, Isabella can't stop thinking about Panama. She's so distracted that she almost walks right past her apartment building, her mind like a mouse in a maze.

"I'm home," Isabella calls out. She hangs up her coat on the hook by the door and enters the room, but Alex is nowhere in sight.

"I just got out of the shower," Alex says, emerging from the bathroom, stark naked. "Welcome home."

Alex's naked body is so enticing that Isabella forgets the conversation she wanted to have about her exchange with Brian. She takes off her clothes to join him.

After a blissful hour of lovemaking, they are lying in bed, when Alex unwraps himself from their embrace. He rolls over and reaches into his nightstand drawer to pull out a tightly rolled joint and lights it, then begins lamenting his current writing crisis.

"My editor says my main character isn't consistent and my plot line is erratic, but what does she know?" Alex sneers. "She's never even written a book, just likes to criticize those of us with the creativity and grit. Easy enough to judge from the bleachers, but harder to get into the ring."

"Maybe you should think about getting a new editor if that's how you feel?" Isabella says, a little bored with this tired conversation. All Alex seems to do lately is complain.

"Easy for you to say," Alex grumbles. He gets out of bed and grabs a sort-of-clean pair of underwear off the chair in the corner and pulls them on, then stands, one hand on his hip. "It was a fucking nightmare of hoop-jumping and ass-kissing just to get the editor I have. I'm not starting down that road again." He huffs, blowing out smoke through his nostrils. "I don't know why I try to get some support from you. You can't possibly relate, being a server and a yoga instructor."

"Wow, that stings," Isabella says. She doesn't bother to remind him that she is an artist too, just one who creates with pencil and paint, not words, and who hasn't had the recognition he has, with two books published already.

"Whatever, let's forget I said anything," Alex says, changing the subject abruptly. "I'm starving. What do you say I go pick up some sushi?"

"Yeah, sure," Isabella says. "I'm crazy for those vegan yam and avocado rolls."

"Oh yeah, I keep forgetting, you don't eat anything anymore that once had a face," Alex mocks her. He makes a face; his eyes open wide and then he bats his eyelids.

Isabella cringes and has to fight back tears that are welling in the corners of her eyes as she gets dressed. She swipes her eyes with the back of her sleeve and takes a deep breath.

"I'll get some cash," Isabella says as she reaches for her purse.

"Oh, put that away, it's all good; I've got this," Alex says, suddenly all honey-sweet again. He kisses her on the cheek and pinches her bum.

***

Over the next several weeks, Isabella attempts to have a meaningful conversation with Alex about travelling to Panama together, but somehow it never materializes. It seems like overnight, Alex's attentiveness shifted to total distraction. The long conversations they used to have feel like a distant dream, and more often than not, Alex is either working or out with Fahad and Cory.

Christmas comes and goes without much fanfare or celebration. Over the holidays, Alex moves deeper into his writing process and becomes more and more impatient, sharp, and critical of her. He still wants frequent sex, but even that has shifted. He's more demanding, sometimes a little rough, and often Isabella feels triggered and unsatisfied.

In the new year, Isabella can't shake the strong, persistent yearning she feels that it's time to make a change. She's just finished *The Alchemist* by Paulo Coelho and is inspired by Santiago's travel adventures. Just as he felt compelled to leave his flock of sheep in search of treasure, her soul calls her to switch things up, to give up her dual yoga and restaurant gigs, and seek something more fulfilling. Santiago's words, "it's the possibility of having a dream come true that makes life interesting," keep turning around in her head.

During her weekly FaceTime with her parents, Toni agrees that getting out of her relationship is past due, while Sylvie worries that picking up and moving on again will only bring more instability into Isabella's life.

While Alex is busy working on his novel, Isabella gets out her laptop and googles information about Panama. She finds an Airbnb in the hip-looking neighbourhood of Casco Viejo for a cheap price and books a plane ticket from Victoria to Panama, with a connection through Toronto, leaving the return date open. She gives notices at the café and yoga studio. The only thing she has left to do is break the news to Alex that she's leaving . . . and she's going alone. Part of her knows it will feel so good to finally get it off her chest. The other part of her is terrified of how he will react. She procrastinates until there are only two nights before her departure.

"How's it coming?" Isabella asks, referring to Alex's manuscript. He is bent over the computer at his desk, hard at work, as usual.

"Fine, fine," Alex says, clearly focused.

"I know you're busy, but I wonder if you could take a few moments to have a conversation with me?"

"Now?" Alex says, as if it's the most ludicrous request ever.

"Yeah, now," Isabella says. "I've been trying to tell you something important for weeks now, but you keep blowing me off."

Alex closes the lid of his computer and stands up, a dark shadow crossing over his face.

"Sounds serious."

"I suppose it is," Isabella says. "I've booked myself a plane ticket to Panama. I, I, just need to get away for a few weeks, clear my head, think about my future. I'm tired of drifting along and, like you've said more than once, I need to get a grown-up gig." Isabella rambles on.

"What?" Alex says. "A plane ticket? What the fuck are you talking about? You can't be serious. You're joking, right? I can't possibly take a vacation at this point in my book, so close to my deadline. You know that."

"Yeah, I do," Isabella says. "I wasn't suggesting you go. This is for me."

"What?" Alex says, his brows turning into a scowl. "That's even worse. I can't believe you're going to pick up and go, just like that." Alex snaps his fingers. "I thought we had something kinda serious developing."

"Of course, we do," Isabella says. "It's only for a few

weeks. It's perfectly normal for couples to take a break from one another now and again."

Alex looks so hurt, it's all Isabella can do not to go online and cancel her ticket. Yet she knows that a big part of her decision to leave is because of him, that she's exhausted by their volatile relationship.

"I just need some time away," Isabella continues. "I love you. But it's not like either one of us is ready to make a commitment. Besides, you're so busy, you'll barely notice I'm gone."

Isabella moves closer to him and wraps her arms around Alex's neck. He lowers his head to kiss her.

"Maybe you're right," Alex says. "I am super busy. Sometimes I feel guilty about how little time I have to spend with you. How long did you say you're going for? I might be near the end of my book by the time you get back."

"I left the return date open," Isabella confesses. "I wanted to wait and see if I like it there or not. I've got accommodation in the city for a week, but I'm thinking of exploring other areas of the country. I thought it best if I leave it open."

"That sounds like a rather stupid plan," Alex says. He pulls away and turns to step into the kitchen, grabs a beer from the fridge, and pops it open. "Isn't there a hefty fee for the freedom of not choosing a return date?"

"It was a little more," Isabella admits. "But less expensive than cancelling a flight or rebooking. Anyway, I don't know why you care, it's my money."

"You know what? You're right. I don't give a shit what

you do," Alex says, his mood shifting again. He turns his back to her and picks up the remote for the TV, then plops down on the couch with a huge sigh. While he scrolls through the channels, Isabella quietly grabs her purse and her sketchbook and slips out, careful to close the door softly behind her.

———

Isabella walks toward the Cowichan River. She's taken this path so many times, her body knows the way without her having to think. Her mind spins with anxious thoughts. She questions her decision, wondering if Alex is right, that going to Panama is a crazy idea. In the next instance, she feels certain that staying with Alex is even crazier, and definitely more of a problem than she's been willing to admit, even to herself. She's known for a long time she should end it, that his energy is toxic, his moodiness unsettling, but just when she starts to explore her options, he does something incredibly sweet, like make a candlelit dinner or bring her roses. She laughs to herself, remembering the time she came home from the yoga studio to find him cutting up vegetables to roast in the oven, naked under his chef's apron. As she was washing up to help out, he got a hard-on so massive, he almost singed himself. She'd bent down to kiss it better. She knows their awesome sex has been a reason why she's stayed. But what started off strong has only continued to deteriorate since then. She thinks again of Santiago and the intoxicating sentiment from *The Alchemist*: "When you want something with all your heart, that's when you are closest to the Soul of the World."

Isabella tucks away her dreams of connecting with her soul to discover her life purpose as she descends the uneven terrain, slick with newly fallen rain, to the river's edge. She pulls her coat collar up high and fastens the button at her neck to block the cool winter breeze, puffs of condensation forming on her lips. She takes a seat on a flattish rock and digs in her purse for her drawing pencil, then opens her sketchbook to a clean, crisp page.

More than an hour later, just as the sun is beginning to set, Isabella's drawing is complete. She feels lighter. She looks down and smiles. She has drawn an ocean scene, again. Another version of the photo of the ocean she has on her vision board, but this time she has added in two women, walking alongside the water, holding hands. The lines are blurred, the view from behind them, but she feels a tingling of her intuition, knowing one of the women is her, but the other woman is unknown. Somehow, she feels certain that she hasn't met her yet, but she will, perhaps in Panama. She closes her book and feels reassured. She can feel it in her bones. She's about to make a life-changing decision that's going to switch things up for her, in a positive way. Isabella stands up and brushes the dirt and dead leaves from her pants, then walks back home, a smile on her face.

When Isabella enters the apartment, she spots the note on the counter right away. She picks it up and reads it over.

"I decided to go meet up with Fahad and Cory at Craig's Brew Pub. Don't wait up."

That's par for the course, Isabella thinks to herself. She puts her things away and takes a long, hot shower, then crawls into bed.

Isabella dreams that she's walking along the ocean, holding hands with the woman in her sketch. She can't make out her face, but her energy is bright, confident and easy. In her dream, Isabella feels so happy and at peace.

She's wakened by the sound of Alex as he stumbles into the room, clearly wasted. She sneaks a look at her phone. It's two in the morning. Isabella pretends to be asleep while Alex brushes his teeth.

"Izzy?" Alex says softly. He shakes her shoulder as he crawls into bed beside her. "Are you awake? I want to be with you."

"Mmfh," Isabella mumbles. She rolls closer to the edge of her side of the bed, her back to him.

"Wow, how the tables have turned," Alex says. "It wasn't so long ago that you couldn't resist me."

Isabella doesn't bother to respond. She doesn't have the energy, and besides, what is there to say? It's true. Even their lovemaking has lost its appeal.

The sun is just beginning to peek in the bottom of the drawn shade when Isabella slips stealthily out of bed, careful not to wake up Alex, then tiptoes from the room. It's only just past six, but she doesn't mind. She puts on a pot of coffee, then gets out her computer to confirm her flight and accommodation information. She can hardly wait to leave. Only one more night. She has a final shift at the café, a yoga class, and a few last-minute errands to run.

When her shift at the cafe is over that afternoon, Isabella walks over to the drugstore to pick up some mosquito repellent, sunscreen, and a fresh tube of toothpaste. She grabs a box of granola bars and a bag of roasted tamari almonds—snacks for the plane—at the grocery store. She arrives at the yoga studio with just enough time to change into her gear and set up the space with her speaker, candles, and mat. She dims the lights to low and sits cross-legged, her wrists on her knees, her hands in *mudra* - the tips of her index fingers lightly touching the tips of her thumbs - as she waits for everyone to arrive.

As each person files in and takes a place, Isabella opens her eyes and greets them.

"*Namaste*, welcome to tonight's Mysore offering, and my final class. It has been such a gift to lead you in practice, but my heart is calling me to new things."

There is a murmur of disappointed voices. After ninety minutes of deep engagement, her focus on the primary asanas, her *pranayama*, and her fellow yogis, Isabella feels grounded and present. She's ready. All she has to do is finish packing. One more sleep.

After class, Brian, who has been attending her yoga classes regularly, offers to drive her to the airport, instead of Isabella catching the bus all the way to Victoria. He promises to arrive at her place by five the next morning. Everything is falling into place, and Isabella can feel the familiar tingle of excitement, deep in her belly.

When she gets home, she finds the apartment is empty, no sign of Alex, not even a note. Isabella feels grateful, and yet, she didn't want to leave with things so sticky. She finishes packing, then handwrites a long letter to say goodbye.

Dear Alex,

I'm sorry to leave like this, without so much as a face-to-face conversation or kiss goodbye, but maybe it's for the best. I've been feeling us drift apart, and I'm sure you must feel it too. Perhaps this time away will end up being a good thing for us, but I don't want to leave on a promise that I can't follow through with. You have your writing career, and even though I love teaching yoga, I know it isn't my life purpose. My heart is calling me to Panama, and I trust my intuition, that there is something there for me to discover. I know you don't believe in that kind of thing, but I do. Just another example of how we're so different. I love you, Alex, but in the end, I don't think love is enough. There needs to be compatibility and shared values in a committed relationship. I feel like we'll both end up having to make too many compromises and create too many regrets if we stay together. I don't want that for either of us.

I'm leaving early in the morning, and you will

most likely still be asleep. I wish you every happiness and success with this next book.

Love, Izzy

<hr>

Isabella sets her alarm for four o'clock and sets it to vibrate so as not to awaken Alex, then tucks it under her arm. As it is, the alarm doesn't have a chance to go off. Isabella is too excited to sleep, waking in fits and starts. At three thirty, after checking her phone for the thousandth time, she slips out of bed, Alex asleep beside her. She showers and gets ready in the bathroom. Her suitcase is packed and at the front door. After she locks up, she slips the key underneath the mat, then takes the stairs down and out the building entrance. Brian is waiting in his faded silver Volkswagen, the engine idling.

"Hey, let me get that for you," Brian insists, coming out of the car to join her on the sidewalk. He hefts her bag and sets it in the compact trunk.

"Thank you, Brian, you're a rock star," Isabella says.

Isabella turns to walk around to the passenger side when she hears Alex.

"What the hell do you think you're doing, just slipping out without saying goodbye?" Alex yells. He is already bounding down the front steps, clad only in his boxers, his hair in rooster tails that stick up at all angles.

"I, I'm sorry," Isabella says. "I wrote you a note."

"A note is all I get?" Alex says. He's standing beside

her now, the crumpled note in his hand. His face looks stricken. Then he sees Brian.

"And who the hell is this clown?" Alex says with a sneer.

"There's no need to be rude," Isabella says, mortified. "Sorry, Brian, just get in the car. I'll be right there."

Before she knows it, Alex grabs her and pulls her to him. He kisses her, hard, on the mouth. He pulls away, a maniacal look on his face, then walks around to the driver's side of Brian's car and shouts through the closed window.

"Just so you know, she's mine," Alex says. He kicks the bumper of the car and walks off in a huff, a cloud of heavy energy in his wake. "And Izzy, this isn't over; just you wait and see."

"I'm so sorry," Isabella says as she climbs in and closes the door. "It's embarrassing how possessive he can be."

"You're not kidding," Brian says. "I never realized it was so bad. I was feeling sorry for myself, that you're leaving without the chance for us to get to know one another better, but now I'm just relieved you've made this decision for yourself."

"Thank you so much, for your friendship and support," Isabella says. She moves her hand to pat his thigh, then changes her mind, not wanting to send a mixed message.

Isabella is quickly drawn away from her thoughts and into conversation as Brian tells her a story about the first time he hailed a taxi in Panama City, only to discover three other people squished in the back seat.

"So how does that work, sharing a cab with strangers all going to different locations?" Isabella asks.

"I know, it seems ludicrous, but somehow it works," Brian laughs. "Each person ends up going a little out of their way, but because the cost is shared, they don't seem to mind the extra time added. I don't like to quote stereotypes, but for the most part, the Panamanian people are way more chill than us Canadians."

"Well, I can't say that would suit me," Isabella says.

"Sounds like you need to work on your *mañana* attitude," Brian says. His infectious laugh alters the sour mood of Alex's outburst, and before Isabella knows it, they are through Goldstream and within the Greater Victoria limits.

"Nature is so amazing here," Isabella sighs, looking out the window on the final stretch, parallel to Elk Lake.

"Yeah, well, hold on to your socks, because in Panama, it's like nature on steroids," Brian says. "There's got to be over fifty shades of green, not to mention all the tropical birds and iguanas that you see commonly, even in the city. Granted, it's far more abundant as you move into the countryside and beach areas. Did you say you have an Airbnb in Casco?"

"Yeah, it looks like a very vibrant community, at least from the photos online."

"You won't be disappointed," Brian says. "And as an artist, I'm sure you'll appreciate the plethora of graffiti throughout the neighbourhood. And another great thing, you won't have to endure these chilly winter temperatures either. Being so close to the equator, it's hot all year there, with only two seasons: rainy and dry."

"I could talk with you for hours, Brian, but it looks like

we're almost there," Isabella says as Brian merges into the first of three complicated traffic circles before the airport.

"Me too," Brian says. "Let's stay connected, and please, if you need any advice along the way, just reach out."

"Thanks, I really appreciate you," Isabella says.

***

After saying goodbye to Brian and checking her bag at the Air Canada counter, Isabella makes her way to the small coffee shop on the other side of security and buys a tall soy latte.

It isn't long before she hears the boarding announcement. Isabella takes her seat near the back of the plane, squished between two large men. She doesn't feel like small talk, so she puts in her earbuds and presses play on a podcast, then closes her eyes. She ends up falling asleep until the flight attendant is tapping her shoulder.

"Time to put on your seat belt and return your seat to upright," the attendant says. "We're going to be descending shortly."

Isabella tries to peer out the window for a glimpse of the city. She's never been to Toronto before. But the guy in the window seat takes up too much space.

In the Toronto airport, Isabella has several hours to wait for her connecting flight. She decides to walk a few laps to stretch her cramped legs and then finds a quiet spot in a corner to practise a few yoga poses. On her tour of the impressive, modern terminal, she gets a kick out of the hall of echoes, then is thrilled when she finds a kiosk with vegan options. She purchases a few snacks and tucks them into her carry-on before she makes her way to the waiting area where there is internet access. She chooses a spot on a high bench, sort of like a bar stool, then reaches out to her parents for a FaceTime. She sends messages to Mark, Chuanna, Anita, and Brian, until it is time to board.

The flight isn't as full as the one before, and Isabella lucks out with a window seat near the front and no one in the two seats beside her. She looks around the bare-bones cabin, a little surprised to find there are no entertainment screens for an international flight.

"Hello, *bonjour*, and welcome on board today's Air Canada Rouge flight to Panama," the flight attendant announces. A large woman with curves to spare, Isabella is intrigued by her tattoo of a jellyfish on her collarbone. "For today's flight, we are pleased to offer our selection of in-flight movies that you can access through our app on your iPad or computer. If you don't have a device, we have iPads available for rent for a small fee of ten dollars. We'll be coming around shortly, so if you're interested, please have your credit card ready."

Isabella feels grateful that she has her laptop stowed in her carry-on and fishes it out to log in. There isn't much of a selection, but with a flight duration of five hours, Isabella chooses a drama based on real life featuring one of her favourite actresses, Jessica Chastain, called *Molly's Game*. It turns out to be a well-done film that captures Isabella's attention and has her rooting for the main character right to the last scene.

As she anticipated, the on-board menu features an uninspiring selection. Isabella is glad she thought to purchase snacks at the kiosk and chooses to stay hydrated, accepting water refills whenever offered. She rereads her favourite sections from *The Alchemist*.

Before she knows it, the seat belt light comes on and they are preparing to descend. Sunlight is filtering through the clouds outside her window, and Isabella looks out with anticipation, remembering how Brian described his experience.

Minutes later, the city comes into view. The skyscrapers that line the oceanfront sparkle in the late afternoon sun. It is a pristine and picturesque scene, and Isabella's heartbeat quickens.

The plane passes over the dark blue waters of the Pacific Ocean, then glides over lush green fields and a canopy of trees. The wheels hit the tarmac with a slight jolt and the aircraft slows down, the brakes on full, before meandering to the terminal where a team adjusts the ramp to fit over the plane's doorway. Isabella grabs her carry-on and purse and stands in the queue. She can already smell the hot, sticky air as she steps into the tunnel that leads to the arrivals level. There is a buzz of activity, a hot dog cart to her left, and a sign with an arrow pointing downstairs to the baggage claim and customs.

A long lineup snakes its way to the customs booths, five in a row. It takes about twenty minutes, but then Isabella is being waved over for her turn.

"*Buenos tardes*," the officer says. "*Bienvenido a Panamá; viene por negocios o placer?*"

Isabella isn't certain about the translation, but between her fluency in both Italian and French, she determines he is asking if her trip is for business or pleasure.

"*Placer*," Isabella answers.

"*Ah, muy bien*," the officer says with a smile, clearly pleased with her attempt to speak the language. "*Dirección de dónde se va a quedar?*"

"*Casco Viejo, gracias*," Isabella says.

The officer stamps her passport and points to the baggage claim area. Isabella walks down a wide hallway that features floor-to-ceiling wall art of local attractions, then enters the small baggage area with eight carousels. She finds the one from Toronto and waits patiently for her luggage, then goes through the final line where she presents her customs paperwork that she filled out on the plane. She steps through the sliding doors and walks to the left, a sea of faces all along the roped-off area, people holding signs and families scanning the passengers for their loved ones. Isabella walks past the car rental booths and follows the throng to the exit, then makes her way to the bus shelter to wait for the shuttle to Casco. She's sweating already and pulls her hoodie off to stuff it inside her backpack. She fans herself with her book, and takes pause for more gratitude when she enters the cool air-conditioned bus.

The bus is packed, a stranger in the seat beside her too close for comfort, but Isabella chooses to look out the window, lost in her own little world. The bus merges onto the Corredor Sur highway and drives along the ocean, the sun now set, the sky a charcoal grey. They pass what looks to her like low-income housing and then into the downtown, the tall buildings looming overhead. Traffic is a nightmare, and there are several tolls to pass through in the lane reserved for public transportation.

At the bus stop, Isabella disembarks and walks the short distance to her Airbnb accommodation using Google Maps, lugging her heavy suitcase. She notices a large wall of graffiti and guesses it is making a political statement of some kind, judging by the image of a man who looks to be a rebel with his fist in the air and the bubble-letter phrase in Spanish, *"no a la tirinia, si a la Liberta."* On the other side of the street, rows of shops selling everything from souvenirs to party supplies, clothing, and convenience food crowd together in a mishmash display of commerce.

Ten minutes later, Isabella is at her destination, passing through a worn wooden door that creaks onto a crumbled stairwell and going up one level. An old woman sits on a stool, stroking the fur of a cat curled up in her lap.

"Es usted, Isabella?" the woman asks. She gets up slowly. The cat jumps to the floor.

"Si, soy Isabella," Isabella confirms. *"Tienes la llave de mi cuarto?"*

The woman pulls a key out from the pocket of her smock and passes it to Isabella, then grabs a clipboard from a shelf on a bookcase and passes it to her to fill in her information. Isabella jots down her name and email address, then follows the woman as she shuffles along and leads Isabella to her room. She disappears back down the dark corridor as soon as Isabella unlocks the door and crosses the threshold.

With a click of the light switch, the studio apartment comes into view. It is even smaller than the four-bed room she'd shared at the hostel in Bangkok. At least that's how she remembers it. To her left, there is single daybed, covered in a clutter of cushions of varying fabrics and designs that looks anything but comfortable. Straight ahead is the scant living room, featuring one lumpy loveseat and a wooden coffee table that needs refinishing. Just behind, there is a kitchenette, which turns out to be little more than a bar fridge, hot plate, single-basin sink, and one tall, narrow cupboard with no doors. The mismatched pots and dishes are stacked in disorganized piles that look ready to topple over at any moment. She guesses the bathroom is to the right, where a curtain that looks like it's meant for showers is draped across the doorway, not quite reaching the floor. A rusty fan with peeling paint hums on a table, in the centre of it all.

Isabella sets her heavy traveller's backpack on the floor by the bed and sighs. *I'll give this place a good scrub and it will do just fine,* she thinks to herself, her last thought before she drifts off into the exhausted sleep of travellers.

Chapter Five

Isabella wakes up to the sound of Latin music drifting through her partially open window, the room black as the depths of a deep cave. She yawns and stretches, then takes her phone out of her purse to check the time. The neon numbers show 8:11. Isabella is surprised she's been conked out so solidly for almost an hour.

Isabella gets out of bed and pulls back the gauzy curtain to peer out the living room window onto the street below. Rows of mini twinkle lights drape amongst clothes lines, colourful shirts and dresses hung row after row. A group of children are crouched together under a street light, playing some kind of game; rocks and sticks are in an unusual formation in the centre of their circle. Isabella's tummy rumbles as unknown, enticing, aromas greet her, and she inhales deeply.

Isabella doesn't bother to flick on the light switch. She slides into her sandals while combing her hair with her fingers, then grabs her purse and walks out the door, closing it behind her and locking it with her key. She's intent on finding a cheap place for dinner, and perhaps a grocer after, to stock up on a few basics for the days ahead.

Out in the street, one of the children gathered in the circle sees her and runs over, holding out her hand.

"*Me regala una moneda?*" the little girl asks, her face streaked with dirt, her hair pulled back in a messy ponytail.

"*No, lo siento,*" Isabella says. She pats the girl's head, hoping she will take no for an answer without too much fuss. Brian had warned her that if she gave money to every local looking for a donation from what they perceive to be a rich gringo, her savings wouldn't last long. The girl's smile turns into a frown of disappointment, but it returns as soon as she skips back to rejoin her friends.

Around the corner, Isabella takes another deep inhale. She can smell the salty ocean. The wide cobbled road leads to an intersection where Isabella turns right. She walks towards the waterfront, then enters the next restaurant she sees that looks like a local establishment, a lit-up Panama hat shining brightly over the entrance.

"*Buenas noches,*" an older woman, apparently the hostess, says. She has a tired, unenthusiastic expression, her voice monotone. "*Una mesa?*"

"*Si, gracias,*" Isabella says. She's led to a small table in the corner, covered in a woven tablecloth in a bright array of colours. The woman hands her a stained paper menu and disappears, only to return moments later with a silver water jug and a glass.

"*Le gustaría un vaso con agua?*"

Isabella says yes and takes a huge sip of her water before she sets the glass down on the table. As she swallows the cool liquid, she wonders if the water is safe, or contaminated like it was in Thailand, but it's too late for second guesses. She studies the small menu, all in Spanish, then chooses what she hopes is a dish of local cuisine: beans, rice, and fried yuca, for only five dollars. *It's so convenient that they use American currency here,* Isabella thinks to herself, remembering how confusing it was to convert baht in her head. Everything seems to dredge up old memories. She thinks of the night in Ko Samet and a shiver runs down her spine.

"*Tiene frio?*" asks the server, who has materialized out of nowhere again.

"*No, gracias, estoy bien,*" Isabella says, hoping she is using the proper Spanish words to convey that all is well. She points to the menu to indicate her order, then sits in quiet contemplation, observing the other patrons. They all look Panamanian, not like tourists, despite it being a diverse group of men and women of different skin tones; to her ear, they all seem to have a similar accent. Isabella signs onto the restaurant Wi-Fi, the password written on a plastic laminated sign that is taped to the wall, then turns on her phone to discover a message from Alex.

I must have read your note a hundred times. I can't believe you're considering ending our relationship. I love you, Izzy. I was seriously thinking of taking things further, saving for a ring and everything. I know I can be a little moody, but it's all part of the introverted author gig. I can change. I want to change, for you. For us. Please, please, give me another chance? Take this time to cool off and explore Panama, as long as you need, but don't give up on us, okay?

He adds a bunch of heart emoticons after his message. Isabella feels conflicted, but then her meal is delivered to her in record speed, not more than ten minutes after she ordered it. She's too hungry to give much pause for thought and devours the simple but satisfying fare, scraping every last grain of rice with her fork. As soon as she finishes, Alex's words return to swim in her head, in a confusion of feelings.

The next morning, Isabella awakens refreshed, though a little stiff in her lower back and neck, all thoughts of Alex forgotten. She heads into the bathroom to take a hot shower. It takes a few moments for the water to heat up and it turns cold halfway through, when the shampoo is still lathered in her hair, then scalding hot, just as she is rinsing the soap off her body. She is reminded, again, of her time in Thailand.

Isabella walks barefoot into the kitchen, cringing at the feel of sticky grime on her feet. She's grateful that she found a few things at the Rey market, including a bottle of cleaning liquid. She hunts around for a kettle to make instant coffee, but finding none, resorts to boiling water in a silver pot on the hot plate. She chooses one of four mismatched ceramic mugs and scoops instant coffee granules into it, then pours in the hot water and gives it a stir. She takes a sip, longing for a dollop of coconut milk, the hot liquid bitter on her tongue.

After a simple breakfast of peanut butter on toast,

Isabella pours a generous amount of all-purpose cleaner into the sink and begins to scrub down all the surfaces, including the floors. By mid-morning she's finished and ready to go exploring, her sketchbook and pencils tucked into her purse.

The neighbourhood has a whole new vibe in the light of day. The streets are quiet, only some piles of garbage and empty cans and bottles here and there to indicate the vibrant energy of the night before.

She hasn't been walking long when Isabella stumbles onto an impressive church, white stucco gleaming in the sun, with massive wooden doors at least ten feet high, perhaps more. She takes the cement steps to the entrance and pushes the door.

Inside, it's dark and cool. Isabella is transported back to her childhood, to the church she attended growing up, although this one is far more grandiose, with its elaborate stained glass windows lining each wall of the sanctuary, the ceilings that seem as high as the heavens, and the richly sculpted dark wood furnishings. The familiarity comforts her, and she takes a seat on a smooth wooden pew, closes her eyes, and says a prayer. She picks up a Bible from the shelf in front of her and thumbs through the pages. She reads one of her favourite passages from Matthew 6:26: "Do not worry about your life. . . . Is not life more than food, and the body more than clothes? Look at the birds of the air; they do not sow or reap or store away in barns, and yet your heavenly Father feeds them."

Isabella closes the book. This particular teaching from Jesus resonates with her even more in this moment than it has before because of its reassurance that she is safe and protected, that she doesn't need to worry. She feels lighter as she rises from the spot and rummages in her wallet for a dollar bill, then places it in the collection tray before taking a tour of the temporary haven and heading back out into the heat.

———

Over the course of the morning and into the early afternoon, Isabella discovers so many objects of beauty, she knows she won't be spending much time inside her cramped, dingy rental. She loves the feel of the sun and the humidity on her skin. She takes photos of the graffiti, and selfies outside market stalls and shops. She finds her way to the walking path that begins at the bottom of a set of stairs at the entrance to Casco and leads under a bridge to a huge park that sprawls for miles along the oceanfront.

Families are congregated at the swing sets and young men are kicking a ball around in an open field. Isabella passes two couples playing tennis, then finds a bench under a massive canopy tree that provides protection from the sun. There is an impressive, expansive view of the ocean and Casco in the distance. Isabella retrieves her sketchbook with enthusiasm. As she draws, time seems to stand still, she's so immersed in the process. With each pencil stroke, she relaxes into her comfort zone. She draws a collage of images from her morning walk: the church doors, the graffiti art, and the view from her park bench. The energy of Panama feels captured on the page, a crazy beautiful mix of freedom and tranquility she's never felt before.

"*Hola,*" says one of the soccer players Isabella recognizes from earlier as he takes a seat on the bench next to her, a nice-looking boy-man, perhaps eighteen or so. "*¿De dónde eres?*"

"*Lo siento, hablo poco español,*" Isabella says, unable to recall what *donde* means. She is about to close her journal when he reaches out his hand, grazing her forearm.

"*No lo hagas,*" he says emphatically, shaking his head. "*Es muy bueno.*"

Isabella knows enough Spanish to gather the overly confident young man is saying he likes her drawing. She suspects he is interested in more than her sketches, that he is likely only flirting, and even though she would like to meet some new people eventually, she's not in the mood for games.

"*Gracias,*" Isabella says, closing her book. She stands up and tucks her pad into her purse. "I was just about to leave."

"*¿Hasta luego?*" the soccer player says, looking deflated, but still determined.

"No, *adios,*" Isabella says, in the most assertive voice she can muster.

———

On the walk back to her rental, Isabella stops at the fish market. She purchases a freshly caught, whole sea bass, ignoring her commitment to being vegan, to embrace being in a city on the ocean. The large, full-breasted woman behind the counter wraps the fish in a paper bag and scoops some ice into a plastic Ziploc bag to keep it cool. Isabella thanks her, hoping the ice won't completely melt before she gets back. She wonders, as she walks home, if she even remembers how to cook fish; it's been so long.

Well, I wanted to step out of my comfort zone and spice things up, so I guess I'm doing just that, Isabella thinks to herself. She smiles as she takes the steps to her room two at a time. She opens the paper package, salvaging her dinner just before the last of the ice has disappeared. Her stomach does a bit of a tumble when she slices the head off the fish and discards it in the garbage under the sink. But she's seen her mother fillet a fish enough times to know the drill. Soon the apartment is filled with the pungent scents of sea bass, lemon, dill, and butter.

***

The next day, Isabella is at her neighbourhood coffee house, browsing the internet, when she notices a posting on LinkedIn for an English instructor. *It's so creepy how the internet knows I'm in Panama,* Isabella thinks to herself. She's intrigued by the possibility, and although she imagines her TESL course isn't going to get her the position, she decides she has nothing to lose by submitting an application. She writes a message and attaches her CV, then releases her intention to God.

Isabella is surprised when she finds a reply in her inbox the next day, inviting her for an interview. She stresses and fusses about what to wear, having no idea what the protocol is for such things in Panama. She ends up choosing a flowery sundress with a high-ish neckline that flows to her knees and the only pair of somewhat dressy closed-toe sandals she owns.

The bus ride to the neighbourhood of El Carmen is a bit of an affair, Isabella not knowing the fare or having the correct change, and unsure which stop is the right one for her connection. But she left plenty of time built into her schedule for delays and ends up arriving at the bus stop a block from the school with half an hour to spare. She stops to purchase a bottled water from a convenience store.

"*Me presta el baño, por favor?*" Isabella asks the cashier, hoping to quickly freshen up, the heat and humidity creating rivulets of sweat that trickle down her spine.

"*Sí,*" the cashier says, pointing to the back of the store.

The washroom is the size of a small closet and not very clean, but Isabella takes advantage of the cool water running from the rusty taps and the stiff paper towels. She dabs at her eyes, her melted mascara creating black smudges. She brushes her hair and applies a little more lip gloss. She tries to smooth out the wrinkles from her dress, then goes back outside and makes her way to the ESL Language Centre.

"Good morning, I'm here for an interview, for the English teacher position," Isabella says with a smile at the receptionist's counter immediately inside the entrance. "I believe Ms. Gomez is expecting me?"

"Yes, she is," the stone-faced receptionist says. "Please, take a seat, and Ms. Gomez will be right with you."

Isabella waits on one of the four uncomfortable plastic chairs that line the adjacent wall. She doesn't feel nervous at all, just hopeful. While daydreaming on the bus, she decided that she wants to get to know Panama better and find a more appropriate place to live, but in order to do that, she'll need to have an income.

"Hello, thank you for coming," Ms. Gomez says, striding toward Isabella, her red manicured nails, long and filed into points, catching Isabella's eye as she extends her hand in greeting. "Please, follow me to my office."

Ms. Gomez leads Isabella down a hall, her skin-tight black pencil skirt restricting her gait. She leads Isabella to a small office without a window and indicates the chair by the desk.

"Please, take a seat," Ms. Gomez says as she does the same. She looks over at her computer screen. "I see here that you not only have your international TESL requirements but also a full two years of experience, along with a glowing referral, from your time teaching English in Thailand. I must say, I never imagined such a unique resumé. And you're from Canada?"

"Yes, I do, and I am," Isabella says. "I loved Thailand,

and in fact, I might still be there if it hadn't been for my father's illness."

"Ah, yes, family is the most important of all," Ms. Gomez says, clucking her tongue. "I hope your father is okay?"

"Yes, thank you for asking," Isabella says.

"I see here that you also speak some French and Italian?" Ms. Gomez continues. "I must say, that is very impressive."

"Well, it's not as impressive as it sounds," Isabella laughs. "My parents are both immigrants. My mother was born in France, my father in Italy, so I grew up with three languages being spoken and mingled together."

"That will be very helpful for you here, I'm sure," Ms. Gomez says. "If you haven't discovered for yourself already, the American influence in Panama, going all the way back to the building of the canal, has resulted in all kinds of interesting slang. And Spanish, Italian, and French are all Latin derivatives. Here at the school, we are committed to providing our students with a formal American English course of studies. Many Panamanians are quite ambitious, and to be successful in today's global economy, English is certainly a huge asset."

"Yes, I agree, and I feel so fortunate that it is one of my first languages, and of course the language I learned as part of my own education," Isabella says. "By the way, your English is very good. Did you learn at a young age as well?"

"Ah, yes, I too am one of the lucky ones," Ms. Gomez smiles. "My father was determined I have the best private school education. I think he had grander plans for me than the director of an English school, but it is my passion. I like to follow my intuition, and I feel a very positive energy from you, Isabella. I'd like to offer you the position. Are you able to start in one week?"

"Absolutely, and thank you so much. This is fabulous," Isabella says, rising from her chair to shake Ms. Gomez's hand.

"There will be a two-week trial period, and if it turns out to be a good fit, we'll offer you a permanent contract and help you sort out the paperwork for a work permit."

———

Isabella practically floats across the tile floors as she leaves the building. She can hardly wait to find an apartment and embrace her new life. The first thing she does when she gets back to her room is message Mark.

I got the job! Can you believe it? I'm so excited! I start in one week. I will let you know the deets then. Take care, my friend. I hope you are well, xxoo Izzy

———

Things continue to unfold in an energy of flow, despite daily messages from Alex begging her to return to Duncan, which she chooses to ignore. On a flyer taped to the bus shelter, Isabella stumbles upon an advertisement for a month-to-month sublet in the central neighbourhood of El Cangrejo, just one neighbourhood over from her new job.

The studio apartment is in a modest older building, a huge upgrade from the Airbnb, and much cheaper. The space feels larger than it is, due in part to two large portrait windows with sand-coloured sheers that let the light in. The walls have been painted white, and the compact kitchen has a full-size stove and fridge, with bright turquoise cupboards accented by shiny silver handles. It comes furnished, albeit sparsely, but Isabella prefers the minimalist look to clutter. She doesn't hesitate to grab the opportunity and agrees to sign the landlord's month-to-month lease at the end of the brief tour.

The first Sunday after her move, Isabella dials up her parents for their weekly FaceTime and surprises them with a video tour of her new digs.

"It looks lovely, *mi Cara*," Toni says, all smiles. "A huge improvement from the temporary place you took, what it's called again, an Air Baby?"

"Oh, Papa," Isabella laughs. "You need to get into the twenty-first century. They're called Airbnbs, and they're very popular. People rent out their space so travellers can have more room for less money than a hotel. It's a great concept."

"Well, your father and I don't plan on staying in anyone else's 'digs' as you call them," Sylvie says.

"We're both so proud of you, getting hired for this teaching position," Toni says, changing the subject.

"Yes, we are," Sylvie agrees. "But I must say, the more settled you get down there, the more I worry I'll never see you again. It's been way too long already since you've been home."

"Now, Maman, don't worry so much," Isabella says, trying to lighten the mood. "I miss you too. But now, with this new job, I should be able to save enough money for airfare home to come and visit you, sooner rather than later."

"Oh now, that would be the best news," Toni says. "In the meantime, these FaceTime chats are such a great way to feel connected."

"Yes, they are," Isabella smiles. "I love you. I suppose I should get to bed so I can have a good night's sleep before my first day of work. We'll FaceTime again next week, same time." She blows them a kiss and signs off.

Isabella purchases a few decorative items—cushions and a framed mirror—to make her space feel more like home. She explores her new community and finds coffee shops and bars that are always full, where expats and locals alike mingle over coffee and beer.

Her first day of work, Isabella is introduced to the other teachers before her shift. They each have their own station, a crescent-moon-shaped table that seats three students in a semicircle around the teacher. Each student is at a different place in the levelled course, and Isabella rotates through one-on-one instruction with each of her students over their one-hour study period, with very little support or assistance. She remembers how stressed out she felt when she was left to figure things out on her own during her first teaching assignment in Thailand, and feels grateful that the experience taught her how to be adaptable and think on her feet.

After five hours and five groups of three students, one right after the other, Isabella is completely drained and ready for some relaxation. She's heading toward the staff room to collect her belongings when she hears her name.

"*Hola*, Isabella, *bienvenida*," one of the other teachers says, an attractive woman Isabella guesses to be Panamanian. "My name is Catalina. How did you enjoy your first day?"

"I have to admit, it was intense," Isabella says with a laugh. "But honestly, it was so engaging, the time just flew by. I didn't realize how exhausted I was until it was over."

"That's par for the course," Catalina laughs along, a smile that reaches her gorgeous eyes, framed dramatically by thick fake eyelashes. "I'm glad you had a positive experience. I was getting worried that if Ms. Gomez didn't find a replacement for the last guy who didn't survive the trial period, I'd be stuck taking on an extra workload indefinitely. Have you been in Panama long?"

"No, actually, not quite two weeks now," Isabella says. She can't help but feel something familiar about her co-worker, but she can't quite place it. "I love it here. I hope I pass the trial period. The people are so friendly, and the city is amazing. I never anticipated it would be so modern, despite a friend back home giving Panama glowing reviews."

"Trust me, it isn't all as clean and safe as this neighbourhood," Catalina says. "And some of the locals can be either disgruntled at their lot in life or, in the case of many of the young men, too cocky for their own good."

"I'm afraid I have been on the receiving end of some unwelcome catcalls and whistles," Isabella agrees, shrugging her shoulders. "But it all seems to be in good fun. At least I haven't had any problems so far."

"That's good to hear," Catalina says. "I don't mean to sound judgmental or dissuade you, but the men here can act, how shall I say it . . . entitled?"

"That doesn't sound critical at all, more like friendly advice," Isabella says. "I imagine someone as gorgeous as you must be a prime target. I appreciate you taking the time to share your insights with me. If there's one thing I've learned, it's that sometimes I can be too trusting in human nature."

"I'd be happy to talk more, maybe over dinner," Catalina says. "What do you say, are you hungry?"

"Famished," Isabella says, just as her stomach growls loudly to confirm. "And I'd love some company for a change."

Catalina has what she calls her "vintage" red Kia parked in the staff parking lot behind the building. Isabella hops into the passenger side after shuffling the stack of miscellaneous items on her seat into the back. There is a cross dangling from the rear-view mirror, along with a crystal tied to a scarlet silk ribbon. Catalina merges into the heavy traffic, then navigates the roads with an easy confidence.

"One of my favourite restaurants nearby serves authentic Lebanese food. It's run by an Israeli family I've gotten to know. They're the real deal. Do you like Mediterranean food?" Catalina asks as she shifts into second gear to enter a travel circle.

Isabella glances down at Catalina's hand on the gear and has a flash of the woman in her dream. She feels her intuition burning, excited at the possibility that she and Catalina are destined to become good friends.

"Oh, I go crazy for shawarma, pita bread, and hummus," Isabella says, coming out of her reverie to answer Catalina's question. "I was eating totally vegan back in Canada, but it doesn't seem a very popular choice here."

"Oh God, say it isn't true!" Catalina says with drama, reaching her free hand to her forehead. "We Panamanians don't understand this American privilege of not eating meat, many of us having to settle for daily rice and beans because we can't afford it. I've known some people who've even stooped to cook up an iguana here and there, just for the thrill of the taste."

"Ew, that sounds disgusting," Isabella says, making a dour face.

"Well, it's all just cultural, what you grow up with, I think," Catalina says. "Eating meat is just part of eating a varied diet. There's no judgment. I mean, do you think sloths are somehow superior to jaguars because they're naturally vegetarian?"

"Well, no," Isabella flounders. "I suppose not, but they aren't conscious beings; we are."

"Oh, you're one of those New Age spiritualists?" Catalina teases.

"Truthfully, I'm not really against eating meat in principle," Isabella says, a serious tone in her voice. "My parents are both huge meat eaters and I grew up eating it without qualms. It's more about how we treat animals these days, with practices like factory farming, that I really object to. And it's not always easy to discern."

"I must admit, I don't agree with forcing animals to live in crowded conditions either," Catalina says. "That's one of the advantages of living in a country that's not so advanced. We still do things so old-fashioned here. Most farmers raise a variety of crops and animals. Chickens literally run around free, no cages or coops. Anyway, enough of that. Have you been to the countryside yet?"

"No, I haven't," Isabella says. "But I'd love to."

"Maybe we can go together sometime?" Catalina says. She pulls over and parks the car. "C'mon, the restaurant is just a few blocks up this street."

———

Before Isabella knows it, she and Catalina have become close friends. Catalina is easy to be with, not to mention funny and intelligent. They hang out almost every night after work at one or the other's apartment, and most weekends as well.

One Friday after work, near the end of February, Catalina comes over to Isabella's for dinner and a Netflix movie. Isabella is preparing a local dish called sancocho soup, thanks to Catalina, who provided the recipe.

"Remember when we first met and you told me that I really should head out of the city, into the countryside, to get a different perspective?" Isabella asks, stirring freshly chopped garlic into a pot where a whole chicken simmers.

"Yeah, sure," Catalina replies lazily, sprawled out on the area rug, thumbing through glossy magazines.

"Well, what do you say we plan a weekend getaway?" Isabella says. She puts the lid on the tin pot and turns the burner to low, then goes over and plops down beside Catalina on the floor.

"Yeah, sure, I think it's a great idea. Let's sort out all the arrangements for next weekend. Should we see what we can find in Coronado? It's a favourite destination for locals, especially rich Panamanians, but I know a few people who rent out their space for a decent price."

"Okay, I'll see if there's anything on Airbnb," Isabella says. "And I know you warned me, when I asked about those crazy-looking converted school buses I've seen around, that they're stuffy, stupid hot, and unreliable, but I'm just dying to experience a road trip on a *diablo rojo*, as you call them."

"If you insist," Catalina says, rolling her eyes. "But don't cry to me after about what a bad idea it was. I'll only say I told you so."

Chapter Six

The first weekend of March, Isabella and Catalina head out Friday night, as soon as their shifts are over, their bags already packed and stowed in the staff room. It is a bit of a hike along the choked artery of Via España to the city's main bus terminal, but the city lights and Catalina's confidence guide the way.

Rows of converted school buses are plastered in visually busy artwork that has Isabella captivated. Catalina finds their bus, with the hand-painted Coronado sign propped on the dash. On the side of the bus Isabella spies a drawing of an animated female warrior, bare-breasted, wearing nothing but a loincloth, wielding a sword. She's instantly propelled back in time, to when she sketched similar drawings in the pages of her sketchbook, after the night in Ko Samet. She shakes away the disturbing memories with a shrug, shifting her attention to the cartoon depictions of Sylvester and Tweety Bird, from the bygone days of Looney Tunes. She reads script advertisements for local restaurants and shops, interspersed amongst the graffiti art, as loud reggae music blares from the speakers that dangle from each of the four corners of the bus.

Isabella follows Catalina up the three steps and inserts her four quarters into the slot of the payment box at the front, then smiles politely at the driver, a man who looks to be in his late forties, wearing a wrinkled white tank top and faded jeans. He smiles back with a lewd grin and an enthusiastic, "*Bienvenidos*," followed by a low whistle. Isabella chooses to ignore him, but Catalina turns around to give him the finger. They push down the aisle, past a young woman dressed in skin-tight jeans, a middle-aged woman in a floral dress wedged in between stuffed paper grocery bags, and an old man, a wide-brimmed hat pulled down over his eyes, asleep despite the noise and confusion.

"I'm already questioning my decision," Isabella says loudly, the stuffy air settling in her lungs.

"I tried to warn you," Catalina says. She takes the next available seat and squishes in next to the window while Isabella sits next to her on the aisle.

"Oh, look at the bubble lights all along the roof," Isabella says, her neck tilted back, her eyes aglow. "This feels more like a roving party than a means of transportation."

As if on cue, the guy across from them in khaki shorts, hairy legs sprawled out in the aisle, lights a joint. Then the driver starts the bus, and with a loud grinding of the gears, a cross between a growl, rattle, and rumble that erupts over the blare of the music, they pull out of the station and onto the busy street.

The drive to Coronado takes much longer than it normally would by car because the bus makes several stops along the way and the traffic on a Friday night is bumper to bumper. At one point the driver gets out and takes a piss on the side of the road, Isabella inadvertently getting flashed as she faces Catalina, with a view out the window, illuminated by the light of a nearby *casa*.

"Ew, that's just not right," Isabella says, averting her gaze.

"Hey, c'mon, it's a free show," Catalina teases, turning her head to see what Isabella is referring to. "Did you see the size of it? Maybe you should give him your number. After all, he was ogling you."

"Oh, please," Isabella groans. "He's old, and besides, I've had it with men. I'm still trying to get rid of my last boyfriend, remember? He's so full of himself, he won't let go. Even though I broke up with him more than two months ago, he still sends me messages almost every day."

"Yeah, well, it's tough to be so desirable," Catalina says, giving Isabella a playful nudge on the shoulder.

"That's the conductor speaking to the choir," Isabella says. "You are the most beautiful woman I've ever known. Which reminds me, I've been meaning to ask you, what is your background anyway?"

"My parents are both of mixed race, which I suppose makes me a complete mishmash," Catalina says. "Mamá is from Columbia, but she is part Colombian, part Indigenous, of the Guna tribe. Papá grew up here in Panama, but his father is originally from Jamaica and *mi abuela* is an immigrant from France, whose father came over to help build the first attempt at the canal, if you can believe it."

"Wow, that is such a cool history," Isabella says. "My *maman* is from France too. Do you know whereabouts your—how do you say it in Spanish? *Abuela*? Where in France is she from?"

"I can't say I recall. I never met her. Oh, hey, there's the sign for Chame. We're almost there," Catalina says, pointing out the window to the brightly coloured letters, standing four feet high on the grass adjacent to a pedestrian bridge and lit up by a pot light planted in the ground.

Twenty minutes later, the bus is pulling up to the stop outside the Coronado Village shopping centre on the right side of the highway. Catalina and Isabella disembark and stand off to one side.

"Well, we made it, all in one piece," Isabella laughs. "But it was touch and go when we ploughed through those gigantic potholes near Gorgona."

Catalina nods in agreement, then puts two fingers in her mouth and whistles, a piercing shriek. A car that looks like it should be towed to the junkyard pulls up to the curb. Catalina conducts a quick exchange in rapid Spanish that Isabella can't follow and then tells her to hop in.

The rusted-out vehicle smells of dirty feet and old cigarette butts. The floor mat is missing, as is any sign of seat belts. Isabella tries to hold her breath, grateful that the apartment Catalina booked is only a ten-minute drive down Avenida Roberto Eisenmann. They rattle their way through the security check, the green sign that reads, "*Coronado es Vida*" on the right, lit up by a spotlight planted in the grass, then down a few blocks past Picasso, a local restaurant and bar, where there is a party in full swing.

"That place looks like fun," Isabella says. "Maybe we can go there later, for a late supper?"

"Yeah, Picasso is a landmark, known for good times. They support local musicians and run community events too," Catalina says. "But if you want really amazing food, we should go to Luna Rossa for authentic Italian cuisine that's to die for, and to Picasso after, for drinks and dancing."

"Oh, you've been here before?" Isabella says.

"So many times, I've lost count," Catalina laughs. "Oh, there's our place." Catalina pokes the driver on the shoulder to pull over, the house number barely visible in the soft glow of the lantern outside the front door.

"*Gracias*," Isabella says, as she hands over a five-dollar bill before turning to Catalina. "I'll get this."

"Okay," Catalina agrees. "I'll get it next time."

The room Catalina has rented is a few doors down from a huge condominium tower, just blocks from the ocean, in an old house that has been converted into four units. The owner has left the key under a ceramic flowerpot by the door, as agreed.

Inside, the air is dank and hot. The first thing Isabella does is locate the switch for the air conditioner and turn it on full blast. It creaks and croaks in protest as she walks into the living room and opens the window a crack to let some fresh air in. The kitchen is brightly decorated, with an eclectic array of multicoloured knick-knacks: ceramic parrots adorning the walls, bowls of glass fruit, wooden sculptures, and fake plastic flowers in a vase.

"Hmm, the owner said it was a two-bedroom, but I only see one," Catalina says after a quick tour of the space.

"Maybe this old lumpy couch is a pullout?" Isabella wonders aloud. But upon investigation, it proves to be only a couch. "Oh, well, I don't mind sleeping together, do you?"

"No, although it might be hot and crowded. It is only a double," Catalina says, her hands on her shapely hips.

"We'll just have to make the best of it," Isabella says. "But first things first. Let's change out of these sweaty clothes and walk over to Luna Rossa. I'm starving."

Luna Rossa is packed, inside the restaurant and on the spacious patio too. The friendly hostess who greets them manages to locate a table for two in the outside dining area. The thatched roof has mini lights draped all around the perimeter as well as wrapped around the wooden beams and columns.

After being poured tall glasses of water and given menus, Isabella reads through the extensive options.

"I can hardly decide what to choose," Isabella says. "Everything sounds so amazing. Do you have a favourite dish?"

"I love the grilled octopus," Catalina says. "But I imagine that's too much of a stretch for you, after so recently adding chicken to your diet. The owner is Italian, but she serves a mean Greek salad, with creamy feta that is out of this world. She imports the buffalo mozzarella from Italy too, if you fancy caprese. We'll probably come back here again, so you can try something else then."

"The Greek salad it is," Isabella says, closing the menu. "And I think I'll order a glass of white wine too, unless you want to share a bottle?"

"No, *gracias*, I'm dying for a tall, cold *cerveza*," Catalina says.

After an incredible meal that Isabella suggests would pass her mother's high standard, the girls walk hand in hand up the road to Picasso, where the music is pumping out into the street and the sounds of people having a great time permeate the night air.

"Too bad there's no live band tonight," Catalina says as they walk up and she spots a DJ. Just then, the owner of the bar walks onto the stage and grabs the microphone.

"As promised, karaoke is all set to resume in just a few minutes, so all you wannabes out there, it's your time to shine."

"Oh, God, not karaoke," Catalina sighs, rolling her

eyes. "I swear every second Panamanian you meet wants to be a rock star, and the expats are almost as bad."

"I happen to love it," Isabella says with mock indignation. "It was all the rage in Bangkok too. I'm definitely going to be one of the wannabes."

"Are you serious?" Catalina laughs.

"Totally," Isabella admits.

"Okay, then I'll clap the loudest to cheer you on," Catalina says. They find a table near the road and take a seat.

The atmosphere of fun expands as Catalina and Isabella switch from wine and beer to margaritas, then shots of tequila. They stay until closing, Isabella getting into a bit of a friendly competition with a middle-aged expat who is a huge Bruce Springsteen fan.

"Lucky for us, our accommodation is so close," Isabella says, slurring her words a little as she weaves down the road, her arm around Catalina's waist.

—

Isabella wakes up with a huge hangover. She squints open her eyes and sees Catalina's arm draped over her. She can feel her, stark naked and spooned up behind her. She feels a shock of sensual longing. Her nipples harden at the feel of Catalina's full breasts pressed up against her back. *What the hell?* She stifles a groan, totally surprised to find herself aroused. She's never felt anything sexual toward a woman before and feels completely confused. She pulls away, brushing off her feelings as after-effects of the alcohol. She slips quietly from the bed and tiptoes down the hall to take a shower. The jets of water pelt against her breasts. She reaches her hand between her legs and strokes herself, the picture of Catalina's naked body in her mind as she moans and climaxes, all the while wondering what on earth has caused this sudden, unexpected shift.

When she emerges from the steamy washroom, naked, with the terry towel wrapped turban-style around her head, she almost bumps right into Catalina.

"Good morning," Isabella says. "I didn't know you were up."

"I'm dying to go pee," Catalina says, doing a little jig for emphasis while scooting past her. "I was going to barge in on you if you didn't come out soon."

"Oh, sorry," Isabella blushes, ripe with her recent activity. "Go ahead, it's all yours."

———

After drying off and throwing on a sundress over her bikini, Isabella pokes about the kitchen cupboards, hoping to find some coffee, still unnerved. There is a Mr. Coffee machine on the counter, but she doesn't see any coffee, only a few half-used spices and a fingerprint-smudged bottle of olive oil. She opens the fridge, and there, on the top shelf, is the trademark yellow-and-brown Duran coffee package. She fills the coffee machine compartment with water and scoops in two large spoonfuls of the coarse grinds into the filter, then plops down in one of the two rattan chairs in the living area to wait for it to brew.

"Phew, that's better," Catalina says as she emerges from the bathroom. "I had one hell of a full bladder."

"Yeah, we knocked back a few, that's for sure," Isabella says, her head throbbing.

"I had a great time," Catalina says, taking a seat on the other chair. "I think you win the prize for the most fun friend. I love how we can go from just shooting the shit to discussing the big issues in a split second."

"Me too," Isabella says. "My life seems to be in flow ever since I arrived here, what with scoring the great gig at the ESL centre, finding an apartment for such a good price in a convenient location, and then meeting you. I can't help but wonder what's in store for me around the corner."

"Well, for now, I'd say a trip to the beach is in order," Catalina says. "What do you say we head down, straight after coffee? We can stop at a super-mini later and pick up a few groceries for lunch."

"That sounds perfect," Isabella agrees.

Isabella is rinsing out their coffee mugs at the sink when Catalina comes out of the bedroom, dressed and ready for the beach in a coral-red thong bikini, her bum cheeks totally exposed. The top is even more scandalous, the knitted fabric with holes so large Isabella can see Catalina's dark nipples poking through.

"Wow," Isabella says, her jaw dropping. She feels uncharacteristically attracted again, noticing, for the second time that morning, Catalina's ample breasts. She looks down at her own modest barely-B-cups, then back up into Catalina's eyes. She feels a stirring in her groin and feels confused again, then suddenly embarrassed. "I, I, mean, um, that's a really pretty colour on you," she stumbles.

"Oh, this old thing?" Catalina says, plucking at the waist of the string-tied bottoms. "I've had it for ages. It's practically falling apart, but it's all I have. I keep meaning to buy a new one, but somehow, I never get around to it."

"I feel you," Isabella says. "Bathing suit shopping has to be one of my least favourite tasks. They always seem to have mirrors and lighting that give the worst impressions."

"Oh, please," Catalina says. "You could rock a paper bag in a closet."

"Well, that's kind of you to say," Isabella says, blushing again.

Isabella throws her sunscreen and a towel into a burlap beach bag, then stops to grab her oversized purse.

"Will we pass a super-mini on the way?" Isabella asks. "I'd like to pick up a few bottles of water, to stay hydrated in this heat and after overdoing it last night."

"That's a good idea, and no worries, there's a super-mini on every block in this country."

The two friends pass a group of construction workers on the way to the beach, and despite having thrown on wraps to cover themselves, they are subjected to a barrage of catcalls.

"Ba, ba boom, *muy bo-ni-ta*," yells one of the guys closest to them, followed by a long whistle. "*Vengan a casa conmigo después de mi trabajo y les haré pasar a ambas un buen momento.*"

"*Vete a la mierda,*" Catalina shouts back.

"What did he say? What did you say?" Isabella says, quickening her pace, the exchange in Spanish far too rapid for her to keep up.

"He offered to show us both a good time when he's done work," Catalina says with contempt. "What did I tell you about the guys here? Anyway, don't worry, I told him to go fuck himself."

"What? Catalina, you didn't!" Isabella keeps her gaze forward to avoid eye contact, the men still shouting lewd comments.

"You bet I did," Catalina says. "You've got to be firm with these guys. Most of them don't know how to take no for an answer."

"I'm glad I'm with you and not on my own then," Isabella says with a shiver, remembering again the night on Ko Samet Beach. "I suck at being assertive and I never know who to trust."

"Stay here long enough and you'll learn," Catalina says. "But let's not allow their negative energy to ruin our weekend getaway. C'mon, this pathway leads straight to the public beach."

Isabella laughs as she reads a sign out loud. "*No sofás o basura en la playa.* Who the heck would leave their sofa on the beach?"

"You'd be surprised," Catalina scoffs, then takes Isabella's hand and leads her down the crooked path, strewn with dead branches, leaves, and pop and beer bottles, despite the sign.

Isabella gets quite the surprise when they emerge from the pathway onto the pristine beach, which is an unusual combination of black and beige sand.

"What's with the black sand?" Isabella says. "I've never seen anything like this before."

In her mind, she suddenly remembers the scene of a beach on her vision board, as well as in her sketchbook journal. Goosebumps pop up on her forearms.

"Isn't it beautiful?" Catalina says. "It's unique to the Pacific coast beaches of this area, created by volcanic ash. There used to be active volcanoes, once upon a time."

"How interesting," Isabella says. "And there's hardly anyone else around, not crowded at all, like the beaches in Thailand, where you can barely squeeze into your own spot amidst rows and rows of tourists. Is it always so quiet?"

"Pretty much," Catalina says. "It will pick up a little later in the day, but that's one of the things I cherish about the beaches here. They haven't become all commercialized. Although it has its negatives too. There are no handy restaurant-bars offering cold drinks or food, no comfortable plastic recliners for rent. Just the sand and the ocean."

"I'm in love already," Isabella says, feeling inside like the beach isn't the only thing she's falling in love with.

After a full morning basking in the sun, Isabella has a bit of a sunburn to show for it. She's managed to plough through her latest book, *A New Earth: Awakening to Your Life's Purpose* by Eckhart Tolle, despite finding the abstract concepts a bit deep for a beach read. She does resonate with his eclectic approach to spirituality, which includes quotes from Jesus, Buddha, and ancient proverbs, along with his own take on things. She feels like her spiritual journey is expanding, that she's getting closer to knowing her inner self as well as her life's purpose.

When they get back to their accommodations, Isabella strips out of her swimsuit and surveys herself as best she can in the rust-speckled bathroom mirror, assessing the damage. She's looking over her shoulder at the spot she missed along the line of her bikini top that is siren red, when Catalina pops her head in.

"Ooh, that looks painful," Catalina says. "C'mon, let me apply some aloe vera gel I brought with me. It will help soothe it a bit."

Catalina takes Isabella by the hand and leads her to the bedroom, then plucks the jar of green jelly from the dresser.

"Go ahead, lie down on the bed," Catalina says. She sits down beside Isabella and undoes the tie of her bikini top, then sets it aside and begins to gently rub a large dollop of gel into Isabella's bright crimson skin.

Isabella can no longer resist her urges or ignore her desire. On an impulse, she turns over onto her back, reaches up, and kisses Catalina on the lips, her hands around her neck, pulling her closer. Catalina seems to resist, if only slightly, then kisses her back, matching her passion and then some.

"I'm glad you're feeling it too," Isabella says, pulling her lips away breathlessly while taking her hand and sliding it from Catalina's back to her breasts. She caresses each one in turn, slowly, lovingly, then moves her hand lower, stroking between Catalina's legs.

"Oh, God," Catalina moans, ripping off Isabella's bottoms while kissing her and grinding up next to her. Somehow, this unknown territory feels completely natural for both of them.

Isabella loses all track of time as she and Catalina make love, seeming to know all of each other's desires without saying a thing, both coming to a climax again and again.

"Wow," Isabella says, hours later, covered in sweat and lying on the bed beside Catalina. She kisses her lover on her hard, flat stomach. "When I said earlier that I wondered what life had in store for me next, I certainly never imagined this. I've never been with a woman before. I thought I was a straight-up heterosexual."

"Me neither," Catalina says. "I've always felt so drawn to the masculine form, crazy for a hard, erect penis. I must say, this is a complete surprise. You are my best friend, and I love you. I just never thought we would end up expressing our love like this."

"How do you feel about it?" Isabella asks, propping herself up on one elbow. "I hope I didn't cross a line? I'd hate to lose your friendship. It means everything."

"You crossed a line, that's for sure," Catalina giggles, then reaches across to kiss Isabella on her still-erect nipple. "But in case you didn't notice, I crossed it too. Even though I didn't see this coming, in this moment, I feel deliriously happy."

"Me too," Isabella says with a sigh. "Me too."

Later that day, Isabella sends a text to Mark to share her big news.

It would seem your best friend is a bisexual. Yeah, I said it. I had sex with a woman. I know, it's crazy. But this is the most natural and happy I've felt in a long time, maybe ever.

She presses send, and only a few minutes later, she sees the three bouncing dots indicating Mark is composing a reply.

What? My Izzy? That is the craziest news I've heard in a long time. But to be honest, I'm not that surprised. I've certainly caught women noticing you before. Regardless, if you're happy, I'm happy. I have some big news to share too. Filipe and I have been talking about getting married, maybe this summer, when I finish my master's! But I told him I don't want to plan anything until I have a chance to talk with you. It would be so amazing if you could be here, and be my best woman.

Isabella is so excited for her friend; she writes back immediately.

You've definitely outdone me in the big news department. Congratulations! I'm so happy for you. And I would SO love to be there. I don't know if I can make a commitment right now. Let's talk more about this over FaceTime when I get back from my weekend getaway. Xxoo

Isabella is relieved when she discovers that it doesn't feel awkward at all for her or Catalina. They seem to fall into an easy flow, both of them completely relaxed with one another and interested in getting up to the same things. They catch a lift with strangers up to the shopping area to look for bathing suits together, trying them on in squished cubicles, giggling as they cop a feel with glee, the shopkeepers impervious to their secret pleasures. They pick up some groceries to prepare an evening meal at home, which is how the little rental feels for both of them.

The weekend flies by all too quickly. When Isabella and Catalina check out on Sunday morning, they head down to the beach for one final afternoon in the sun before they have to make their way to the bus terminal. They've already agreed, the converted school bus known as the "red devil" was an experience to remember, but they're going to opt for the air-conditioned comfort of the modern coach line for the return trip.

Once Isabella has her towel spread out on the sand, she fishes her sketchbook journal out of her bag and begins to draw a portrait of the lovely Catalina, her body like a goddess reclined on her towel, spread out on the unique sand, a craggy rock where the ocean waves beat against it in the background. She's just shading in the area below where Catalina's breasts create a dark shadow against her skin, when Catalina lifts her head and opens her eyes.

"What, are you sketching me?" Catalina says.

"Yeah, I am. I hope it's okay?" Isabella says. "I wanted to record this moment, forever."

"Of course it's okay," Catalina says, her voice soft with emotion. "In fact, I'm flattered and honoured. May I take a look?"

"Sure," Isabella says, holding out the page in the sun for Catalina to see. "What do you think?"

"I think I love how I look from your eyes," Catalina says. She stoops down and kisses Isabella on the top of her head. "C'mon then, *mi amor*, we best get going if we want to make it in time for the last bus back to the city."

"Yeah, I know," Isabella says. "It's time, but I don't want it to end. I'm afraid the magic will disappear when we return to reality."

"There's no need to worry on my end," Catalina says. "I'm not going to make any promises or pledges; I don't operate like that. But I will love you and be good to you, as long as we choose to be together."

Isabella smiles, feeling as though her heart in her chest is about to burst open. Her soul lightens as she discovers the truth, that this is her authentic self, a newly excavated part of herself she never knew existed, that feels like a gift worth treasuring.

Chapter Seven

Back in the city, Isabella returns to work on Monday still radiating from her weekend away. She feels like her emotional and spiritual fuel tanks are so full, they're spilling over. She has a renewed zest for life. Even the five hours of intense instruction at work seems like an opportunity to make a difference.

"Sanje, you've made so much progress since last week," Isabella says at the end of one of her student's sessions. "You must have been studying all weekend."

"Thank you," Sanje blushes. "I took your good advice, of watching English movies on Netflix without the subtitles. I think it helped my pronunciation. My mom didn't believe me, though, when I insisted it was my homework."

"Well, keep up the good effort, and see you next week."

At the end of her shift, Isabella is rinsing out her coffee mug in the staff kitchen when one of her Panamanian colleagues, Julio, approaches her. He is one of those Eeyore-type personalities, always walking around with a gloomy perspective, but the heaviness of his aura is even more intense than usual.

"Hey, Isabella, you've got quite the tan going on," Julio says, a sour sound to each syllable. "By the way you and Catalina have been carrying on, all goo-goo-eyed, I bet you got more than a little sun on the weekend."

"I don't know what you're talking about," Isabella says, doing her best to sound unruffled. She turns from the sink to look Julio in the eye. He has dark rings under his eyes and his cheeks look sunken, his skin sallow. He stares back at her with pupils so large his eyes look like deep, endless pools of dark water. "You know very well that Catalina and I are best friends, but if you're suggesting anything else, well . . ."

"Save the denial for someone more gullible," Julio interrupts, unable to conceal his contempt. "I know a *tortillera* when I see one. Besides, I saw you two holding hands out in the parking lot the other day. I'd have to be *muy estúpido* to think it was a gesture between friends, and I'm not. Take some free advice from me. You best try harder to tone it down around here. I know for sure that Ms. Gomez is a strict Catholic who takes offense to homosexuality. She might fire you if she finds out."

Julio slinks from the room, just as Catalina comes in, having overheard their exchange.

"I can't believe Julio was so rude to you," Catalina says, coming over and reaching her arm around Isabella to pull her in for a hug.

"Shh," Isabella says, her finger to her lips. She takes a

step back and brushes away Catalina's arm and looks up and down the hall for prying eyes and ears.

"I'm not going to let a jerk like Julio intimidate me," Catalina says, her voice louder.

"Catalina, please, lower your voice," Isabella whispers. "I know you don't let people push you around, and it's one of the things I admire about you. But, if what Julio says is true, I suppose we're lucky in a way that he's forewarned us about Ms. Gomez. I never would have pegged her to be like that, but then again, I'm not that surprised. Most people here are very traditional and conservative."

"I guess you have a point," Catalina says, taking her voice down a few notches to match Isabella's whisper. "It just feels so natural. It hurts that we have to hide our relationship."

"I sure hope my parents are going to be more open-minded. You know they're strict Catholics too," Isabella says, her bottom lip quivering.

"Oh, are you ready to introduce me to your parents already?" Catalina teases, trying to lighten the mood.

"Actually, I would love to introduce you to them," Isabella says. "I wish I could shout out my love for you from the rooftops. But after that exchange with Julio, I think it would be best if we keep our feelings to ourselves."

"Yes, I agree. That's a good decision, for now," Catalina says. "This job matters way too much to jeopardize it in any way, and besides, how we choose to live is nobody's business but ours."

For the rest of the week, Isabella and Catalina go out of their way to be a little more distant with one another when they are at work and when they're out in public. They take turns staying at each other's apartments on the weekends, where they can be totally open about expressing their feelings.

The last weekend in March, Catalina is at Isabella's, and they are curled up together on the couch, having watched another less-than-enthralling movie on Netflix. The credits are scrolling across the screen when Isabella grabs the remote, turns off the television, and looks at Catalina.

"We had so much fun, that weekend away in Coronado. I think we should make it a goal to save enough money to explore the country together, maybe once a month, instead of sitting around inside watching lame movies. What do you think?"

"I love that idea," Catalina says. She moves in closer and kisses Isabella on the top of her head. "Adventures are so exciting, and when we're somewhere no one knows us, we don't have to be so careful. It makes me sad, that just because you're a woman, we can't share our joy with family or friends. After your encounter with Julio, I've been totally petrified to tell anyone. What about you?"

"I admit, I feel apprehensive too," Isabella says. "The only person I've told is Mark."

"I suppose he gets it, since he's gay," Catalina says.

"Yes, but gay or not, Mark is a true friend, and supports me totally in everything I do," Isabella says.

"Well, for now, let's just enjoy our lives as we choose," Catalina says. "We can figure out the rest in time."

Isabella and Catalina decide to make a road trip to El Valle de Antón their next adventure, and they book a room at a cheap hostel for mid-April.

Instead of driving at night, like they did when they went to Coronado, and missing out on all the breathtaking scenery, Catalina suggests they get up super early Saturday morning, when the roads will be deserted. On Friday night, Catalina sleeps over at Isabella's. They crawl into bed early, their alarms set for five a.m.

Isabella scrolls through the internet, reading articles and blogs about things to do in El Valle, then switches over to reread a few sections from *A New Earth*. She thumbs through the well-worn pages until she finds the sentence she's looking for: "In essence, you are neither inferior nor superior to anyone." She closes her eyes and sits with that wisdom in silence. Something shifts inside her; she feels a softening. She turns toward Catalina, who is deep into her Spanish romance novel, and touches her cheek.

"I love you," Isabella whispers.

Catalina closes her book and sets it on her nightstand. She reaches her arm around Isabella's waist and pulls her close. "I love you too."

They open themselves to one another, fully present and in the moment. It isn't long before their worries about what other people think disappear completely from their minds.

When the alarms buzz, one after the other, Isabella groans and sighs.

"Eight hours of sleep somehow feels shorter at this ungodly hour," Isabella says, swinging her legs over the side of the bed and stretching her arms over her head with a huge yawn.

"Good thing I set the coffee maker on a timer," Catalina laughs. "A strong cup of Duran will have the cobwebs gone soon enough."

"You're so thoughtful and organized, thank you," Isabella says. She takes a quick detour to the washroom, then pads barefoot into the kitchen and pours them both full mugs to go.

"I'm glad we decided to pack last night, when we were fresh," Catalina says. "I can hardly wait to hit the road."

Catalina merges onto Balboa Avenue, and Isabella realizes she was right; it's a ghost town on the usually jam-packed streets. When they cross the Bridge of the Americas, there are only a few other cars.

"Wow, I couldn't fully appreciate at night how vast this view is," Isabella says, gawking out the passenger window. "I can't get over how many boats, yachts, and ocean liners are in the canal. It's really beautiful. Oh, and is that the Amador Causeway?" she asks, pointing to the left.

"Yes, and yes," Catalina laughs. "We'll have to check

out the biodiversity museum one of these days. It's that multicoloured building with the unusual architecture."

"That sounds interesting," Isabella says. "But for now, I'm super jazzed about El Valle de Anton, and seeing the waterfalls I researched, not to mention the hike up La India Dormida."

"It's all going to be spectacular." Catalina grins.

Catalina navigates the winding highway, through small villages and towns, where the speed limit drops to sixty kilometres per hour, then back along the highway at eighty, two lanes in each direction. The road is surrounded by thick trees one minute, expansive valleys the next. Chickens, dogs, and even the odd pig or goat dart out onto the road and Catalina has to swerve quickly on several occasions to avoid an incident.

They drive through sleepy Coronado, still with few people about, then turn right to begin the ascent up the road that goes to El Valle. It curves past brightly coloured Panamanian homes tucked in amongst a canopy of trees. At a roadside turnout, they pull over to take a few selfies with the incredible views as a backdrop, then hop back into the car until Catalina spots the sign for their hostel.

"There it is," Catalina says. She pulls over and parallel parks next to the sidewalk, just a few feet down from the hostel entrance.

"This place has a really great vibe," Isabella says as they walk through the door together.

"*Hola!*" A chill-looking guy with curly, caramel-coloured hair greets them from behind the wood-panelled counter, setting his phone down.

"We're checking into the large dorm room we reserved," Catalina says in rapid Spanish.

The hostel employee scrolls through an old-school, paper-and-pen register to find Catalina's name, his forearms covered in tattoos and rows of colourful woven bracelets. She passes him her Visa card and passport.

"*Ah, lo siento, efectivo no tengo tarjeta de crédito,*" he says with a shrug of his shoulders.

"*No hay problema,*" Catalina says. She tucks her card back into her wallet and fishes out a stack of worn bills, then slides the money across the counter.

"Hello and welcome," an older English-speaking woman with crazy, fly-away grey hair says as she enters through a curtained-off area at the back. "We offer a free pancake breakfast, including fresh local fruit, and the best coffee for miles, all included."

"Yum, that sounds delicious," Isabella says.

"How long are you staying with us?" she asks, coming around the counter to greet them with a soft shake of their hands.

"Just one night," Catalina says.

"That's not much time to explore everything the valley has to offer. I've been living here for nine years now, and I still don't think I've seen it all."

"Yeah, but what to do? We both have work on Monday," Isabella says.

"*Así es la vida,*" the young man says with a shrug of his shoulders.

After stowing their bags in their room, Isabella and Catalina order take-away cappuccinos that are as delicious as the woman claimed, then head back to the car. Isabella has loaded the directions for their first attraction, Chorro el Macho, using a map app, and she gives Catalina directions. Soon they are pulling up to a gravel clearing outside an enclosure with a thatched roof.

"Here we are," Catalina says, shifting the car into park. "Mmm, I can already smell the humid, fresh air of the waterfalls."

"I'm so excited," Isabella says, taking Catalina's hand in hers as they walk over to where a bored-looking park ranger is standing behind a wooden counter inside the enclosure. The glass-topped cabinet showcases a variety of souvenirs, including ceramic mugs and T-shirts.

"It says here the waterfall is thirty-five metres high," Catalina says, reading the large map on the wall while waiting for her change for the admission.

"*Si, es muy alta y muy bonita*," the ranger says in a rehearsed monotone. "*Te gustaria un bastón?*"

"*No, gracias*," Catalina says. "At least, I don't imagine either of us needs a walking stick for this beginner-level hike," she says to Isabella.

Isabella and Catalina begin the descent down the stone stairs embedded in the hard clay earth, then cross a worn pathway. They follow the trail across a shaky, moss-covered suspension bridge, through dense forest.

"Wow, these tree trunks must be at least three feet wide," Isabella says, gawking at the giant bases of the famous multi-rooted square trees.

"Yeah, these special trees are very old," Catalina says. "They are particular to this area and protected by the government. Aren't they cool?"

"I just love them," Isabella says. "And these signs with the Inspector Gadget character are hilarious too."

"We Panamanians love our *chistes*, or 'jokes' as you call them in English," Catalina says. "Although in my experience, most people from other cultures don't get our sense of humour. Oh, watch your footing there; it looks quite slippery."

Isabella grabs onto the railing just as her foot slips on the rocks, worn smooth and slick with the humidity and rainfall, then steadies herself. They take a ton of photos in front of the waterfall, then continue the short half-hour hike that leads down to a still pool, where families are enjoying picnics and swimming in the dark water.

"Do you want to take a dip?" Catalina says, already pulling her T-shirt up and over her head, her coral bathing suit underneath.

"Ooh, I don't know, it looks awfully murky," Isabella says, hands on her hips, as Catalina removes her denim cut-offs.

"Aw, c'mon in, it's beautiful and so refreshing," Catalina says, already lowering herself in. She splashes Isabella playfully, then dives into the water. She shakes her wet hair enthusiastically and Isabella can't resist joining in.

After drying off on the rocks and putting their clothes back on, it is a short walk back to the car.

"I'm starving," Isabella says, fishing her phone out of her handbag. She googles restaurants in the area. "There's a cool-looking South American café with three stars and reasonable prices on the main strip. Let's go check it out."

Lunch is followed by another outing, this time to the Pozo Azul waterfall. They drive past lush farmland to arrive at a series of crystal-clear waterfalls. The mood is tranquil, but the rest of the landscape isn't very exciting, and it isn't long before they are switching gears, back in the car and ready to head out to a nearby zoo.

"I can see why they only charge two dollars," Isabella says, turning a corner to view an endangered frog species. "This attraction isn't getting a good review from me."

"I agree," Catalina says. "I think it's bordering on inhumane, how they have large animals, like the coyotes and jaguars, in such cramped enclosures. They are probably used to being very active hunters."

"And the exotic birds must feel claustrophobic in those small wired cages," Isabella adds, her heartstrings tugged taut, a tear in her eye.

"Even a total non-activist like me feels bad," Catalina agrees, noticing the change in Isabella's happy-go-lucky demeanour. "But who knows, maybe they are rescues that would have ended up dead, eaten by some other prey, if they hadn't been taken in by the zoo?"

"Maybe . . ." Isabella says, clearly unconvinced.

By the time they've taken in all the exhibits, both women are exhausted from their day out in the heat and sun.

"Let's drive back to the hostel for a short siesta before dinner," Catalina suggests.

———

After a solid hour-long catnap, they both wake up. Catalina heads in first to take a shower in the shared washroom, but Isabella follows close behind, and, after looking around and seeing no one else in sight, she enters the steamy enclosure. She quickly removes her clothes, leaving her shorts in a lump on the floor, then pulls back the plastic curtain to step inside and join her lover. She doesn't say a word as she lathers soap from the dispenser on the wall into both hands, then rubs Catalina down, head to toe.

———

"I'm past ready for a bite to eat," Isabella says, dressed and ready in a cute sundress. "Shall we walk up the street and see what jumps out at us?" She pushes the door to the hostel open and steps out onto the sidewalk, the air a little cooler, tempered by the setting sun and the high elevation.

"Sure, I'm easy," Catalina says, taking Isabella by the hand.

They aren't far along the main drag when Catalina spots a food truck. They order greasy, thick-battered fish and chips, then plop down at a wooden picnic table at a park just up the street. When they've finished, Isabella suggests they walk over to an outdoor bar where there is live music, a local trio with a guitar and tambourine crooning Latin bossa nova tunes.

"I'm having way too much fun," Isabella laughs. She takes a big sip from her glass of sangria, then pulls Catalina to the makeshift dance floor, undulating her hips in a sultry figure eight.

"With moves like that, I think we should take this party home," Catalina says under her breath, her mouth pressed close to Isabella's ear. When the song is over, Isabella agrees she's ready to leave. They make love for the third time that day before falling asleep, spooned up tightly next to one another.

Isabella is wakened early to the sound of her phone alarm, the second time in two days.

"Ugh, what were we thinking staying up so late when we'd planned this sunrise trip to the Sleeping Indian trail?" Isabella says. She wipes her sleep-crusted eyes with the back of her hand and squints, the sky outside their window still black as squid ink.

"I know, we should have gone straight to sleep, and maybe held off a little on the drinks," Catalina says. "But trust me, you don't want to miss this."

"I'm sure I won't regret it after. It's just mustering the energy to get my butt in gear," Isabella says. "I'll go grab a quick shower; that ought to perk me up."

After two minutes with the water running hot, then cold, Isabella is wide awake. She throws on a pair of khakis and a light sweater over her tank top, the morning air crisp in the valley, only fifteen degrees. She joins Catalina and they creep on tiptoes past the other hostel occupants, then through the front entrance and out to the car. Catalina drives to the summit, then parks the car under the shade of a cluster of trees.

The loop trail takes them right to the top where the sun is just beginning to peek through the slight cloud cover. Isabella takes the brightly coloured woven wool blanket she purchased in Coronado from her backpack, shakes it out, and spreads it on the ground.

"I don't think I've ever seen anything so scenic in my life," Isabella says, a peaceful note to her voice as she stares out at the view. "Do you know the history of this place and how it got its name, other than the obvious fact that from a distance the mountain ridge looks like a sleeping person?"

"The legend is that La India Dormida is named after the youngest daughter of Chief Urracá of the Guaymí tribe. I think her name was Luba? But I can't recall the specifics."

"How fascinating," Isabella says. "I want to learn more about the history of Panama. But, for now, I'm going to get out my sketchbook and draw this amazing view."

Isabella ends up falling asleep, her head in Catalina's lap, her sketchbook open and her drawing half-finished beside her. She's been out for a while when the heat of the new day wakens her.

"Hey, sleepyhead," Catalina says, who has been wide

awake and is staring at Isabella with love in her eyes. She strokes Isabella's cheek.

"I'm not used to this go, go, go," Isabella says as she sits up. "I think we should consider a slower pace today. What do you think?"

"That's fine with me, Izzy," Catalina says. "Do you want to grab a light breakfast and then go for a drive?"

"That sounds great," Isabella says.

During their driving tour, Isabella spies a sign for a butterfly haven.

"I've never been to a butterfly museum before. Want to check it out?" Isabella asks.

"Sure, I'm game," Catalina says. She follows the road to the parking area. There is a sign out front that advertises a five-dollar entrance fee that includes an informative tour, a short video presentation, and a life cycle exhibit.

Isabella is infatuated with the seemingly unremarkable large brown butterflies that are a surprising electric blue on the inside. She thinks the markings in the bottom corner of their wings look like eyes, and almost falls into a trance staring at them for so long. Catalina isn't quite so enamoured with the tour, but she waits patiently while Isabella stops to sketch a few butterflies perched on a tree branch.

"I want to spend some time at the market and maybe choose some fresh fruit and vegetables to take home with us," Isabella says as they leave, crunching over the gravel back to the car. "But we don't want to get away too late if we want to beat the weekend traffic, so let's just go for a quick pit stop."

"Sounds good to me," Catalina agrees. "Last stop, the market. Then it's homeward bound, back to the hustle and bustle of the city."

———

Catalina drops Isabella off outside her apartment complex just after the sun has set.

"I had an amazing time," Catalina says, rolling down her window as Isabella steps around the car and onto the sidewalk.

"Me too," Isabella says. She leans over and bends in for a kiss. "Thank you, for everything. I'll see you tomorrow at work."

Once Isabella has unpacked her bag, she puts in a small load of laundry, grateful for the decrepit but functioning apartment-sized washer and dryer, stacked one on top of the other in a pantry next to the fridge. She curls up on the couch with her phone and spots another message from Alex. She decides to respond to hopefully get some closure and end the incessant messaging.

Hi Alex, I just got back from an amazing weekend in an incredible place called El Valle de Anton. I'm loving my job at the language centre, making good money, and I've decided I'm going to stay in Panama, indefinitely. I'm really sorry, but I think you need to move on and stop messaging me all the time. It's over, Alex. Thank you for all the good memories. I wish you the best and all the success I know you are dreaming of with your writing. Izzy.

After she presses send, Isabella dials her parents on FaceTime. She shares stories of her adventures in El Valle and gushes about how much she loves the diversity of Panama.

"Sounds like you and Catalina get on so well," Toni says. "Maybe someday you can call us up when she's over and introduce us?"

Isabella decides it's the perfect opportunity to break the news about her relationship.

"That's a good idea, Papa," Isabella says. "But before I do, there's something I need to tell you." She pauses and takes a deep breath, terrified, but wanting to be open and honest with her parents.

"Well, go ahead then," Sylvie says. "No need to be so dramatic."

"It's just that, well, Catalina and I, we're, more than friends," Isabella blurts out in awkward starts and stops. "I, I never knew I had this, um, tendency, I guess you might call it, but . . ."

"Tendency?" Toni interjects. By the tense look on his face, Isabella knows he suspects what's coming.

"Yes, Papa, Maman, Catalina and I are in a relation-ship. An intimate relationship."

"Intimate?" Sylvie says. She looks incredulous, her eyes stretched wide. "You mean to say you've turned into a lesbian down there?"

"Well, I don't know if I turned into one exactly . . ." Isabella begins.

"This can't be true," Toni says with a sob, his hand to his heart. He looks at Sylvie, then back at the camera. "Izzy, please tell us you're only teasing."

"I'm not teasing," Isabella says. "I wouldn't joke around about something as important as this. It doesn't have to change anything between us. I'm still your daughter, the same Izzy I've always been."

"Clearly you're not the same," Sylvie says. "At least you've never mentioned this before. Or have there been other women in your life?"

Isabella thinks her mother looks ready to faint.

"No, Maman," Isabella says with another sigh. "You know Alex and I dated for two years, and I never had a long-term, serious relationship before him. Like I said, it just kind of happened. But truthfully, I'm the happiest I've ever been in my life. I hope you guys can be happy for me too."

"It's a lot to take in," Toni says.

"I suppose this means we will never get to be grandparents," Sylvie says with a sniffle. She grabs a Kleenex and dabs at the corners of her eyes.

"Let's not jump ahead of ourselves," Isabella says. "I never said anything about marriage, or a committed relationship, and I've never been certain about whether or not I want to have children anyway. Can we please just take things one day at a time? I'm in love and I'm happy, settled in my job, and living my life with authenticity. Isn't that what you've both always said matters?" Isabella wipes her hand across her cheek as her tears fall, unbidden. She knew this conversation wasn't going to be easy, but she never imagined it would hurt this much. "I'm going to hang up now," Isabella says when she gets no response to her question from either parent. "Maybe you should call me when you've had a chance to absorb and process what I've shared with you."

Isabella ends the conversations, then sends a text to Catalina.

I told my parents about us. They didn't take it well. Understatement.

I'm so sorry, mi amor. Do you want me to come over? Catalina texts back instantly.

Thanks for offering, but I'm too exhausted and emotionally drained. Good night, babe. We can talk more tomorrow.

Isabella turns off her phone and plugs it in to charge, then crawls into bed, not even bothering to take off her makeup or clothes, and cries herself to sleep.

Chapter Eight

Several weeks go by, and still Isabella receives no word from her parents. She tries her best to put it out of her mind, but it's always in the background. Isabella feels caught up in her grief and loss, unable to focus on anything.

"*I broke the news about us to my family over dinner last night. They didn't take it very well either. Want to get together to commiserate?*" Catalina writes in a text.

"*Yes, please,*" Isabella replies. "*But I don't feel like being cooped up inside.*"

"*Okay, why don't I pick you up? We'll go hang out in Amador, by the beach.*"

The beach at Amador is crowded with families enjoying the last hours of a holiday weekend. Isabella and Catalina have to squeeze into a spot amid the throng. They spread their towels out, crammed in between two lively groups—music blaring out of speakers on one side and children crying, laughing, and generally being emotional creatures on the other.

"What do you say to a dip in the ocean?" Catalina says, not long after they've laid out their towels on the sand.

"It looks almost as busy out there," Isabella says, her hand shading her eyes as she peers out at the shoreline. "And what about our things? I don't feel comfortable leaving my purse and wallet unattended."

"Good point," Catalina agrees. "Let's switch it up, pack up our gear and walk along the top deck. It looks quieter."

They roll up their towels and tuck them away, then traverse the long cement pathway that overlooks the wharf, where everything from luxury yachts to disintegrating wooden fishing boats are lined up in rows. They find an unoccupied bench and spread out their towels to cover the dirt and seagull droppings. Catalina opens her beach bag and retrieves two bottles of sparkling water, then passes one to Isabella.

"To the truth biting you in the ass," Catalina says. She clinks her bottle to Isabella's, then takes a sip before she continues. "I feel like my parents are being total hypocrites. They've always taught me to be truthful, but when I opened up to them about falling in love with you, they blew a gasket. *Mamá* had the nerve to ask me not to tell anyone in my family, and *Papá* insists that this is only a fling, that I'll come to my senses when the right man comes along."

"I know, right?" Isabella says. She joins in on the venting session. "My father thinks I'm only reacting to having been in a negative, controlling relationship with a man, that I'm confused. But what does he know? I haven't lived in the same city as them since I left for Thailand, other than the few months Papa was battling cancer. And even though we used to FaceTime most weeks, it isn't the same. It's been three weeks now, with no word from them."

"Well, my family is just as blind and unaccepting," Catalina says. "They only see what they want to see, what makes them comfortable inside their values of what is right and wrong. They think God is judging me when it's them. At least, I can't believe a loving God would condemn something as beautiful as what we have together."

Catalina reaches her hand out and places it over Isabella's, then pulls it away quickly. She glances around to see if anyone noticed.

"It sucks, so much, to have to pretend all the time," Isabella says, as a lone tear trickles down her cheek. "Maybe we should pick up and move somewhere a little more civilized, like New York or Paris."

"Wouldn't that be amazing?" Catalina sighs. "But not very practical. The cost of living is through the roof in both of those cities. And, despite everything, I love my family and my country too."

"Yeah, you're probably right," Isabella says. "Running away won't solve anything, and perhaps the adage is true, that time heals all wounds? It's still early days. But I'm tired of moping. And this hot, busy energy isn't working for me at all. Do you want to come over to my place and stay for dinner?"

"Okay, sure. Let's go, *mi amor*."

Catalina and Isabella decide the best remedy to deal with their painful emotions is to distract themselves with another adventure. They research things to do and places to stay in Boquete, a city in the northwestern province of Chiriqui. They each put in a request for an extra day off work the first week in May, to extend the Cinco de Mayo holiday weekend to four days. Ms. Gomez decides to close the centre so all her staff and students can take an extended break.

"Road trips are so epic," Isabella says, looking over at Catalina as she jots down a list of items to bring. "I remember when I hitched a ride from Winnipeg to Vancouver Island. I thought it would be sheer drudgery at twenty-six hours door to door, but I ended up loving it."

"Wow, are you serious? Twenty-six hours?" Catalina says. "That's something I've never done, nor plan to. Panama is such a small country, and I've never been anywhere else. I guess this trip will feel like a breeze in comparison."

"That's for sure," Isabella laughs. "I'm interested to see how the landscape changes along the way, once we get further west than we've been yet." She stops to write down "mosquito repellent" on her list. "My research showed it's mostly coastline for the first half of the journey, then it becomes quite dry and sparse in Santiago, but as you get closer to Boquete, it becomes more like a lush jungle."

"I'm so excited about the coffee plantation tour you

booked for us," Catalina says. "I've never been to one before, have you?"

"No, I can't say that I have," Isabella says. Her smile turns to a frown. "The only thing close to that was on my first date with Alex. He took me for a cider tasting. We ended up in a big fight. I knew, somewhere deep down, right from the start, that it wasn't a smart move to get involved with him, but I ignored my intuition because he was so damn charming and good-looking."

"Charming and good-looking?" Catalina says, getting up from her chair at the kitchen table and coming over to sit beside Isabella. "But surely not more than me, right?"

Catalina feigns being jealous, then tips her head to nibble playfully at Isabella's neck.

"No one has ever come close to being as beautiful as you," Isabella giggles. "But what I love and appreciate most is that you are beautiful inside and out."

The light banter turns sultry, and they end up in a passionate embrace that has Isabella dropping her pen and taking Catalina by the hand, over to her daybed in the corner.

On the morning of their big trip, Catalina and Isabella pack a cooler with sandwiches, several bottles of water, some assorted fruit, and roasted almonds. Isabella has her sketchbook journal and a stack of freshly sharpened charcoal pencils in her oversized purse. They load their suitcases into the small trunk of the Kia and crank up the stereo. Isabella selects the road trip playlist that Catalina put together, a crazy mishmash of Latin, American pop, and classical music. It's a seven-and-a-half-hour drive from Panama City to Boquete, but Isabella and Catalina are up for the challenges and unanticipated rewards of a new adventure.

Catalina is pleasantly surprised to find the two-lane paved highway continues past Coronado and the turnoff for El Valle. They stop at roadside turnouts along the way to take selfies. Isabella rolls down her window to take a few shots of the massive windmill farms. Near Santiago, they stop for gas at a public washroom with no hot water or paper towels, glad they thought ahead and brought their own tissue and hand sanitizer. They find a decent place to stop for lunch in a Va y Ven gas station parking lot.

Isabella breaks out laughing when, along the way, she sees signs depicting monkey, armadillo, and sloth crossings. Her laughter erupts when, instead of exotic wildlife, they spot an ambitious, stubby-legged dachshund attempting to hurdle himself over the cement meridian with Herculean effort.

They pass the hours during the long drive talking about their dreams of the future. Isabella shares how much she wishes she could become a famous artist, or at least well-known enough to make a decent living off of her paintings. She tells Catalina about her portfolio, in storage back in Winnipeg, and all the rejections she's suffered over the years.

"I think you should give it another go," Catalina says.

"That was so long ago. I know you draw regularly in your sketchbook journal, but I never knew you had an interest in becoming a bona fide artist. Maybe it's time to invest in yourself and purchase some proper artist tools, like an easel, some canvases, and paint?"

"Do you really think so?" Isabella says.

"Yeah, I really do," Catalina says. "You've got talent and ambition, which I think are the two most important elements of making any dream come true. And you know, come to think of it, I do have an uncle who owns an art gallery. I can't believe I never thought of it before, but I could introduce you."

"Wow, really?" Isabella says. "That would be so cool, thank you."

When they arrive at the city of David, Catalina turns right at the turnoff for Boquete. The temperature drops from thirty-two to twenty-two as they drive along the steep road into higher elevation. The wind picks up and the cloud cover is dense and dark. Just before sunset they arrive at the villa accommodations Catalina booked online.

Bright pink canopies cover the decks of all the rooms, and a quaint, flower-lined pathway made of coral-coloured tiles leads them to the main building. Inside, a big man dressed casually in beige shorts and a black tank introduces himself as Alejandro. He writes their names in his guest book and gets them each a set of keys, then shows them to the top-floor suite.

"This place is incredible," Catalina says, her sandal-clad feet literally sailing across the ceramic tile floors. "No wonder you earned a 4.9 rating on Tripadvisor."

"Oh, come see the view from the balcony!" Isabella calls out, one step ahead. "It's absolutely stunning! Look, there's the Caldera River!"

"I'm so glad you like it here," Alejandro says. "Although your booking didn't mention there were two of you. This room only has one queen bed."

"That's no problem for us; we're *together*." It's out of her mouth before Isabella has time to think or retract.

"Oh, I, um, *comprendo* . . ." Alejandro stumbles over his words.

"*Lo sentimos*," Catalina says. She looks embarrassed.

Alejandro makes a quick departure, mumbling under his breath about checking in with him if they have any questions.

"Izzy, you shouldn't have just dropped that bomb on that poor, unsuspecting man," Catalina says as soon as he closes the door behind him.

"I know. I don't know what came over me," Isabella says. "I guess I just felt like being upfront for a change. This is so new for me. I really don't know what's expected or accepted. Straight people don't know how lucky they are, that they are always free to express themselves, without fear of repercussions or judgments."

"Yeah, well, I think you caught him off guard," Catalina says. "But what's done is done." She turns to see a towel folded into a swan at the foot of the bed and laughs out loud, plucks the towel, and takes it to the bathroom with her, making strange noises that sound sort of like a swan and moving her bottom in an exaggerated waddle. "I'm going to wash off the grime from our long day on the road. Want to join me?"

Isabella doesn't answer; she's already taking off her clothes.

———

After making love, they are spooning on their queen bed when Catalina turns to Isabella with a serious expression on her face.

"Izzy, can we talk?" Catalina says. She props herself up on one elbow to look Isabella in the eyes.

"Of course," Isabella says. She reaches over and takes Catalina's hand in hers. "It sounds serious."

"I suppose it is," Catalina says. "I know I brushed it off earlier, but it actually felt a bit uncomfortable for me, when you said we were together. He definitely got your meaning, and the thing is, I don't identify as a lesbian. That probably sounds totally strange as I lie here, naked with you, but for me, I don't think of myself as gay or straight. I'm in love with your spirit. It wouldn't matter to me if your spirit manifested as a man or a woman. I'm in love with who you are, inside."

"Hmm," Isabella says. "That's actually how I feel too. I never felt attracted to females before you. I admit, I don't know that many gay people, except Mark. He said he repressed his true feelings out of fear of rejection and criticism, but that he knew he was gay when he was only, like, nine years old or something. What I feel for you seemed to come out of nowhere. I honestly fell in love with you. You just happened to be a woman. I guess if we wanted to label it, that makes us bisexual. I'm just not sure."

"Well, neither one of us is much for labels," Catalina says. "Let's not overanalyze it. If anyone asks, I am your best friend, and partner. How does that sound?"

"Of course, my love," Isabella says. She strokes Catalina's hair. "In the future, I'll be more discerning and thoughtful about how I share our relationship, and with who."

"Thank you," Catalina says. "I appreciate that."

Catalina drifts off to sleep a few minutes later, but Isabella is too full of emotion to relax. She slips quietly from the bed and digs out her sketchbook journal, then takes it outside. She plops into one of the two wicker rocking chairs and starts to draw. The only light is from the moon and stars, and the street lights from the town in the distance. With each stroke of her pencil, Isabella feels a release.

By the time an hour has gone by, she feels at peace. She looks down at the page. She's drawn a Biblical-looking scene inspired by a Renaissance painting she saw in a museum once. Two naked women are entwined in a lover's embrace, trapped in purgatory. The devil has an outstretched hand below, while God reaches out a hand from the clouds above, both vying for their souls. She remembers a story in Genesis, about the sinfulness of homosexuality, that describes how two towns called

Sodom and Gomorrah are destroyed with fire and brimstone by God. She shivers as she closes her journal, sensing Catalina's presence behind her.

"I was totally out," Catalina says. She takes a seat in the empty rocker. "It's seven thirty already. Have you been out here drawing the whole time?"

"Yes, I have," Isabella says.

"Was it good therapy?" Catalina says. Each line in her brow expresses her concern.

"I still feel a little heavy and confused, but I'm confident that I'm on a road toward healing and acceptance, and being okay with the fact that not everyone is going to be comfortable with our relationship," Isabella says. "What I'm finding the most difficult is not being in communication with my parents. We've always been so close."

"Yes, well, let's hope they come around soon," Catalina says. "In the meantime, I'm so hungry my stomach feels like it's eating itself. What do you think, should we get dressed and go find a place to have dinner?"

"Yeah, that sounds good," Isabella says. "And since our room has a fully equipped kitchen, let's stop for a few groceries on the way back, so we don't have to eat out all the time."

Back inside, they both get dressed, Isabella choosing a flowing floral sundress and Catalina donning a skin-tight red skirt with a frilly black blouse.

Isabella is craving something hearty and simple, so they head over to a café that serves up generous portions of local favourites. They share an appetizer of fried yuca stuffed with chilies and cheese, followed by big bowls of seafood-and-vegetable soup with bottled mineral water instead of their usual white wine and beer.

"I'm not in the mood to party tonight, I'm afraid," Isabella says, placing her spoon in her empty bowl. "And with that morning coffee plantation tour, I wouldn't mind tucking into bed early with my book."

"Okay, *mi amor*," Catalina says. "Do you want to walk off dinner with a stroll around the area and stop in for some groceries before we head back?"

"Oh, that's a great idea," Isabella says. She asks for the cheque and pays the bill, then takes Catalina by the crook of her arm.

Outside, the blue-black sky is lit up by a thousand twinkling stars, the crescent moon curled up like a smile. They amble along in silence through the pothole-riddled streets, each lost in her own thoughts.

A few blocks from their accommodation, they are about to cross the street when a black SUV that seems to come out of nowhere barrels into the intersection.

"Catalina! Watch out!" Isabella screams. She grabs Catalina by the arm with all her strength and pulls her aside in seconds.

"What the fuck!" Catalina yells, more angry than concerned for her welfare after such a close call. "That asshole is driving like a maniac! Izzy, can you see his license plate?"

"Not a chance," Isabella says, still holding on to Catalina's elbow. "He's long gone. What about you? Are you okay? Did he hit you?"

"Yes, but luckily it was only a slight graze," Catalina says, pointing to the large black smudge the dirty vehicle left across her chest. "But that was way too close for my comfort. I'm just so mad he's going to get away with this."

"Yeah, me too," Isabella says with a huge sigh. "But I'm just so grateful you're all right. For a minute there, I thought I was going to be taking you to the hospital, or worse."

Isabella pulls Catalina in close and hugs her gently, conscious of her injury. They remain in an embrace on the sidewalk for several long minutes before they feel calm enough to resume their walk back to the villa.

"I can't get over how tired I am, even after that big nap," Catalina says, not long after they've put their groceries away.

"It's no wonder," Isabella says. "Maybe you weren't physically damaged too much, but emotionally, it was a big deal. I think heavy emotions can make us feel sleepy. And on top of almost getting ploughed over, we've both been processing so much. I'm so worried I'm going to lose the relationship I have with my parents, and you're obviously still coming to terms with the fact that being in love with a woman isn't always socially accepted here."

"You're so sensitive," Catalina says. "It's one of the many things I love about you."

"You are too," Isabella says. "You just don't wear your feelings on your sleeve like I do."

"That has got to be another one of your crazy Canadian expressions," Catalina says. "But you're right, I am more guarded than you, but I am sensitive, and I feel everything deeply."

"And speaking of your stoicism, I think we should take a closer look and make sure you really are as okay as you say."

Isabella moves closer to Catalina and helps her remove her blouse and bra.

"Oh my God," Isabella says, a tear in her eye and her hand to her heart. "You've got a serious bruise forming already!"

"It's nothing, *mi amor*. Don't worry. I'm just a little tender."

Catalina shrugs it off and goes off for a shower, but Isabella can't stop thinking about what could have happened. The whole incident has her more aware than ever of just how much she loves Catalina, and that she never, ever wants to lose her.

Neither Isabella nor Catalina thinks to set an alarm. They've slept so soundly that it's already past eight the next morning when Isabella stirs and reaches for her phone on the nightstand.

"Oh my goodness, look at the time!" Isabella says, darting out of bed like a startled gecko. "We're going to have to hurry."

"What? Where?" Catalina says, waking up, disoriented. She shakes her head. "Oh right, we're in Boquete. The plantation tour."

"I'm not going to bother with a shower," Isabella says as she throws on a pair of linen pants and a loose cotton blouse with long sleeves. "It will be hot and humid, so I'll just get all sweaty anyway."

"Good point," Catalina says. "I'll skip it now too and take a shower later, when we get back." She grabs her purse and throws in mosquito repellent and sunscreen, then gives her teeth a quick brush.

"Thank goodness a coffee tasting is included in the tour," Isabella says. "And who knows, maybe there will be something to eat too."

After turning off the main highway, Catalina skillfully navigates the winding gravel road that ascends a hillside, so narrow that Isabella wonders how on earth a car coming in the other direction would pass. Chubby, well-fed black-and-white cows graze lazily in a lush pasture. There are a few more turns before Isabella spots the sign for Finca Casanga, then another steep incline from the gate to the property.

Catalina parks the car near a hand-painted wooden sign just as a tall, energetic man with short-cropped hair and a trim goatee dressed in jeans and a snug T-shirt approaches. He waves hello as they get out of the car and then shakes both their hands, introducing himself as Enrique, their tour guide. A flock of ducks and two large dogs come to greet them as well. The dogs wag their tails and sit down in the gravel.

"Well, hello there, gorgeous," Catalina says, peering over the top of her leopard-print sunglasses at the smaller of the two dogs who has come forward, head bent down. She gives his ears a scratch. Enrique leads them up a stone path and introduces them to the owners of the plantation, who are gathered around a picnic table.

"Would you like a bottled water, or a glass of our own triple-filtered well water?" Enrique asks. Both women say yes to the well water and he fetches them glasses. He suggests they apply a tea tree oil natural bug spray to protect them from the fruit flies that are attracted to the coffee cherries.

"I always like to begin my tours with an explanation of these brightly coloured signs at the bases of these coffee trees," Enrique says. He points to a row of wooden signs with names painted in bright colours underneath. "It's an interesting marketing initiative, whereby businesses or individuals purchase a single tree and the harvest their tree produces."

"That does sound original," Catalina says. "But also like a lot of extra work, to harvest each tree individually."

"Actually, you're right," Enrique laughs. "It did end up being more work than we anticipated. But with almost two hundred different buyers, it's also been a great opportunity to build connections."

Enrique leads them down the path to the next stop on their private tour, the roasting room. He refers to a chart that depicts the stages of coffee bean growth, then offers them both a ripe bean, one red, the other yellow.

"Squeeze gently to release and two beans should pop out from the skin," Enrique says, clearly jazzed about the entire process. Catalina and Isabella pepper him with tons of questions before he leads them out the back door, where the owners have planted rows of several different varieties of coffee trees to test which are the sturdiest and most resilient. After a thorough explanation of all four trees, the threesome walks up the lane to a grove of coffee trees, the dogs close on their heels.

"Now it's your turn to pick your own pail of ripe coffee cherries," Enrique tells them. "I'll use your cherries to demonstrate the highly intricate process that each cherry has to undergo before it is ready to be packaged and shipped to your local grocer."

It's half past ten by the time they've been taken through the washing station, on to the de-pulping, and then to the drying shed. Tightly woven black mesh trays hold small quantities of beans that will take several days to reach the proper humidity level of eleven percent. Enrique leads them back to the roasting room but stops outside in front of an old school mortar and pestle.

"This contraption removes the silver skin from the dried beans. Have a go at it," Enrique says. He passes the massive pestle, which looks more like a club from pre-historic times, to Catalina.

"Oh, wow, this thing must weigh a ton," Catalina says as she lifts and smashes it down on the beans in the mortar.

"Yeah, it's around ten pounds," Enrique chuckles. "And don't worry, Isabella, I have a job for you next."

Enrique leads them back inside the roasting room and directs Isabella to pour their dry beans into the funnel of the roasting machine.

"Wait for the first crack before turning the dial up," Enrique says. "Precision timing is essential to produce the right roast."

Isabella selects Dark City. Once the beans are roasted and bagged, Enrique leads them back outside. The tour ends at the tasting station. Isabella is delighted to discover small slices of homemade banana bread to accompany the coffee. Enrique prepares them three small cups to taste: Italian espresso prepared in a tin teapot, a French press, and a contraption that looks like something you'd see in a science lab, a glass beaker bubbling over an open flame.

"Um, my favourite is the French press, hands down," Isabella says. She licks the foam on her top lip with her tongue.

"That's the one I prefer too," Catalina says. "I must say, Enrique, I have a new appreciation and deep respect for how much work goes into my morning cup of coffee. Thank you so much for this amazing tour. I never expected to learn so much."

"I'll be sure to give you a five-star review on Tripadvisor," Isabella agrees as she pays Enrique in cash.

The drive back down the hill is somehow less dramatic now that they know what to expect. Soon they are back on the paved road, on their way into town, on the lookout for something fresh and quick to eat for lunch.

Over the next four days of their holiday, Isabella and Catalina get into more deep discussions, each of them processing the challenging and unfamiliar emotions that their relationship has created in different ways.

One afternoon, while sitting on their balcony and enjoying some downtime, Isabella drawing in her sketchbook and Catalina reading her novel, Catalina closes her book abruptly.

"Remember way back, when we were on the bus ride to Coronado, and you said you'd had it with men?" Catalina asks. "I can't help but wonder if what we have is just a rebound relationship for you? Like, a protest against men or something?"

"Are you serious?" Isabella closes her journal and sits up straighter, her body triggered into fight, flight, or freeze mode. "I can't believe, after all this time, after how committed I've been, that you could even ask such a question."

"When you say it like that, it doesn't make sense, but that's what popped into my head, and I want to be open with you that I'm feeling a little insecure and uncertain."

"Uncertain?" Isabella says. She looks like she's just been told the world is flat, her face contorted, her breathing suddenly shallow. At a loss for words, Isabella sits in silence for a few eternal minutes before she continues.

"When I said I'd had it with men, I wasn't communicating what was really going on with me very effectively," Isabella begins. Her bottom lip quivers and she picks anxiously at her cuticles while her foot taps a ready-to-run rhythm and tears pool in her eyes. "I've never told you, or anyone, but when I was in Thailand, I was raped."

"Oh my God, *mi amor*. I'm so sorry," Catalina says. She moves from her spot on the chair adjacent to Isabella and sits next to her as mirrored tears form in her eyes. She picks up Isabella's hand and holds it in hers. "I never imagined, I . . ."

"I know. You couldn't have known, and perhaps I should have told you before, but I thought I'd processed it all and moved on," Isabella says. "It is in the past, and I thought I overcame my fear of trusting anyone again, but in hindsight, when I swore off men then, and after Alex, it wasn't really about men at all. It was about the pain I felt, being gullible, and feeling vulnerable. I lost my confidence. I didn't trust myself to discern whether someone was trustworthy or not. It was about being stabbed in the back and taken advantage of."

"That's so heartbreaking," Catalina says with a sniffle. "I feel like a total shithead for making it about us, for wondering if what we have is real. It's just that what we have is so important to me, and I guess I'm a little afraid to be vulnerable too. What we have feels so much deeper and more tender than anything I've shared with anyone before."

"That's how I feel too," Isabella says. "I love you, so much, as much as is humanly possible, and I don't want my history and mistakes from the past to get in the way of what we are creating together."

"That's what I want too," Catalina says. "Thank you for opening up with me, *mi amor.* It couldn't have been easy to dredge up those buried feelings, but it helps me understand and be more supportive. I would like it if we shared everything with one another, including all the difficult stuff."

"I agree, and to be honest, I feel so much better now,

after getting all of that off my chest. I can't promise that I'll be able to be open all the time. Sometimes I struggle to shift gears and embrace a new mindset. But I want to give you everything you need to feel loved, and I'm willing to try my very best."

"That's all anyone can ask," Catalina says. She pulls Isabella in close, and they hold one another in a deep embrace.

Along with more difficult discussions about past experiences and unresolved trauma, Isabella processes her emotions by filling several pages in her journal with images that convey feeling beyond what words could express.

She immerses herself in more adventures with Catalina, but a jungle wildlife refuge tour leaves them both feeling uncomfortable about the conditions of the animals that the sanctuary has rescued. The tiny cages are crammed in, row upon row, and Isabella feels certain the howler monkeys look depressed, shaking their cages with a crazed look on their faces. She remembers the zoo in El Valle. But when they tour the national park's volcano trail, both women feel present to the healing energy of nature.

By the time they're ready to leave Boquete, Isabella feels better. Her relationship with Catalina feels more solid than ever, a strong foundation to build upon. She's ready to move forward, to be the one to offer up an olive branch to her parents, to try to repair the rift that has come between them.

Chapter Nine

Isabella's stomach is so tied up in knots, it feels like a too-large load of clothes on the high-spin cycle. She's dialled her parents on FaceTime four times, with no answer. On the fifth try, just as she's getting ready to give up and move on with her day, her computer screen lights up.

"Hello, Izzy," Toni says. "Sorry it took so long to answer. I didn't have our iPad ready."

"It's no problem, Papa," Isabella says. "I know I said I'd wait for you to reach out, but I really miss our weekly chats. I'm hoping and praying that maybe you're ready to forgive me and move on?"

"There's nothing to forgive," Toni says, his eyes downcast, unable to look his daughter in the eye. "It's just so difficult. Your mother and I, we're from a different time. And you know well enough that our Catholic faith teaches that homosexuality is immoral. So, we're struggling with that. But it doesn't change how much we love you."

"Do you mean that?" Isabella says, her voice cracking.

"I thought maybe, when you didn't call, that you were going to cut me out of your life, for good."

"It would take a lot more than falling in love with a woman for us to change how we feel about you," Sylvie says. "You're our daughter. You don't know what that bond feels like yet, maybe you never will, but it's the most powerful thing there is."

"I'm so relieved you feel that way and that we're talking again. I need you to know, when we were on vacation in Boquete, Catalina had a close call. A car came barreling through the intersection when we were crossing the road and grazed her. It could have been worse if I hadn't reacted swiftly and pulled her to the curb. It made it even clearer for me how much I love her and want her in my life, always."

"Oh my goodness, that sounds awful," Sylvie says.

"I can't imagine, if that happened to your mother, or you . . ." Toni stops, the words caught in his throat. "I hear how important Catalina is to you, and I'm so sorry I've struggled to be supportive."

"Thank you, Papa," Isabella says. "If you're both willing to put all of this stickiness behind us and move on, I also have great news to share."

"Great news?" Toni says. "Yes, please, tell us."

"Mark and Filipe are getting married," Isabella says. "And Mark wants me to be his best woman, so I'm considering making the trip home."

"What?" Sylvie says, her hand to her throat. "Men can marry men? That is such a surprise, but I guess . . . if they're happy . . ." she trails off. "I must admit, the idea of you coming home is the best news of all. When is the wedding?"

"They haven't decided yet," Isabella says. "Mark wanted to see if I can make the trip, and when might work for me, before deciding. We're going to talk about it more during our next FaceTime."

"Well, be sure to let us in on the details, as soon as you know," Toni says.

The conversation goes on a for a short time longer, and Isabella senses the heaviness of difficult feelings, still at the surface, unhealed. Sylvie makes up an excuse about needing to finish up her ironing.

When Isabella hangs up, she feels a little better, but she can't help wonder if the damage to their relationship can ever be undone. She questions if it's possible to go back to how it was with her parents before. She closes the lid of her computer and lets out a heavy sigh, then puts on the kettle for a cup of tea before picking up her sketchbook journal. She sits down on the lumpy couch and draws a scene of herself, surrounded by walls that box her in, her knees to her chest, with her head tilted toward heaven, searching for answers.

During her FaceTime with Mark and Filipe, they tell her that they would like to get married the September long weekend, if she can get her finances in order by then. Isabella decides to make the commitment, to make it happen, somehow, some way.

When she gives her parents the news the following week, Sylvie and Toni can hardly contain their elation. The fallout from Isabella's disclosure seems somewhat forgotten as the three of them excitedly discuss all the details.

Feeling hopeful for the first time in what feels like forever, Isabella feels motivated to rekindle her yoga practice. She's hasn't made space for it since moving to Panama, and she remembers how grounded she used to feel after spending time in quiet reflection on her mat, present and aware of her body and her breath. She goes online and searches for a store that sells yoga equipment, and while she doesn't find anything local, she clicks on the website for an online company with a huge selection. She scrolls through the choices, then clicks on a mat with a Panama City skyline in shades of blue and green on a white background and adds it to her cart. When she's done filling in her payment information, a message pops up in her inbox, saying her package will arrive in two to three business days.

Isabella checks in at the post office on her corner every day to see if her yoga mat has arrived. She can hardly wait to get started now that she's made the decision. It takes longer than expected, but after a week of impatient anticipation, her new mat arrives.

Her hands shake as she peels off the sticky Cellophane tape of the cardboard cylinder. She unrolls the mat to reveal the beautiful artwork and stares at it for a few moments. Her tiny apartment doesn't have a lot of options for her to set up. She ends up choosing the space directly under the two portrait windows in the hall off the kitchen and rolls out her mat. In her nightstand drawer she rummages around and finds three half-melted votive candles, the vanilla fragrance quickly filling the room. Isabella sits down cross-legged in a yoga *mudra*. She closes her eyes and begins reciting a mantra: "I am safe, I am protected, I am loved." To prepare for her practice, she meditates on the foundational beliefs of non-violence and truthfulness, then surrenders herself to God.

Within a few moments, Isabella sees in her mind's eye a bright blue light with a clear white centre. With a deep inhale, she moves into a seated side twist. As she exhales, the light bursts into a thousand fragments that transform into golden hands that clap before transforming into butterfly wings.

"All is well," she says out loud, forcing herself to stay relaxed through her mindfulness practice. A deep sense of peacefulness washes over her. She rises to her feet to move into mountain pose, her eyes open, but her focus is inward. The pain she's been carrying in her chest, over her strained relationship with her parents, still feels as sharp as a knife.

As Isabella flows into sun salutation, her palms pressed together, she imagines the spirit of the daughter of the Guna chief that Catalina told her about, La India Dormida. The priestess reaches her hand toward her, pointing to a knife with a jade-green handle plunged into Isabella's heart. The spirit-priestess moves toward her, a compassionate and gentle look on her face. She takes hold of the handle and, ever so gently, pulls it free. As the knife releases, the vision disappears. Isabella is left with a feeling of pure joy, her heart feeling whole again. The peacefulness stays with her all through the rest of her practice. When she's lying in *savasana*, she says a prayer of gratitude. She feels a deep knowing that everything is going to be okay.

Despite all the negativity from outside influences, Isabella's relationship with Catalina continues to grow and blossom. Catalina comes over to Isabella's apartment after work most days for dinner and a sleepover. They discuss the idea of Catalina giving up her apartment and making the commitment to move in together, officially, but decide to wait until after their trip to Canada for Mark and Filipe's wedding.

On a lazy Saturday morning, after sleeping in, Catalina is slicing raw pineapple into chunks for breakfast at the kitchen counter when she notices Isabella has her sketchbook in her lap, a look of extreme concentration on her face.

"What are you drawing now, *mi amor*?" Catalina asks.

"I had the most amazing vision come to me during my yoga practice the other day, and I feel inspired to put it to paper."

"A vision?" Catalina says, her eyebrow raised. "You've never told me you have visions before. May I take a look?" She sets the chef's knife down on the wooden cutting board, washes her hands at the sink, and makes her way over to where Isabella is on the daybed, propped up against the wall on a mound of cushions.

"Of course," Isabella says, holding her book out. "I've only just started but—"

"Wow, this is incredible!" Catalina says, interrupting her. She gazes with an expression of awe at the image Isabella has drawn of herself in a side twist on her mat, a flock of luminescent butterflies surrounding her. "You really need to take my advice and start working toward your goal of becoming an artist."

"That's kind of you to say, but it's harder than you think," Isabella says. "And besides, now that we're saving up for our trip to Winnipeg, I can't be spending money on art supplies. Buying everything I need would be way too expensive."

"Hmm, that's a shame," Catalina says. "Maybe after our trip you can start putting away your savings for art supplies? Or it could be a great Christmas gift?"

"You're so generous," Isabella smiles. "But Christmas is a long way off yet, and I don't want to get my hopes up again. I need to be realistic."

Later that same afternoon, Isabella is doing laundry and Catalina is reading her book, the sun shining through the windows after a morning of thunderstorms.

"I'm going to take advantage of this gorgeous weather and head over to the tennis courts," Catalina says, setting her book down on the coffee table. "How about if I stop in at our favourite restaurant for some takeout on my way back?"

"Ooh, that sounds amazing," Isabella says. "And when this load of laundry is done, I'm going to take your lead and head out to the park with my mat to practice yoga in the sunshine."

The sun has set, and Isabella has returned from her yoga practice feeling rejuvenated and centred. There's no sign of Catalina, so she irons the outfit she picked out for work the next day. She paints her nails a shade of pastel pink. She looks at her phone, wondering what could be taking Catalina so long. She sends her a text, but there is no answer. She feels a little restless, and slightly worried too, but decides to light some candles and make a new romantic playlist to distract herself. She's only just pressed play when she hears the key in the lock and walks over to greet Catalina at the door.

"I was beginning to worry you'd been in a car accident or something," Isabella says, opening the door. "Ever since that incident in Boquete . . ."

"Surprise!" Catalina says, her face lit up with excitement. She turns and grabs an artist's easel that is leaning against the wall outside and presents it to Isabella.

"What's this?" Isabella says, her eyes wide. "Catalina, you didn't!"

"I did, *mi amor*," Catalina says. "And wait, there's more."

Catalina disappears into the hallway and returns with three large white canvases and several paper bags.

"What on earth is all this?" Isabella says, her face a picture of delight.

"Open them and see," Catalina says, brimming over with uncontained enthusiasm.

Isabella opens the largest bag, which has the logo of a local art store on the front, and peers inside to discover an assortment of brushes and paints.

"Oh my God, you've absolutely spoiled me!" Isabella says, her face glowing in the candlelit room. "And by the divine aromas, I'm assuming the rest of these bags contain the dinner you promised?"

"Yes, they do," Catalina says, practically purring.

"My darling, you really shouldn't have," Isabella says. "Where on earth did you get the money for all this?"

"That's for me to know," Catalina says with a sly wink. "But don't worry yourself, Izzy. I didn't hit up some sleazy loan shark or anything. It's all on the up and up."

"You're way, way too generous and good to me," Isabella says, choking back tears. She sets the art supplies on the kitchen table, then pulls Catalina to her in a deep embrace. "Thank you, *gracias*. I appreciate you so much."

"*También te aprecio*," Catalina says. She kisses Isabella, long and soft. "And it looks like you've been busy too." She looks around the apartment at all the candles.

"Oh, that was nothing," Isabella says. She takes the clunky easel from the doorway and sets it over against the wall by the window, next to her yoga mat. "I'll set this up later, after a romantic dinner. I think I have a bottle of wine in the fridge we can open."

Dinner turns out to be a long, drawn-out affair. They end up drinking the entire bottle of wine, totally uncharacteristic for both of them, especially on a work night. They talk about their dreams of the future until past midnight, then crawl into bed together. Their lovemaking feels different for Isabella, like there is an undercurrent of a pledge being made.

———

"So, tell me again. Winnipeg is this little dot right here?" Catalina says, pointing to the map on her phone. "And you're not teasing me? It isn't freezing cold in September?"

"Yes, that's it," Isabella says, glancing over while laughing out loud. "And I'm being totally honest. The weather is usually lovely in September, especially at the beginning of the month. My parents used to take me to Assiniboine Park over the long weekend every September for a last late summer picnic before going back to school. Then again, I'm a native Canadian, so I'm used to cold temperatures." She stops, her hands on her hips. "Since I haven't been in Winnipeg for several years myself, I might find I've acclimatized to this heat. It might feel colder than I remember. You better make sure you pack some warm sweaters and at least one decent jacket."

"I don't own a jacket, let alone a decent one," Catalina says. She stops to write down "jacket" on the growing list of things she needs to buy. "How are we supposed to save for our plane tickets with all these unforeseen expenses?"

"Don't worry. I'm sure we'll be able to get a great

last-minute deal for a flight on Expedia, or some other discount site," Isabella says. "I'm glad that I decided not to give my warm winter coat to charity when I came down here. I didn't know then that I was going to find the love of my life and settle down. At the time I thought it was kinda stupid to keep it."

"We weren't looking, but here we are," Catalina says, her scowl turning into a smile. "Now, tell me every detail about your life before me, again, so I'm prepared."

"Again?" Isabella says, feigning a groan as she pulls out the other kitchen chair to sit down beside Catalina. "Where shall I begin?"

"Why don't you start by talking more about what your parents are like?" Catalina says. "I want to know all the details, back to when they first met on your grandfather's vineyard in Tuscany."

"If you're serious about going that far back, let's move onto the daybed where it's more comfortable."

Isabella isn't far into the history of how Sylvie came to work at Toni's father's vineyard as a farm hand, fresh out of high school, when the closeness of their bodies has them both aroused.

"I thought you wanted me to tell you the whole story?" Isabella laughs, as Catalina pulls her closer and begins to unfasten her bra.

"I do, I do, I just want you more," Catalina says with desire. "Tell me the rest later, when I can concentrate fully."

⸻

It's Friday, the last day of the workweek and the beginning of Isabella's shift. She has just retrieved her stack of student resources for the first group and is making her way to her workstation when Catalina comes over and whispers in her ear.

"My aunt Frieda called last night to invite us to a huge fiesta she has planned for tomorrow, for my cousin's eighteenth birthday."

"Us?" Isabella says, almost dropping her pile of textbooks on the floor. Catalina reaches out to help steady her. "Tomorrow?"

"Yes, us, and yes, tomorrow," Catalina says. "Apparently my aunt asked *mi mamá* if I had a boyfriend yet, while complaining that I hadn't replied to the invitation, when my mother broke down and told her the story of us and how she hadn't told me about the party because she was terrified, I'd say yes."

"Well, what did you say?"

"I said I would get back to her as soon as I had a chance to talk to you. What do you think?"

"I don't know," Isabella says, setting her books on her desk and looking at the clock. "I have to admit, I feel a lot of conflicting emotions. Let's talk about it more tonight, after work."

Isabella has a hard time concentrating on her lessons for the rest of the day. She steals furtive glances over at Catalina and her mind races. On her break, she spills half a cup of coffee on the floor, missing the sink entirely. When her last group of students finishes, she can hardly wait to talk to Catalina. She hurries to meet up with her in the parking lot and bumps right into Julio.

"Watch where you're going," Julio growls.

"Oh, I'm sorry, I didn't see you there, I . . ."

"Don't bother with another one of your stupid lies," Julio interrupts. "I overheard Catalina talking with you earlier, and I've followed you both as you sneak off to your lady lover's den."

"Julio, I don't know what you think you know," Isabella says, trying her best to sound casual. "But I wish you'd just live and let live. Neither Catalina nor I have ever done anything to you to deserve this rude treatment, and honestly, I think stalking is illegal."

"Illegal?" Julio snorts. "I highly doubt that. Following you around is nothing compared to what you and Catalina do, which is immoral." By this time Julio has blocked the doorway preventing Isabella from leaving.

"I'm sorry you feel that way," Isabella says. "I don't want to make trouble. Please, Julio, just move out of the way."

"I'll warn you again. You should watch your back. People in this city don't put up with *hombres con hombres y chicas con chicas. Comprendes*?? It's not natural. You could end up getting hurt, or worse."

Julio skulks away. Isabella tries to brush off his cloud of negativity, like a sticky spiderweb, but as she climbs into Catalina's car, her heart is still racing.

"Hey, babe, what took you so long?" Catalina asks.

"It was Julio, getting in my face again," Isabella says, her hands visibly shaking as she reaches for her seat belt.

"That motherfucker," Catalina says, her lightning-fast temper rising to the surface. "I could just smack his hater, prejudiced face."

"He was being super creepy, threatening me almost," Isabella confesses. "He basically admitted to following us home after work. I wouldn't be surprised if he's one of those creeps who gets off on peeping in on other people. Oh, I just had a thought. What if he has been taking photos of us, for evidence to blackmail us?"

"I never thought of that," Catalina says. "But I'm not about to let him bully me. And I won't put up with his negativity. Please, let's just drop the whole thing. What I want to discuss is if you want to go to my cousin Nic's birthday party."

"Well, I have to admit, I wasn't able to think of much else all day, until Julio confronted me that is," Isabella says. "I really would love to go and meet your family, but I can't deny, I'm scared to death of the possible drama. I don't know if I can handle more judgment and rejection, or someone making a big scene."

"No worries there," Catalina says with a half-hearted chuckle. "Most of my family is so passive-aggressive that even if they don't accept us, they'll be all sweet and fake to our faces. Although my aunt and uncle are way more modern thinkers than my parents. My uncle Eduardo is the one I told you about who owns two art galleries. I could introduce you and maybe the two of you could share artsy conversation?"

"Okay, that seals the deal," Isabella says. "Let's go."

The day of the party, Isabella frets and stresses over what to wear. She's changed her outfit at least six times and is standing in her bra and panties, a pile of discarded clothing on the bed, when Catalina arrives to pick her up.

"Oh, my, is it seven already?" Isabella says, glancing quickly at her phone as Catalina enters the apartment. "I totally lost track of the time. I still haven't finished styling my hair and . . ."

"Relax, *mañana*," Catalina says. She pulls Isabella toward her and holds her close. "Take a deep breath. It's going to be fine, and you will look amazing in whatever you choose to wear. It won't matter a lick to anyone if we're a little late. Remember, timings in my family are more like guidelines. Would you like some help deciding?"

"Yes, please," Isabella says. She stops to look Catalina up and down. "It's going to be hard to keep up with you in that beautiful red dress that hugs all your gorgeous curves." She goes over and sifts through the pile of clothes on the bed, then picks up a slinky silk blouse in a deep shade of gold that brings out the amber flecks in her eyes in one hand, a classic white button-down in the other. "Which do you think goes best with my favourite black skirt?"

"The gold one, hands down," Catalina says. "And that black skirt is such a great choice. It looks amazing and shows off your strong, lean legs."

"Thank you, it's decided then. I'll go give my hair a quick brush. I won't be long."

Isabella chatters non-stop during the twenty-minute drive to Catalina's Aunt Frieda and Uncle Eduardo's apartment in a modern condominium in the stylish neighbourhood of San Francisco. Catalina pulls up to the security gate and flashes her smile and identification, but the guard clearly knows her by the familiarity of his greeting. He waves her through, and she pulls into a visitor space in the underground parking lot.

"Wow, this looks like quite the posh establishment," Isabella says. She notices the details in the elevator area: a leather wingback chair, a gleaming glass table with an expensive-looking table lamp on it, the glossy marble floors.

"Yes, my aunt and uncle are both very successful in their chosen careers," Catalina says. She pushes the button with the up arrow. "I already told you that my uncle owns two flourishing art galleries, but my aunt also owns a large home furniture store."

"I hope they don't think I'm too much of a hick."

"I don't know what a hick is, but don't worry about what anyone thinks," Catalina says. "Remember the age-old wisdom: 'What other people think of you is none of your business.'"

"You're right," Isabella laughs. "But for your information, a hick is a backcountry, uneducated person."

"Then no one can call you that," Catalina says. "You're the most intelligent, wise person I know."

The elevator dings as they arrive on the fourteenth

floor. They emerge and walk hand in hand down to the corridor to the left, the noise of music and conversation drifting from the apartment, where the door is ajar. They've barely stepped across the threshold when Frieda, who must have been watching for them, comes over to greet them, the epitome of style and grace in a striking off-white silk pantsuit.

"*Bienvenida, pasa,*" Frieda says. She looks at Isabella, then slips easily into English. "It's such a delight to finally meet you, Izzy, I believe?" She extends her petite and exquisitely manicured hand, her fingers adorned with a collection of stunning gold rings.

"It's my pleasure, or how do you say in *Español, estoy encantada*?" Isabella says, taking Frieda's hand and pressing it firmly in her own.

"Your Spanish is perfect, my dear," Frieda says. "And your accent is divine. I'd never guess you'd only been living here for, what was it you said, Catalina? Six months?"

"*Gracias,*" Isabella says.

"Izzy's mom is French and her father is Italian, so learning Spanish has been quite a breeze for her," Catalina adds. "Although once you get to know her, you'll soon discover she has a quick intelligence and many gifts."

Isabella blushes, but Frieda pays no attention.

"Well, I mustn't keep you all to myself, and I'm sure you'll be wanting to pay your respects to Nic, but come on over to the bar, ladies, and let's get you a drink."

Frieda leads them away from the front entrance, through the huge open concept living and dining room area that is packed wall-to-wall with guests. The bar stretches from the far wall into the middle of the room and separates the space from the kitchen. The granite counter is an attractive mosaic of black, grey, white, and silver tones. Two professional-looking bartenders dressed in formal black-tie are busy, one shaking a silver canister and the other expertly pouring from a sleek spout into a crystal glass. Isabella feels a little overwhelmed amidst the opulence. She notices an intriguing piece of art that takes up almost an entire wall of the living room—an abstract featuring bold, geometric strokes in black, grey, and red.

"Wow, I've never seen anything like this before. I wasn't expecting—" Isabella is whispering in Catalina's ear as they wait for a place at the bar, only to be interrupted by an attractive man in his forties with a dark head of wavy hair and a trim moustache and beard.

"Catalina, *mi sobrina favorita!*"

"*Hola, Tío,*" Catalina says with a smile. "Izzy, this is my uncle, Eduardo. Eduardo, Izzy."

"How lovely to meet you," Eduardo says, taking Isabella's extended hand and raising it to his thin lips for a kiss. "Catalina tells me you are quite the gifted artist? I would so love it if you would drop by and let me have a look at your portfolio."

"I left it in Canada, at my parents' house," Isabella says. "And Catalina just gifted me my first set of paints and canvases a few days ago. But when I finish something, I would love to take you up on your offer."

"She may not have anything to show at the moment, but you should see her sketchbook, Tío. It is amazing."

"Yes, yes, I'm sure," Eduardo says. "Have you seen

your cousins yet? Your *madre y padre* are on the balcony I believe, but I can't say I've seen your sister or brothers."

"*Gracias*," Catalina says. "As soon as we have our drinks, I will take Izzy on the rounds to meet everyone."

"Enjoy, enjoy," Eduardo says, then turns when he hears his name being called out. "Excuse me, but a dear friend beckons."

Out on the balcony, people are crammed tightly into small groups. Catalina spies her sister, Kamila, standing next to her cousins, Nic and Javier, and leads Isabella over to where they are grouped together near the glass railing with white steel columns overlooking a spectacular night-time view of the city.

"*Feliz compleaños*," Catalina says when she is close enough for her cousin to hear her over the din. She leans in for a big hug, then steps back.

"Nic, Javier, and Kamila, this is my girlfriend, Isabella. Isabella, this is Kamila, my younger sister, and my cousins, Nic and Javier."

Isabella is surprised at how night and day Kamila and Catalina are in appearance. She guesses Kamila to be several inches shorter. She has striking high cheekbones, narrow eyes, and a massive black Afro that frames her face like a lion's mane, with golden hoop earrings the size of saucers dangling from each ear. Nic looks very much like his father, tall and slim, but he has a goatee, no moustache, and his long hair is pulled back into a fashionable bun. He looks very hip, dressed in designer jeans with an open button-down shirt worn untucked and a thick gold chain with an ornate cross around his neck.

Javier seems uncomfortable and out of place, his eyes downcast to his feet, clad in athletic trainers, stamping an impatient rhythm.

"It's a pleasure to meet you all," Isabella says. "And happy birthday to you, Nic. I hear this is your big eighteenth and that you just graduated from high school? That's a lot of big life transitions all at once."

"Yeah, I guess so," Nic says. "I still haven't decided what I want to do with my life, despite constant pressure from my parents. I told them I just want to have a little fun, while I'm young and in my prime. I don't see what the rush is all about, but they want me to choose a career and start working toward it right away."

"I was the same," Isabella says. "Although I suppose I always knew I wanted to be an artist, but I also knew it wasn't very realistic to expect I could make a decent living, so I've always felt a little lost—until I met Catalina, that is."

"It's so scandalous," Kamila says. "I don't think there are any other gay people in our family, at least none that have come out of the closet. And even though Nic and Javier's family are a little less traditional than ours, I'm sure they're all a bit taken aback. What do you think, Nic?"

"I think you're being very rude," Nic says. He looks directly into Catalina's eyes with compassion, then turns to Kamila. "It's not good manners to discuss one's sexual orientation at social gatherings. And I doubt Catalina is the only gay person in our family."

"And what about you, Javier? Do you know what you want to do with your life yet?" Isabella asks, hoping to change the subject.

"Oh, I've no doubt. I'm going to be a soccer player," Javier says. "My coach told me I totally have what it takes to make it professionally, and I'm already training."

"Wow, that's so cool," Isabella says. "How old did you say you are?"

"I'm fifteen," Javier says. "But I'm mature for my age."

Just then Catalina's father waves them over. Catalina gives her sister and cousins a quick peck on the cheek, then takes Isabella by the crook of her arm as they make their way through the crowd to where Luis is standing at the opposite end of the balcony with Catalina's mother, Ciara, and oldest brother, Lorenzo.

"*Mamá, Papá, ella es* Isabella," Catalina says as she pulls away from her mother, whose head reaches just to Catalina's chin.

"*¡Estamos felices, al fin te conocemos!*" Ciara says, extending her hand out to shake Isabella's in greeting.

"Our mother is saying she is happy to meet you," Lorenzo says. He's the spitting image of his father, both men tall and broad. "She doesn't speak much English."

"*No hay ningún problema,*" Isabella says, surprising them all with her fluency in Spanish. "*Puedo entender la mayor parte del español conversacional.*"

"*Tú hablas muy bien,*" Luis says, his thick mane of hair so like Kamila's. His beer belly strains against the buttons of a bright floral shirt, untucked over khaki trousers.

"*Gracias,*" Isabella says.

The three of them engage in polite conversation. Isabella tells them a little about life in Canada. Lorenzo shares some great stories about drunken antics in the club where he works as a bouncer, his massive biceps flexed and popping out from his tight, bright orange T-shirt during his animated soliloquy.

Dinner is served, starting at nine, in a series of tapas. During the second course, Frieda's youngest, Danny, who is the baby of the family at three years old, and who Isabella knows from an earlier conversation with Catalina was an accident, becomes the object of everyone's attention. He puts on a bit of show, singing into a makeshift microphone fashioned out of a broom handle. His thick head of curly hair bounces as he walks up and down the room on chubby legs, belting out lyrics in Spanish and moving in rhythm to the music.

Isabella meets Catalina's other brother, Geovani, who is the soft-spoken one in the family, but he doesn't stick around past midnight. Frieda and Eduardo's other son, Abelardo (or Abel), who is only twelve, disappears to his room early too.

The evening stretches into the wee hours of the morning, with guests trickling out in groups after midnight. By three, Isabella feels about ready to keel over, the combination of too much to drink and endless conversations all a bit much.

"Please tell me it isn't impolite for us to say our good-byes now," Isabella says to Catalina after Luis excuses himself to go back to the bar. "If I drink one sip more, I might not be able to walk back to the car in a straight line."

"*Mi amor*, I honestly had no idea it was so late," Catalina says, looking at her phone. "It's absolutely acceptable for us to go. You've outdone yourself, and I dare say you've won over almost everyone you've met."

"Almost?" Isabella says. She's too tired to make a big deal of it, but she's curious. "Who do you think was unaffected by my charms?"

"I wasn't referring to anyone in particular. Don't start worrying," Catalina says with a light laugh. She takes Isabella in her arms and pulls her close, then kisses her, ever so briefly. "We must say thank you to our hosts and to Nic, plus goodbye to my parents before we go, but I promise to keep it short."

Isabella looks over her shoulder to see Ciara and Kamila glaring over at them. Kamila leans in to whisper in her mother's ear, her hand held up like a stop sign, and Ciara lowers her brows into a scowl. When Isabella and Catalina pass by on their way out, they quickly adopt broad smiles.

It's the end of June, the middle of the rainy season in Panama, and Isabella and Catalina are both feeling gloomy, cooped up inside. They are committed to saving money for their upcoming trip back home to Canada for Mark's wedding, and they aren't able to afford eating out, let alone going on any more adventures.

On a Sunday morning when the two of them are both schlumping around Isabella's apartment, still in their robes at almost noon, Isabella is about to download a podcast when she spots a notification on WhatsApp. She opens it to find another message from Alex.

Hi Izzy, I hope you are well. I'm missing you so much. All I seem to do lately is stare at the photo I framed, of you and I the night we met. Remember how in love we were back then? I think we can restore that; we just need to put in a little effort. I've decided that since you are averse to coming back here, I'm going to book a flight to come and visit you. Panama sounds beautiful and now that my book is at the editor's, I have some free time. I know you've told me that what we had is done and gone, that we're through and you've moved on, but I just can't accept that. I want you, Izzy, and I'm never going to let you go.

"Wow, can you believe this guy?" Isabella says. She passes her phone across the table for Catalina to read.

"He gets top grades for his perseverance," Catalina says. "What's this asshole's problem?"

"I don't know," Isabella says, with a shrug of her shoulders.

"At the very least, why don't you delete him from your contacts?" Catalina says, getting up off the couch to fix them some lunch. "That way at least you won't be affected by his negative energy."

"What a great idea," Isabella says, already swiping her phone. "I can't believe this never occurred to me."

Catalina's tennis game that afternoon gets cancelled due to thunderstorms that have been raging all day. Between the weather and the nerve-rattling message from Alex, neither one of them can muster up the energy to do much. They watch old *CSI: Crime Scene Investigation* reruns and then Catalina leaves to go back to her place after dinner.

Isabella is ironing a shirt for work the next day when a movement over by the window catches the corner of her eye. Not two feet from her, a scorpion clings to the folds of her drapes. She backs away slowly, terrified, never having seen a live scorpion before. Moving cautiously, she never once takes her eye off the intimidating creature, scanning about for something to use as a weapon, but then decides that trying to swat something so dangerous could end in disaster. She grabs a glass jar from a kitchen cupboard and the broom from the closet and steps gingerly back into the room, the invertebrate's striking dark orange shell like a siren. The broom out in front of her like a sword, she knocks the scorpion from his hold within the folds of her drapes. She lets out a slight shriek as it falls to the floor. Isabella sweeps him into the jar quickly, pressing the broom bristles tightly against the opening as hard as she can, then slides the contraption to one of the floor-to-ceiling windows, which is luckily already open a crack. Using her foot to pry it open further, she dumps the contents of the jar onto her small Juliette balcony. The scorpion scuttles away, across the balcony floor and over the side. Isabella closes the window and lets out the breath she'd been holding with a massive sigh of relief. She pours herself a strong dark amber *Abuelo* rum and coke.

Isabella can't shake the ominous feeling of seeing a

scorpion for the first time, right after receiving the disturbing message from Alex.

After a few sips of the sweet liquor, she feels a little calmer. Isabella settles in on her daybed with her journal to continue working on the sketch currently in progress. As her hand moves up and across, she remembers the two-faced drawing she'd made of Alex, and flips through her sketchbook to find it. Her heart beats faster. She knows suddenly, her intuition in overdrive, that the scorpion is an omen. She sets down her pencil and book on her bed, then goes to the kitchen table and opens her laptop to google the meaning of scorpion totem energy. The article claims they rarely appear alone, preferring to travel in groups. Suddenly, the solitary rogue scorpion that intruded her space seems like even more of a message. Isabella reads on, about how scorpions are very intelligent and their spirit energy teaches self-protection. She reads the spirit message to rid yourself of people and situations that keep you down or create psychic clutter. The author of the website asserts that every spirit animal has its own motto, and that for the scorpion, it's "I create my own reality." She hopes that her decision to stop all contact with Alex was a good choice. She prays that she will create a reality that is safe and life-affirming.

Chapter Ten

A week later, Isabella still feels an ominous energy deep in the pit of her belly, despite her hopes and prayers. At work, she is distracted and totally off her game. When Catalina suggests she come for a sleepover, Isabella blows her off, feeling like she needs time to herself. When Catalina persists, she breaks down and agrees to go out dancing with her Saturday night.

That afternoon, Isabella feels inspired to paint. She sets up one of the new canvases from Catalina on the easel, then pencils out a rough sketch of the rogue scorpion in the embodiment of a strong female goddess-warrior. She mixes bold, bright colours and paints strong turquoise, siren red, and glowing yellow hues. Time goes by like in a dream, she's so focused and intent on her creation. By the time she is done, her arm almost ready to fall off with the exertion, it's nearly nine, way past dinner and only an hour until Catalina is supposed to pick her up.

She's tidying up, washing her brushes carefully at the sink, when a loud series of knocks rattles her front door.

She walks over to open it, still drying her hands on a dish towel, expecting Catalina, but is shocked to see Alex. He barges in before she can close the door on him.

"I can't believe you betrayed me like this," Alex says, a wild expression on his face. Isabella doesn't have time to respond before he pulls back his arm and punches her in the face, knocking her flat to the ground. "I never would have taken you to be a lesbian whore." He leans down and spits on her, then straightens up, wiping his upper lip with the back of his hand.

"I don't know what you're talking about, how you . . ." Isabella mumbles, her ears ringing as the room spins.

"Shut the fuck up," Alex says. He kicks her in the stomach. She brings her knees up to her chest with a groan. "I did some detective work, showing your photo around, and my trail led me to your work colleague, Julio. I couldn't believe my ears when he told me you were with that other woman . . . *with* her!"

"Ju-l-i-o?" Isabella stutters, still stunned. "But why?"

"Never mind that. The point is, Julio told me all about you and your new lesbian lover, the real reason you've been ignoring me."

Alex turns on his heels and moves toward the door, then turns back around, his face contorted in agony. "I hope you both rot in hell." He lets out a wail. "Was it ever real, Izzy? Did you ever love me? Or was it all just a game to you?" He doesn't wait for Isabella to reply before he stalks out, slamming the door behind him.

Isabella's insides feel like a bowl of mashed potatoes and her head like it's about to explode. She slowly pulls herself up and limps her way into the bathroom. She leans against the sink and looks in the mirror. Her cheek is already starting to swell, and there is a deep gash where Alex's ring sliced through her skin and blood is dripping down her face. She grabs a face cloth from the stack under the sink and soaks it with cold water, squeezes it, then places it under her eye. She hobbles over to her daybed and lies down, curled up in the fetal position. She's in such a state of complete shock, she doesn't shed a single tear, but instead feels a hollow emptiness in the pit of her stomach. Every muscle in her body feels heavy. She feels unable to do anything but lie there in a daze, in the dark. She has no idea how much time has elapsed when she hears a brief knock, followed by the sound of the key in the door.

"I'm here," Catalina calls out. "Izzy?" She turns on the main light switch and sees Isabella scrunched up in a ball on the bed. She rushes over. "My God, Izzy, what the hell happened?"

"It was Alex. He showed up here and pushed his way in before I could stop him," Isabella says, each word an effort. She winces. "Apparently, he's been hanging out with Julio, who told him about us. He totally freaked out." Isabella starts to cry as the reality of what just happened finally hits her.

"That fucking shithead," Catalina seethes. She softens as she looks at the massive bruise forming under Isabella's eye. "God, he really nailed you. *Mi amor*, I'm so sorry. And I'm so livid, I could spit." She sits down on the bed beside Isabella and puts her arm around her. She caresses the swollen flesh on her cheek. "This might need stitches."

"No, I don't want to go to a clinic," Isabella objects. "I have some of those butterfly bandages that work just as well as sutures in my medical kit in the bathroom cabinet."

Catalina switches into action, jumping off the bed and fishing her phone out of her purse, while heading into the bathroom to retrieve the medical kit. "Do you know where he went, where he's staying? I'm going to call Lorenzo right now and . . ."

"No, Catalina, don't," Isabella says, sitting up on one elbow with concerted effort. "I have no idea where he is, and I don't want anything to do with him. I don't wish for this to escalate any more than it already has."

Catalina stops pushing the buttons on her phone and pauses while she rummages for an alcohol pad from the kit to disinfect the cut before continuing the conversation.

"Izzy, I know you're against the whole eye-for-an-eye attitude, but we can't just do nothing. That prick has to pay for what he's done."

"This isn't we, it's me, and you're right. That's not how I roll," Isabella says. She reaches out her hand to pat the bed, and Catalina comes back over to take Isabella's hand in hers. "You know I'm not a fighter or an avenger. Alex will get what's coming to him as a natural consequence of his choices. He will suffer from bad karma. I don't want to stoop to his level."

"Well, that's all kind and good Samaritan-like of you," Catalina says. "But I don't think it's safe. He could turn up again at any moment."

"You make a good point," Isabella concedes.

"I know we'd talked about me moving in here with

you after Mark's wedding. We both like your space more than my dark cave. But I think at the very least, we need to move you in with me, right away, as in right now, immediately."

"You're probably right," Isabella says. She sits up and then rises slowly to her feet. "I'll pack a bag with the basics. We can come back tomorrow for the rest of my things."

As Isabella goes over to the wardrobe to select some clothes, Catalina sees the finished painting on the easel for the first time. "Oh my God, this is absolutely jaw-dropping!"

"Thank you," Isabella says, following Catalina's gaze. "I'd just finished it when Alex busted in."

Catalina goes over to Isabella and takes her gently by the arm and turns her around to face her. "What you've painted is fucking incredible. You've got to show this to Eduardo. I just know he's going to be all over this, that he'll want to showcase it in his gallery."

"That would be amazing," Isabella says, feeling a bit better despite the circumstances. "But first things first. Let's grab my things and get out of here as quickly as possible."

"I agree, but what about your painting? We can't just leave it here."

"It's still wet," Isabella says. "We'll have to wait to pick it up in the morning."

"But what if Alex comes back and breaks in?" Catalina says. "I wouldn't put it past him to trash your whole place, including your painting."

"If he trashes my place, replacing the painting will be

the least of my worries," Isabella says. "But he doesn't have a key, and I don't think he'll want to get into trouble with the law by breaking and entering. We're just going to have to risk it and trust in the process of life."

"*Vale, mi amor*," Catalina says. "It's your call. Let's finish packing some of your things and go."

Catalina pulls onto Via Argentina and drives southeast towards her place in La Cresta. She lives only a few blocks from the university in an apartment that is smack dab in the residential area popular with students. She parks the car on the street, then comes around to the passenger side to help Isabella, who is still a little off-balance. Together, they take slow, stilted steps to the front doors, where Catalina keys in her code. She opens the door to her basement studio suite, the air thick with the dank, musty humidity.

Once they are inside, Catalina switches on the main lights and leads Isabella to the couch, a broken-down futon with one missing panel.

"Would you like some tea? Or a glass of water?" Catalina asks, walking briskly into the kitchen.

"Some water, please," Isabella says. "My throat feels so parched and constricted, like the walls are closing in."

"It's likely inflamed," Catalina frets as she retrieves a glass from the cupboard. "I've been spending so much time at your place; my fridge is looking pretty sparse. But I have plenty of water and coffee, and a couple of bananas, so we'll be okay until we get a chance to go grocery shopping. Maybe tomorrow? After we move your stuff over, hopefully we'll have some time."

"That all sounds good," Isabella grimaces. She takes a small sip of water and almost chokes. "Thank you so much for taking such good care of me. I've never had someone treat me so kindly since Chuanna, but that was so long ago." Isabella leans in to rest her head on Catalina's shoulder. "I'm so tired, I could fall asleep standing up."

"Come on then, *mi amor*, let's get you into bed."

Catalina gets the futon ready with fresh sheets while Isabella brushes her teeth. She tucks Isabella in. It isn't long before Isabella is snoring lightly, curled on her side, the bruise on her face a dark purple, even in the dim light that the bathroom night light casts into the room. Catalina sighs and makes the sign of the cross—to the Father, the Son, and the Holy Ghost—then turns out the light and crawls into bed beside her beloved.

When Catalina wakes up just after nine the next morning, Isabella is still sound asleep, which is so out of character. She creeps quietly into the kitchen and puts on a pot of coffee, then sits at the table scrolling through social media. She's into her second cup when she hears Isabella stirring.

"Good morning, *mi amor*. How do you feel?" Catalina asks, looking up from her phone.

"Like I've been smashed in the face with a fist,

then kicked in the stomach," Isabella says with a half-smile, half-grimace.

"Ooh, that's really turned into a shiner," Catalina says, coming over to examine Isabella's face up close. "That's not going to be easy to explain at work tomorrow."

"Damn, I never thought of that," Isabella says, her grimace now a frown. "Well, I don't like to lie, so I'll just have to tell Ms. Gomez the truth, but only if she asks."

"That seems reasonable," Catalina says. "In the meantime, we have a busy day ahead of us. Can I pour you some coffee?"

"Oh, that sounds absolutely heavenly, yes please," Isabella says, swinging her legs over the side of the bed.

It takes longer than either of them anticipated, four full carloads and six hours, with Isabella sore and bruised, but by late afternoon they've managed to pack up the entire contents of Isabella's apartment.

"Phew, that was intense," Catalina says, plopping down on the futon after stacking the last box in the corner.

"I know, right?" Isabella says, wiping the sweat from her brow with a towel. "I never realized I'd accumulated so many things in such a short time." She looks around the now overcrowded space. "I think we're going to have to plan a sidewalk sale. We're never going to be able to find a place for all my stuff and still have room to move around."

"I agree, although I think it will be easier to just drop off everything we don't want at a local charity," Catalina says.

"You're probably right. I remember my parents complaining after a full day of sitting out in the hot sun on our front lawn. The miniscule amount of money they made from our yard sale was hardly worth the effort."

"I hope you can handle living in this state of chaos for a week, because I'm done," Catalina says. "I need some relaxation time before I get back to the work grind."

"No problem. Let's plan to do a big cull next Saturday," Isabella says. "For now, it's past happy hour and time we poured ourselves a drink. Can I bring you a cold beer?"

"Yes, please," Catalina says. "And let's order takeout too. Every muscle in my body is protesting that I pushed it too hard. I can't imagine how you must feel. But I'm so relieved it's done, Izzy. I couldn't handle the thought of you in that apartment, alone and vulnerable."

"You know how I've resumed my regular FaceTime chats with my parents, every Sunday evening?" Isabella says. They've finished dinner and she is washing their plates and stacking them in the dish rack.

"Yeah, sure, except for those few weeks after you told them about us, you guys are religious about your commitment," Catalina says. She's squished in beside Isabella at the kitchen counter, busy preparing them both a packed lunch for work.

"Well, since I'm living with you now, I was wondering if you would be interested in joining the conversation and meeting my parents online before you see them in person?"

"I have to admit, I'm not exactly keen on the idea," Catalina says, pausing from her task of cutting carrots into sticks. "It's only six weeks now until our trip, and I prefer in-person introductions. But what the hell, you're here and you've endured the drama of meeting my family. What time do you usually call?"

"At eight our time during daylight savings, seven when it's standard time, so in ten minutes," Isabella says, pressing the button on her phone to check the time.

"Daylight savings? What the heck is that?" Catalina asks.

"Oh right, you Panamanians don't change your clocks," Isabella laughs. "It's a crazy concept. I think it might only be done in Canada, but I'm not sure. I think it started back when most people were farmers and wanted that extra hour of sunlight to plow crops or something like that. Basically, it's a pain in the ass to remember to put your clock ahead one hour in the spring and then turn it back again in the fall, but that's the drill."

"Well, no one can say I didn't learn anything new today," Catalina laughs. "You crazy Canucks sure have a lot of different ideas from us Panamanians, but it's all good. I'll fill both of our water bottles and get your laptop set up while you finish up with those dishes."

Catalina and Isabella have moved the two kitchen stools closer together and the laptop is open between them on the breakfast bar when the FaceTime app rings.

"*Cara mi Bella!*" Toni says as he squints at the camera, leaning forward. "Oh, you have company?"

"Papa, Maman, this is Catalina," Isabella says, turning the computer screen to zoom in on Catalina's face.

"Hello, Mr. and Mrs. Ricci," Catalina says with a wave.

"Oh, hello, Catalina," Sylvie says, combing her hair with her fingers and looking a little uncomfortable. "Isabella didn't mention you'd be joining us."

"It was a last-minute decision," Isabella says. "I ended up moving in with Catalina yesterday, and I thought since I was calling from here, I would invite her to join us. Besides, it will break the ice before we see you in person. It's not long now."

"Moved in?" Toni says. "I thought she was going to move in with you after your trip home?"

"Yes, well, things changed," Isabella says. She turns to look at Catalina and the expression on her face makes it clear she doesn't want to discuss the incident with Alex.

"Well, if you're both happy, we're happy," Sylvie says.

"What's with that massive purple bruise and the bandage on your face?" Toni asks.

"Oh, nothing, I just walked into a wall when we were moving," Isabella lies, not wanting her parents to worry. Neither one of them looks convinced, but Toni changes the subject.

"Your mother and I can hardly wait to see you both in person," Toni says.

"We're excited too," Isabella says. "It will be Catalina's first time on a plane, not to mention her first time setting foot outside of Panama."

"That's a lot of firsts," Toni says. "I hope everything

goes smoothly. Your mother has your old room looking ready for company already."

The mood shifts into one of comfortable inquiry as everyone starts to talk over one another about the wedding, the purchasing of plane tickets, and all kinds of other things each has on their mind. The hour slips by quickly, and by the end of the conversation, it's clear that the four of them are going to get along just fine.

They say their goodbyes and Isabella closes the computer lid and plugs it in to charge.

"You seemed to fit right into our family dynamic," Isabella says, a huge smile on her face. "I can't tell you how happy I am right now. They clearly both adore you already. I knew they would come around."

"It did feel natural," Catalina says. "But I suppose it isn't that surprising. You're their daughter, after all. And you and I are so united in our values and opinions on so many things."

"That's true," Isabella says, coming over to take Catalina by the hand. Catalina stands up and they embrace. "Where there is love, there is always a way."

"*Paso a paso, despacio*," Catalina says.

"That's an expression I've never heard," Isabella says. "What does it mean?"

"It doesn't translate exactly, but basically it means bit by bit, slowly."

They watch a show on TV to unwind before bed, but Isabella still feels wide awake when she crawls in. She picks up her sketchbook journal from the bedside table and draws the scorpion hiding in the folds of her drapes.

She gives it a human face that resembles Alex. Catalina is already asleep beside her when she closes her book and tucks it away, wishing she could make her pain disappear as easily.

———

The next weekend is full, with a total reorganization of Catalina's apartment. Together, they fill five large cardboard boxes with things they no longer need or haven't used in the last six months. Catalina's brothers, Lorenzo and Geovani, pick up the old futon and take it to the dump, then stay for pizza, and Isabella gets to know them both a little better. Another workweek seems to fly by and then there is only one month left until the wedding.

Isabella and Catalina purchase last-minute plane tickets at reduced prices. They make packing lists and get organized. Catalina suggests it's high time Isabella got her courage together to take the painting of the rogue scorpion to Eduardo for his evaluation, and Isabella finally agrees. Catalina calls her uncle to set up an appointment at his smaller, less busy location a few blocks south of their place, just north of Avenida Balboa, in the heart of downtown.

"I'm so freaking nervous," Isabella says. She pulls down the car sun visor and examines her teeth in the small mirror, then applies a fresh coat of lip gloss.

"Take a deep breath and try to relax," Catalina says, her eye on the road, the traffic bumper to bumper across all three lanes of the main artery. "You've met Tío, and you know how lovely and easygoing he is. But most importantly, you have serious talent and you've captured some strong emotion in your painting. I'm absolutely confident Tío is going to love it."

"You're biased," Isabella says. "About both of us. But I suppose the worst that can happen is he rejects it, and I'll be no worse off than I was before."

"That's the attitude of the woman I know and love," Catalina says as she turns left and up a rather steep road, only wide enough for one vehicle. "There it is, just over to your left. Oh, and how lucky, there's a parking spot right out front."

Catalina expertly navigates her car into the tight space and puts it into park, then turns off the ignition and turns to face Isabella.

"You've got this," she says, "Just be yourself. I'll grab the painting from the back so you don't get all hot and flustered in this heat. You go on into the comfort of the air conditioning and I'll be right there."

"Okay, thank you," Isabella says. She opens the door, then presses the creases that have formed in her pale yellow and blue checkered cotton dress.

As she walks up the front steps to the entrance of the gallery, she notices the facade. It is quite impressive. White stucco walls surround three floor-to-ceiling windows framed in ebony wood on either side of the two glass doors, the name of the gallery with Eduardo's name underneath embossed in a simple black font. She steps through the entrance and into the cool air. The space is pristine, with a tasteful, minimalist design. She is scrutinizing a painting of a woman made of fruit, the bright colours and textures a delight to her senses, when she hears the bell ring. Catalina is out front, her arms full with the canvas they've covered in an old faded tablecloth. Isabella turns to open the door and holds it ajar as Catalina crosses the threshold at the same time as Eduardo approaches from the back of the room.

"Catalina, Izzy, you're here, and right on time," Eduardo says, walking toward them with an easy stride. He looks quite dashing in a lilac linen button-down shirt, the sleeves folded up to the elbows, and pressed charcoal-grey trousers. Isabella notices his brown leather shoes are polished to a sheen, and his beard and moustache are meticulously groomed.

"*Buenos dias*," Catalina and Isabella say at the same time.

"*Buenos*," Eduardo returns. "Here, let me take that for you," Eduardo reaches for the canvas. "Come, follow me. We'll go take a look at this in my office in the back."

Isabella and Catalina hold hands as they make their way past attractive displays of sculptures, roped off with red velvet sashes that hang between chrome posts. There is a door at the back of the gallery that Eduardo left open, and as they move inside, Isabella is jolted by the one-eighty inside Eduardo's office. Canvases are rolled up and stacked in piles, leaning against all four walls, protruding from vases and cardboard tubes. Framed works of art are wedged into cubicles, and the desk is covered in a clutter of bills and invoices.

Eduardo puts the canvas on an easel that is set up in

one corner and carefully removes the cloth. He steps back and just stands there, staring in silence, for what seems like an eternity to Isabella.

"This is exquisite," Eduardo says, stroking his beard and stepping back. "Catalina, you didn't begin to do this justice."

"I, uh, really? You mean it?" Isabella says, suddenly tongue-tied.

"I would never say anything untrue about a piece of art," Eduardo says. He turns and takes Isabella by both her hands. "You have a talent for expressing emotion, which isn't easy to do. And your use of colour and form shows maturity and, at the same time, a willingness to be bold and vulnerable. The combination, especially in someone as young as you, with no real formal training, is extremely rare."

"I, um, thank you, thank you," Isabella says, as tears well up in her eyes. "I've never, no one has ever . . ."

"I told you," Catalina says, beaming. "Whatever stories you have about your ability are from the past. You've come into your authentic style, and it shows."

"Isabella, I'd be honoured if you allowed me to display this in my showroom at my other location, which I reserve for up-and-coming artists," Eduardo says. "But first, we need to choose the right frame. If you have time, we can meet up there later tonight, around eight? I'll have my assistant take this over for you and we can discuss options. Does that suit you?"

"It more than suits," Isabella says. "I can't thank you enough, Eduardo. This is all so exciting."

"Please, call me Tío," Eduardo says. "But, for now, I must get back to work." He gestures toward his messy desk. "I will see you both at eight." He walks them to the door of his office and kisses them once on each cheek.

"Oh my God, pinch me, I'm dreaming. Did that just happen?" Isabella says, squeezing Catalina's hand as her feet float across the gallery floor, her mind awhirl with the events that have unfolded. "Do you mind if we stay a little longer and look around? I don't feel ready to rejoin the world."

"My beloved Izzy, take all the time you need," Catalina says. "We don't have anything pressing on our schedules. But I do think, in light of this amazing development, we need to break our budget rules and plan a celebratory dinner. Agreed?"

"Yes, yes, we must, but Catalina, let's make it just you and me. No one else, okay? I don't want to share this with anyone but you."

The following weekend Isabella and Catalina share a romantic dinner out at a posh restaurant to celebrate. Another week seems to fly by at work, only two more weeks until their big trip to Canada. Catalina's mother sends her a text, inviting the two of them for a family bon voyage dinner. Isabella is almost as nervous as she was before Nic's party, even though she's met everyone. She remembers how Kamila and Ciara exchanged disapproving glares at her and feels vulnerable to being hurt again.

"Are you almost ready?" Catalina says, emerging from the bathroom. She looks breathtaking despite being dressed casually in denim jeans and an off-the-shoulder blouse in vibrant colours.

"Almost," Isabella says, clipping the back on her favourite gold hoop earrings. "I just need to brush my teeth and put on some lipstick. What do you think? Is my choice of attire suitable?"

"It's perfect," Catalina says, looking over to see Isabella dressed in a black-and-white animal-print dress with flats.

Five minutes later, they are on the road to the home Catalina grew up in, not far away in the neighbouring *barrio*, El Carmen. The energy shifts as they veer off the main road into the residential area, where neon-painted houses in hues of fluorescent orange, lime green, and bright purple line each side of the road. After a few minutes and a couple of turns, Catalina is pulling into an alleyway and parking the car near a broken-down wooden fence.

Catalina grabs the bottle of wine from the back seat and leads Isabella through the side gate into a cluttered yard. There are ceramic pots of flowers dotted all along the edge of the house, a wheelbarrow overflowing with weeds, hummingbird feeders hanging from the trestle, and wind chimes playing soft chords in the early evening breeze. Catalina opens the back screen door and holds it ajar for Isabella, who is about to slip off her shoes.

"Oh, you'll want to keep those on," Catalina warns her. "My parents tend to pay little attention to the boundary between inside and out, and the floors are perpetually covered in a layer of dirt."

"Oh, okay," Isabella says, wondering just how far she's about to get thrown out of her comfort zone. Fragrant aromas of chilies and onions, fresh tomatoes, and something else Isabella doesn't recognize, fill the air. There is a commotion of conversation coming through the arched doorway to the right, and Latin music is playing in the background.

"*Vamo*s," Catalina says, taking Isabella by the hand. "Everyone will be gathered in the kitchen."

Isabella follows Catalina through the arched doorway and into the bustling kitchen. Ciara is standing over an open-flame stove, her back to the group, stirring something in a massive cast iron pot. Luis is sitting at the head of a long teak table, large enough to easily fit at least ten people around it comfortably, with an odd assortment of different chairs around three sides, the fourth with a bench as long as the table, where Kamila and Lorenzo are sitting side by side, husking corn.

"*Hola, mi familia*," Catalina says. "*Como están?*"

"Cata, Isabella, *¡finalmente están aquí!*" Luis says, teasing them for being late. He gets up from the table and comes over to give them both big hugs.

"*Papá, sólo llegamos veinte minutos tarde*," Catalina replies as she passes her father the paper bag with the bottle of wine inside.

"Isabella must be having a cultured effect on you," Kamila says. "You usually show up empty-handed, or at the most with a six-pack of cheap beer."

"Kamila, don't start in already," Lorenzo says, giving his sister a playful punch in the arm. "Isabella is going to have her work cut out for her if she hopes to have a cultured effect on you as well."

"Where is Geovani?" Catalina asks, changing the subject as she looks about the room.

"Oh, he got called in to work last minute," Luis answers. "One of his co-workers called in sick. But he said to say sorry he missed you."

"Oh, that is too bad, *pero, así es la vida*," Catalina says.

The conversation continues in a mix of Spanish and English. Everyone pitches in to help prepare the meal. When everyone is seated, Luis begins the customary prayer, in Spanish.

"Thank you, Lord, for this meal. We thank you for the food and the farmers, and for our family gathered together. We pray that you guide Isabella and Catalina away from their sin and show them the way to salvation, to enjoy their relationship as friends and seek men to marry, according to your design. Amen."

Isabella knows enough Spanish to understand that Luis is praying for her and Catalina to come to their senses. She blushes red but chooses to act ignorant.

Catalina's eyes narrow at her father and she adds to the prayer. "Amen, Lord, and please forgive my father for his small-minded intolerance."

The air is heavy and awkward over the remainder of the meal. Lorenzo tries to lighten the mood with stories about drunken customers at the club he works at, but isn't successful. Isabella and Catalina help clear the dishes from the main meal away while Ciara torches the *arroz con leche* to caramelize each ramekin before serving the dessert. Isabella is trying to enjoy the creamy smoothness of the rice pudding when Kamila pipes up.

"So, Isabella, Catalina tells me you two are going to Canada for your friend Mark's wedding, and that he is marrying a man?" Kamila says. "Is it very popular to be gay in Canada?"

"Um, I wouldn't say popular is the right word," Isabella begins.

"Don't even honour such a rude question with an answer," Catalina hisses.

"What? I'm only curious," Kamila says, her eyes wide.

"I have to admit, I was a little surprised to learn that homosexuals are allowed to marry in your country," Luis says, coming to Kamila's defence, as usual. "It's against the law here, and frankly, I agree with our government's policy. Marriage is a sacred ceremony that should be reserved for man and wife. It says so in the Bible."

"Homosexuality is unnatural," Lorenzo agrees. "You can't even be blessed with children, which is one of the most important reasons for marriage."

"Actually, many gay couples choose to have children through adoption or artificial insemination," Catalina says, her voice lowered but sharp. "With a world population of over seven billion and millions of abandoned children, I imagine God is quite pleased with how the gay community is contributing by adopting and raising healthy, open-minded children."

"*Suficiente!*" Ciara says, standing up from the table. She

puts her hands on her hips and looks each of them in the eye, putting an end to the discussion.

"*Lo siento, Mamá,*" Kamila says.

"*Si, yo también,*" Lorenzo agrees, looking down at his hands on his lap.

"Well, I'm not sorry," Catalina says. "And I won't subject Izzy to this family's prejudice and judgment one moment longer. C'mon, Izzy, let's go."

Ciara and Luis both start to protest at the same time, but Catalina has already risen from the table and Isabella is close on her heels. They leave out the back door and quickly make their way to the car, Catalina's hands shaking so badly she drops the keys on the ground.

"I'm so angry with them all, but especially that spoiled little brat sister of mine, for instigating all this," Catalina seethes once they are both buckled in.

Isabella stays quiet, creating space for Catalina to vent, listening intently. After ten minutes of heated ranting, Catalina stops and takes a breath.

"Thank you for being such an amazing listener," Catalina says. "I went off on a bit of a crazy tangent, but now that I've aired my feelings, I feel so much better. I'm ready to release and move on. Do you have anything you want to share about how that made you feel?"

"No, not really," Isabella says. "I've already told you how I feel about all this rejection and judgment. It hurts, so much. I hate that something as beautiful as our love for one another is creating tension with your family, but I also know there's nothing I can do about it. These are their demons to face, not ours."

"You say it so graciously," Catalina says. "And you're right. We don't need anyone else's approval. If people don't love us as we are, it isn't true love. I mean, I know my parents and siblings love me, but it clearly isn't as unconditional as I once thought, and that sucks."

"Just because they don't support your choices doesn't mean they don't love you," Isabella says, as tears well up in Catalina's eyes again. "Love is love, in all its messiness and pain. It breaks my heart to see you so hurt."

"How did you get to be so freaking wise?" Catalina asks, grabbing a tissue from the box on the dash and blowing her nose.

"Trust me, it's harder to practice than to preach," Isabella says. "And I'm only just starting down this path. But, just in case there is any doubt, I want you to be clear that I will love you forever. No challenge is too much. I'm willing to fight for us, whatever that means."

"*Si, si sigo asi,*" Catalina says. She reaches across the console and takes Isabella's hand in her own. "Let's go home."

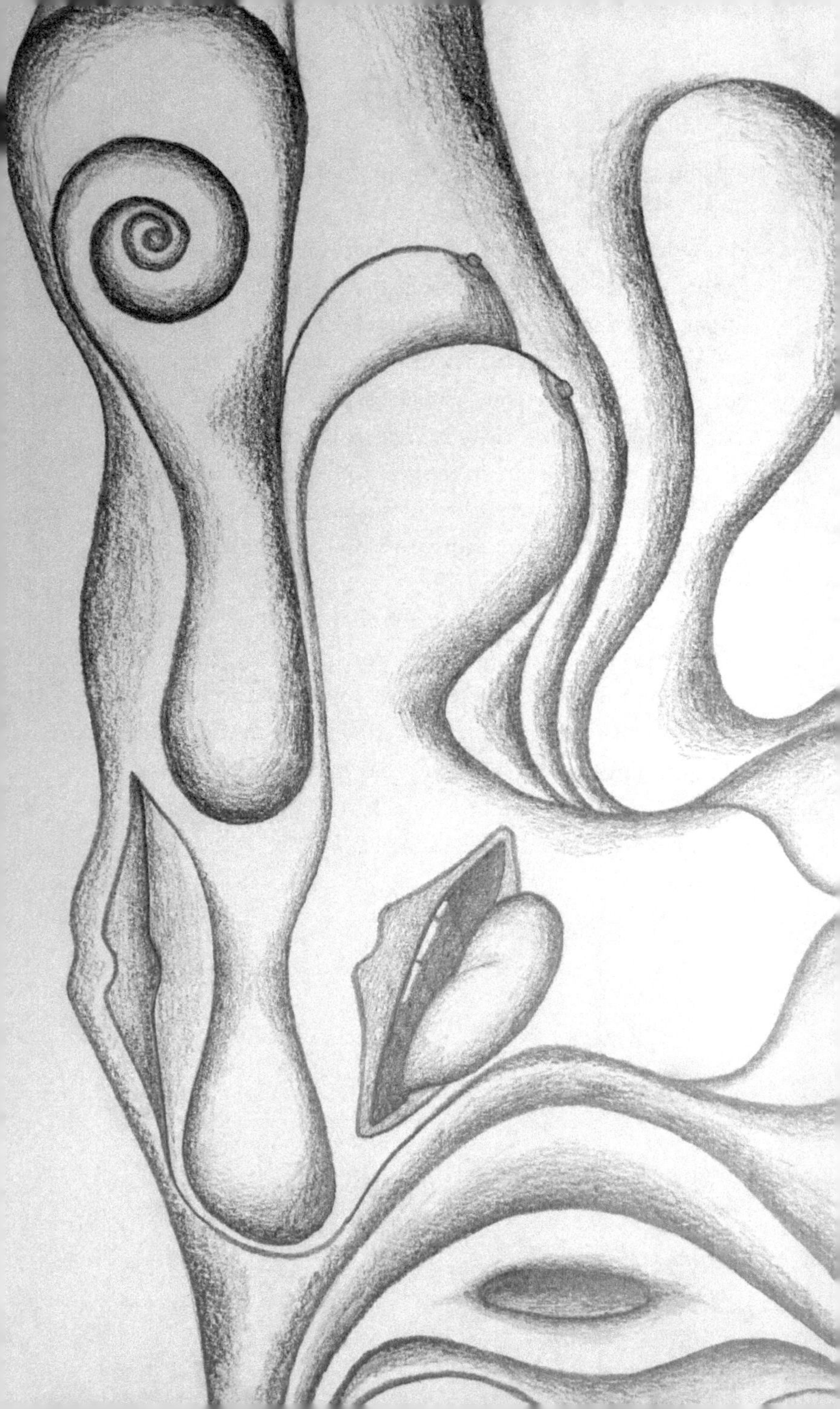

Chapter Eleven

The day of their big trip to Canada, Catalina and Isabella both wake up early. Their flight doesn't leave Tocumen International Airport until late afternoon, and they're already packed, both of them nervous and excited. Isabella is thrilled to be reuniting with her parents, hopeful that the stickiness is behind them. Catalina isn't quite as optimistic, especially after the drama at the dinner party at her parents' house, but what has her nerves frayed and feeling like a million split ends is that she'll be travelling on a plane for the first time in her life, having never left Panama once in her entire twenty-eight years.

"Did you remember to pack your new jacket?" Isabella asks. She's sitting at the breakfast bar, going over her detailed checklist for the third time.

"Yeah, of course," Catalina says. Her luggage is already by the door, and she is sitting on the couch, one foot propped up on the coffee table, applying a second coat of fire-engine red polish to her toenails.

"I don't know why you're bothering to paint your

toenails," Isabella says, glancing over. "You'll likely have your feet covered the whole time. Remember I told you, it could be quite chilly, especially at night."

"Yeah, I remember," Catalina says. "But you also said it could be warm. 'Indian summer' I think you called it? It's best to be prepared."

"You're probably right," Isabella says, looking down at her own plain bare feet. "Maybe I'll get a chance to do mine before the wedding? But at least I packed that cute pair of closed-toe slip-ons, if I don't find the time."

"Ooh, I just love weddings," Catalina says. She tightens the lid on the polish and blows on her toes. "Although, I don't imagine it will get as rowdy as a Panamanian wedding. And come to think of it, I've never been to a gay wedding before. It might be inspiring."

"Inspiring?" Isabella says. She sets her pen down and gets up off the kitchen stool, then goes over to sit beside Catalina. "That sounds like you might be thinking about planning a wedding too?"

"I don't know about that," Catalina laughs. She moves her face in closer. "But if there's one thing that only seems to get clearer every day, it's how much I love you."

"I would like to demonstrate how much I love you," Isabella says as she leans in to kiss Catalina on her mouth. She moves her hand down to stroke Catalina's breast, partially exposed through the opening in her satin robe.

"*Mi amor*, you'll ruin my fresh nail polish," Catalina says. She pushes away and stands up. "You'll have to wait until later for your demonstration, but just so you know, I know."

Not long after, Catalina is the one feeling agitated, pacing the apartment, looking at her phone, wondering where on earth her brother is. She's in the middle of writing him a text when the intercom buzzes, announcing Lorenzo's arrival. Isabella goes to the door and shouts into the intercom that they'll be right out, then grabs the handle of her roller suitcase in one hand and swings her purse over her shoulder. Catalina locks up, and outside their building, they both hug Lorenzo before following him to where his car is parked just a few feet up the road.

Lorenzo drives over the speed limit and swerves aggressively in and out of lanes, impatient with the late afternoon traffic, all the while drilling Isabella for more stories about Canada. He makes the right turn to merge onto the airport roundabout road, and minutes later, he is pulling up to the departures drop-off area.

"Well, here we are," Lorenzo says as he puts the car into park. He jumps out and grabs their luggage from the trunk and sets it on the sidewalk. He squeezes Catalina tightly. "Be safe and have a great time, both of you."

"*Gracias*," Catalina says, tears welling in her eyes, not one for goodbyes.

"I will be waiting for you in the line outside arrivals when you get back. Just don't forget to text me your flight details," Lorenzo says. He waves a final goodbye and hops back into his car, then drives out of sight.

Inside the terminal, the cool air caresses their skin. Isabella shivers, feeling a cocktail of emotions. Catalina is agog, having never been to the airport before, except once to pick up her aunt and uncle, and that had been in the crowded arrivals area. Isabella scans about and sees the signs indicating the Copa Airlines ticket windows are down the hallway to the left, past two sets of escalators.

"This isn't a bad lineup at all," Isabella says, pulling her luggage along through the cordoned-off, makeshift rows. "But I'm glad we chose to come early."

"Is it usually busier?" Catalina asks.

"Well, this is my first time leaving Panama," Isabella says. "But judging from my past experiences, I bet we'll be checked in and through security with over an hour to spare until our boarding time."

"I hope so," Catalina says. "My lack of appetite today is catching up with me. Maybe we can grab a bite to eat at one of the restaurants up there?" She points to the rows of fast-food stalls on the floor above them.

Isabella is about to reply when a woman at the ticket counter with dreadlocks down to her waist, wearing a skin-tight neon orange track suit, starts yelling at the check-in employee.

"What do you mean I can't use my points for an upgrade?" the passenger says, so loud everyone in the vicinity can hear every word. "What's the point of having this reward program if I can't redeem?"

"I feel sorry for that ticket agent," Catalina says, holding her hand over her mouth to whisper in Isabella's ear.

"It must suck to have to deal with disgruntled, entitled people like her."

"Yeah, me too," Isabella agrees. "It's clear she's frustrated, but it isn't the agent's fault. I don't have much tolerance for people who don't know how to exercise any emotional control."

"That's because you're so mindful," Catalina says. "You're always polite to everyone. Sometimes a little too nice, if you ask me."

"Oh, the guy at the next counter is waving us over," Isabella says, grabbing her luggage by the handle.

True to form, Isabella handles the check-in with a cheery attitude, saying thank you for the service and wishing the young man who assists them a nice day in Spanish. Once their checked luggage is weighed and loaded onto the conveyer belt, they make their way to security. There are two lineups with around ten people in each. They show their identification and boarding passes to a security officer before entering another lineup where their carry-on bags are X-rayed.

"*No zapatos*," the security officer behind the conveyer belt says, pointing to their shoes.

They walk in stocking feet through the full-body scan, then collect their personal items on the other side.

"Wow, that was so intense," Catalina says. "You didn't warn me I'd have to endure an invasive pat-down, and that my underwire bra would set off an alarm."

"Sorry, I actually forgot," Isabella says. "Although truthfully, it's hit-and-miss in my experience. You never know when it's going to be a problem and when you're going to be randomly selected. I'm just glad it's over. Let's go relax with something to eat. I think a glass of wine is in order too."

"Now you're talking," Catalina says with a smile, taking her by the hand.

Both the food and wine selections turn out to be rather uninspiring. They each order a hot dog and fries. Isabella sips at her wine, which has a strong flavour of prunes mixed with vinegar, wishing she'd joined Catalina with a beer. The hour goes by quickly and they aren't at their gate long when the boarding announcement is made. Passengers in business class and families with small children are invited to board first. There is yet another security check at the gate, but soon they are comfortably seated on the plane.

The flight attendants are friendly, and Catalina is like a child at Christmas, brimming over with excitement. Even the fold-out tray and safety card in the back flap of the seat in front of her seem to capture her attention.

"Ooh, look at all the movie selections they have," Catalina says, eyes aglow as she swipes through her personal entertainment system. "I can hardly decide what we should watch. What do you think about the latest *Mission: Impossible* movie?"

"Ugh, no thanks," Isabella says, reading the caption. "You know I'm not a fan of good-guy, bad-guy action flicks."

"How about *Ocean's Eight*? I loved *Ocean's Eleven*," Catalina says. She stops to read the plot summary out loud.

"That sounds good," Isabella agrees. "But let's wait

until they're done with the safety briefing and we've taken off. Once they bring us our drinks, we can settle in and watch it together."

"*Vale, mi amor,*" Catalina says. She drapes her headset over the armrests between them and passes the time watching the goings-on out on the tarmac from her window.

A complimentary meal is served during the movie, and even though it's only a packaged sandwich with a fruit bowl, Catalina is impressed with the freebie. When the credits of the movie are rolling, Isabella looks over and sees Catalina has fallen asleep, her cheek pressed against the window.

Isabella digs her sketchbook journal out of her purse, turns to a fresh page, and sets it on her tray. She draws an image of her and Catalina holding hands in front of a church altar, dressed in gowns, exchanging rings. She's just put her book away and has returned her seat to the upright position for landing when Catalina wakes up and blinks her eyes open.

"Wow, I really conked out," Catalina says, rubbing her eyes. "What time is it?"

"Time to get ready to land," Isabella says with a grin. "They just announced that we're about to descend into Toronto."

"Oh, really?" Catalina says. She opens the shade of her window and looks out, but it's pitch-black at midnight, their plane still over the cloud cover, no city lights in sight.

Isabella reaches over and takes Catalina's hand just as

the plane descends enough to see the CN tower lit up in the distance as the plane lowers further, below the clouds.

"The city looks beautiful all lit up," Catalina says. "Bigger than I expected."

"Yeah, it's quite an impressive city," Isabella chuckles. "Winnipeg isn't a tenth of the size. But at least when we arrive there it will be daytime and you'll be able to see how green and clean Canada is. Some of the trees might already be changing colour for fall. It used to be my favourite time of the year."

"Ooh, I've never seen autumn leaves before, except in photos," Catalina says, turning to look at Isabella. "This is all so new and exciting."

After they collect their luggage, they still have hours to kill, their connecting flight on WestJet to Winnipeg not until eight in the morning. Everything in the terminal is closed and it's an uncomfortable wait. They try to catch some sleep, squished together on the hard airport seats, their heads wedged against one set of chair arms and their legs draped over another. When it's almost time to check in, they freshen up as best they can in the washroom, giving their teeth a quick brush, their faces a splash of water.

The flight to Winnipeg is just over two hours. Once they land and collect their luggage at the carousel, Isabella sends Toni a text. When they walk out the entrance, Isabella spots his car parked right in front. Toni literally jumps from the car and onto the sidewalk, then walk-jogs towards them.

"Izzy! *Mi cara figlia!*" Toni says, taking Isabella in his arms and crushing her to him. He hugs Catalina and welcomes her to Canada. He takes both their suitcases, one in each hand, and walks briskly back to the car.

"Where's Maman?" Isabella asks, looking at the empty passenger seat.

"Oh, you know her, she's been fussing all morning—the entire week really—getting your room ready, baking, cleaning, and God knows what else. You two hop on in while I throw these bags in the trunk."

Toni has the air conditioning cranked on high and Catalina shivers.

"I'm glad you encouraged me to wear a sweater," she whispers to Isabella, who winks at her.

The drive through the city on Portage Avenue is scenic. Isabella points out the university campus and other highlights while Toni asks Catalina questions about Panama. Catalina can't get over how clean the city is. There is no sign of poor, run-down neighbourhoods or garbage in the gutters along the side of the road, like there is in many areas of Panama.

When Toni turns east onto the Provencher Bridge, then into St. Boniface, Isabella's heart starts to beat faster as the familiarity of home returns. They pass the grocer on the corner, then turn onto Ritchot Street.

"These homes are so different from what I'm used to, hardly any colour at all," Catalina says. "Everyone seems to favour white and grey here, no neon pinks or lime greens."

"Well, it may not be colourful, but I hope you like it here as much as we do," Toni says, parking the car out front. "Then maybe you'll come visit more often, or who knows, you two might decide you want to change things up and move here."

"Now, Papa, don't get ahead of yourself before we're even in the door," Isabella says. She glances up and sees Sylvie waving from behind the screen. It's all she can do not to run up the sidewalk and burst through the door, but she knows that wouldn't suit her mother's sensibilities, so she forces herself to be calm and walk at a normal pace. She can feel the nervous energy vibrating off of Catalina, like a full pot of popcorn about to blow the lid off.

"Isabella, come, give your mother a hug," Sylvie says, opening the door for Toni to bring the suitcases through. "Dear, carry those up to Isabella's old room please." She turns around. "Catalina, it's so nice to finally meet you in person. Come in, come in."

"Maman, the house looks absolutely spotless, and it is just as I remember," Isabella says. She takes Catalina by the hand, and they follow Sylvie into the hardly used salon, the formal space reserved for entertaining company.

Sylvie has set out a tempting array of plates filled with home-baked goodies and a giant cheese and charcuterie board, overflowing with shaved pastrami, sharp Parmesan, creamy Camembert, and a variety of green, black, and deep red olives.

"This looks amazing, Mrs. Ricci," Catalina says. "And after the meagre breakfast we had at the airport this morning, I'm famished."

"Go ahead, help yourself. Please, take a seat," Sylvie says, gesturing towards the faded rust-coloured velvet sofa. "I know it's just past noon, but would you care for a glass of wine?"

"Wine would be lovely," Catalina says. She fills a plate and then takes a seat on one of the side chairs, crossing her shapely legs as she pops a slice of cheese into her mouth.

Sylvie disappears into the kitchen to pour the wine as Toni returns from upstairs, red-faced from exertion. He sits down in his favourite leather recliner, and Sylvie comes in with a tray of drinks. Soon the room is filled with animated discussion. Toni tells stories about growing up in Tuscany, and Sylvie shares snippets of life in the small village where she grew up in France. Catalina speaks about her family and what it was like growing up in Panama. Time seems to unravel seamlessly, like a spool of thread. Hours later, it's Sylvie who notices the time.

"My Lord, it's already three thirty and we haven't even given you two a chance to unpack or freshen up," Sylvie says, already rising from her seat, collecting empty plates and dirty napkins. "Isabella, why don't you take Catalina up to your room? I'm sure we could all use a little downtime."

"That sounds heavenly," Isabella says. "Do you need any help with anything before we disappear?"

"I've got the sous-chef support role covered," Toni interjects. "Off you go now and take a rest."

Isabella takes the steps two at a time to the second floor. The washroom is to the left at the top of the stairs and immediately to the right is her old bedroom. Toni and Sylvie's room is down the hall, as well as a spare room that Sylvie has converted into a sewing station.

"Well, this is it," Isabella says, flicking on the light. "This is where I grew up. There used to be a single bed and a desk, but it looks like my mother has been doing some renovating. It's pretty tight with this new queen bed, but you can be sure everything is as clean as a whistle."

"It's perfect, *mi amor*," Catalina says, setting her suitcase in the corner by the open window, a cool breeze rustling the vertical blinds. "If you don't mind, I would relish a long, hot shower before a short siesta."

"I don't mind at all," Isabella says. She opens the top drawer of the tall single dresser and retrieves a bath towel and face cloth. "Maman always keeps fresh towels in here. We all have to share the same washroom across the hall; I hope that's okay."

"You've seen my family home. I'm used to smaller, more cramped spaces than this," Catalina says.

After Catalina heads in for a shower, Isabella opens her small suitcase and hangs up some clothes in the closet, then puts some in the bottom two drawers of the dresser. She sets her toiletry bag on top and then lies back on the pillow to reread a favourite section of *A New Earth*. She's drifting off, her book having fallen onto the bed cover, when Catalina slides into bed beside her, naked.

"*Hola*," Catalina says, the word spoken as an invitation.

"Um, you smell divine," Isabella says, breathing in the fresh scent of Catalina's body wash.

Without waiting for a reply, Isabella moves her head

down. Catalina is still vibrating when Isabella lifts her head and kisses her belly button.

"I love you," Isabella says. "Now it's my turn to go get cleaned up. You go ahead and get some rest, my love."

When Isabella returns from the shower, Catalina is asleep. She crawls under the covers and spoons her, soon joining her lover in slumber.

—

"Izzy? Catalina?" Toni says through the closed door, knocking gently. "Dinner's ready."

"Mmfh, what?" Isabella says, lifting her groggy head from the pillow. "Sorry, Papa," she calls out. "We both crashed. We'll be down right away."

"Ugh, I feel so spaced out," Catalina says. "What time is it?"

"It's already eight," Isabella says, picking up her phone. "Knowing my mother, dinner has been ready for a while. C'mon, let's hurry up and get dressed."

—

Over a three-course dinner with the wine flowing, the conversation turns to Mark and Filipe's wedding, starting with the pre-wedding party at the tavern where Isabella used to work. Mark's parents are hosting the wedding ceremony and reception at their new home in Wellington, one of Winnipeg's most upscale neighbourhoods. They moved there after the big boom at Apple, where Mark's father works. Isabella fills Catalina in on the back story of the Andersons, sharing how Mark's dad, Mike, is a successful computer programmer at Apple, then goes on to explain that Mark's mom, Amelie, is a brilliant research scientist employed by the huge pharmaceutical company Bayer.

"I haven't been to their new house," Isabella says. "But I used to walk through the area a zillion times, daydreaming about what it would be like to have enough money to be able to afford to live there."

"I don't know where our Izzy gets that from," Toni says. "Sylvie and I have always been very down-to-earth, happy to live modestly."

"The modesty part is true enough," Isabella laughs. "But c'mon, Papa, you're the biggest dreamer I've ever met."

"Okay, okay, you're right," Toni says, joining in on the laughter. "I'll admit, I do feel a little intimidated by their success and nervous that I might not fit in. I had my old suit I bought for your high school graduation altered—had to take it in a bit after I lost all that weight—and it's fresh from the dry cleaner, but it's only a no-name from Tip Top, not a designer brand or anything fancy."

"Papa, you're going to look absolutely handsome, don't worry," Isabella says. "And you know that despite their financial success, Mike and Amelie are grounded people, whose values are all about family."

"Does Mark have any siblings?" Catalina asks.

"Yes, he has an older sister, but she moved to New Zealand with her partner a few years ago and couldn't make it back for the wedding," Isabella says. "Mark tells me that Filipe is an only child and, sadly, he is estranged from his father. His mother, who lives in Calgary, is the only person from his side of the family coming to the wedding."

"Oh, I didn't know that," Sylvie says. "That is so sad when family relationships fall apart."

"Yes, it is," Catalina says, her eyes misting over. "I've been having some struggles with my own family. They haven't all been as accepting as you two have become about Isabella and I being in a relationship. Is that why Filipe's father abandoned him? Because he is gay?"

"I don't know the details," Isabella confesses. "But I think Mark said Filipe's father was out of the picture when Filipe was quite young, that he left his mother for a younger, prettier woman when Filipe was still in primary school."

"That is so dishonourable," Sylvie says. "But enough of this gossipy chatter. It's getting late, and tomorrow is a big day."

"You're right, Maman," Isabella says. "We'll pitch in to clean up and call it a night."

Isabella wakes up first, sunlight streaming through the half-open blinds, the promise of another beautiful late summer day ahead. She fishes out her sketchbook quietly, careful not to waken Catalina, then throws on her clothes from the night before and heads downstairs, the house quiet. She opens kitchen cupboards to find a bag of ground coffee and filters, still in the same spot, then fills the coffee maker's water reservoir to brew a pot. When it's ready, she pours herself a large mug and heads outside onto the deck, then plops down on a lawn chair to draw.

It's brisk outside, but Isabella welcomes the familiar early morning freshness. She opens her journal, and as she draws, an abstract scene emerges on the blank page that evokes warm, peaceful feelings—wavy lines and curves that resemble breasts, hips, and full lips. She is just writing the date in the bottom right-hand corner when she hears the door open and looks over to see her father carrying a mug of coffee and the newspaper.

"You're up early," Toni says. "I'm glad you remembered where we keep the coffee and helped yourself. How did you sleep?"

"Solid as a rock, Papa, and you?"

"When you get to my age, the days of sleeping like a rock disappear," Toni says. "Your mother and I both wake up several times a night. I usually fall back asleep quite quickly, but your mother often ends up coming downstairs and watching one or two television programs, then coming back up and sleeping until late morning."

"Well, lucky for her, she only works a few afternoons a week now," Isabella says. "Or have you had success in convincing her to retire?"

"No chance of that," Toni says with a chuckle. "I think she's determined to work as long as they'll let her. Other than her sleep issues, your mother is showing no signs of slowing down."

"She always has been a firecracker," Isabella says with a grin. "I'm more like you, Papa; someone who appreciates some downtime and relaxation. But, as Maman pointed out last night, we have a busy day ahead. I promised Mark I would bring Catalina by this morning to help with the decorations, and he's insisting that we go for lunch with him and Filipe. I'd better go wake up my sleeping beauty."

"Yes, well, speaking of beauties," Toni says. He walks over, sets his coffee mug on the outdoor table, and motions to Isabella to get up. "*Vieni qui Bella*; give your old man a hug."

"Umm, that feels so good," Isabella says, melting into the embrace. "I've missed you, Papa."

"Me too," Toni says, a tear in his eye. "And for the record, I think Catalina is an amazing woman. I need you to know, I've fully come around. I've realized what a fool I've been. After hearing Catalina talk about how sad she is that not all her family is accepting you two, I realized that you being in a relationship with a woman is no different than what I share with your mother. It's all about love, and it's clear to anyone with eyes in their head that you two love one another deeply."

"Thank you, Papa," Isabella says. "That means so much, more than you know."

***

Isabella borrows Toni's car and drives to the Anderson home in Wellington. She's a bit rusty behind the wheel after several years of not driving, but she knows the city well, and it is one of those skills you don't forget.

"There it is," Catalina says, pointing her finger at the house number on a stone pillar at the end of a long driveway, her eyes wide. "I'm already impressed."

The house is mostly hidden by rows of poplar and pine trees and a thick hedge that runs the length of the half-acre property.

"It does look opulent," Isabella says, pulling over to parallel park across the street. "At least from what I can see between the trees."

There is a locked black iron gate barring access to the property that spans the black asphalt driveway. Isabella keys in the code that Mark sent her, then opens the gate and pushes it closed behind them. Once they walk a few feet and around a bend, the house comes into full view. A black-and-white two-storey with a three-car garage to the left, a massive double front entrance in the middle, and a large bay window framed by ochre wooden slats to the right.

"Wow!" Catalina says, "This place is massive!"

"It sure is," Isabella agrees. "Oh, there's Mark coming around the side of the house."

"Izzy!" Mark shouts, picking up his gait to run across the freshly mown grass. "You're here!" He pulls her to him in a hug that lasts a good minute before moving away to greet Catalina.

"It's so good to finally meet you in person," Catalina says, returning Mark's friendly welcome. "I feel like I already know you after so many FaceTime chats."

Just then, Filipe rounds the corner and walks over to join them. He's six years older than Mark but is fit and athletic, appearing much younger than his age. He's dressed in a tight pastel pink T-shirt that shows off his muscular torso. He has thick, wavy black hair, down to his shoulders, and a tidy moustache and beard.

Mark's silver-blue eyes sparkle and his smile broadens, cheek to cheek, emphasizing his dimples, as his fiancé approaches.

"Welcome to Winnipeg," Filipe says, stopping to give both women a hug and a kiss on each cheek. "Things are already in full swing around back, and I think Amelie is as stressed as it gets. We should go back and help out."

"What's the drama now?" Mark asks, already following Filipe's lead.

"Something about the florist not getting the delivery right, too many white lilies and not enough red roses or greenery."

"Oh no, say it isn't true," Mark laughs with mock horror. "My mom is a major perfectionist, just to warn you," he laughs again, turning to wink at Isabella.

"I heard that," Amelie says, raising her head as the foursome enters the busy scene. She's bent over a long table laden with flowers under one of the white metal-framed and gauze-covered gazebos, scissors in one hand, a roll of emerald satin ribbon in the other. She sets her things down and wipes her hands down the front of her jeans, somehow looking glamourous even in scruffs with no makeup.

"Izzy, come over here and introduce me to Catalina,"

Amelie says, her smile just like Mark's. "I'm not so stressed that I can't take a moment for a proper welcome."

Several hours later, the flowers are sorted, along with most of the other details. Amelie shoos the "kids" off to go have a little fun, assuring Mark and Filipe that she has everything under control. Filipe suggests they grab a late lunch at The Common at The Forks, and Mark, Filipe, Isabella, and Catalina all pile into Toni's old car.

"This area has really changed since I was here last," Isabella says, pulling into a new parking lot just a block down from the market. "Do they still have that amazing Indian restaurant we used to go to?"

"No, sadly, they went out of business, which is hard to believe. It was always packed every time we went," Mark says. "But there are still tons of great choices, and McNally's bookstore is open too."

"I just might have to pop in for a browse before we go back home," Isabella says. "It's not easy to find English titles in Panama. But not today. I still want to find out more about you, Filipe."

"I'm looking forward to hearing more about how you and Catalina met," Filipe says.

Over a long, leisurely lunch, the foursome falls easily into comfortable conversation, sharing stories from their vastly different childhoods. The afternoon disappears and dinnertime is already approaching when Mark decides they need to get a move on, the pre-wedding party at the tavern only four hours away. Isabella sends her father a text saying that they'll be back soon, then drops the boys back at the Andersons' before driving home.

———

When Catalina and Isabella arrive at the tavern, the party is already well underway, the noise reverberating down the street as they approach. They're barely in the door, making their way over to the group of reserved tables, when Isabella's old manager, Frank, spots her and weaves his way through the crowd to greet her.

"Izzy, my God, it's been way too long, but somehow you haven't changed a bit," Frank says, taking her hands in his. "And this must be the woman Mark told me about, who has stolen our Izzy's heart." He turns to Catalina, a huge smile on his face. Isabella thinks Frank hasn't been lucky with the aging process, his hair now totally grey with a bald spot at the back. The wrinkles framing his lips have become prominent, a classic sign of a heavy smoker.

"You're right, Frank. Catalina is the one for me, there's no question about that," Isabella says, taking Catalina by her hand and giving it a squeeze. "It's so good to see you again. How is life treating you?"

"Oh, I can't complain," Frank says. "My wife left me for a man half my age, but I can't say I didn't see it coming. You know how much she resented all the time I spend here. But business is still booming, and I love this place, so it's all good."

"I'm sorry to hear that," Isabella says. "I had a nasty

breakup before I met Catalina, but that is all in the past too. But enough of all that. Let's go over and join the party." She gestures toward the growing group of people gathered around the couple, Mark and Filipe both clearly in party mode by the look of things.

***

Close to midnight, the group has dwindled down to just Mark, Filipe, Isabella, and Catalina, when the conversation turns to same-sex marriage.

"You two are so lucky to be able to get married," Catalina says. "In Panama, we aren't as progressive. I think it might actually be illegal. At least that's what my family seems to think."

"What a shame," Filipe says. "It became legal in Manitoba back in 2004, after a groundbreaking case in the Court of Queen's Bench."

"Yeah, we Canadians are quite the liberal lot," Mark adds. "By 2005, same-sex marriages were legal across Canada, making us the fourth country in the world to do so."

"Wow," Catalina says. "Maybe we should at least consider moving here, Izzy. What do you think?"

"I don't know, I—"

"Catalina has a great point, Izzy," Mark interjects. "And it would be so amazing to have you two living here. I can totally imagine the four of us becoming the best of friends and hanging out all the time."

"You know how much I'd love to be closer to you,"

Isabella says. "But before everyone jumps on the bandwagon of Catalina and I moving back to this frozen wasteland in winter and mosquito paradise in summer, you two should come and check out Panama. There's something about it that fills me up, heart and soul, that was calling me there before I'd ever laid eyes on it."

"I'm totally on board to come down for a visit," Filipe says.

"Let's leave it at that then," Isabella says, raising her glass. "For now, let's toast to the both of you. I'm so thrilled Mark met someone like you, Filipe. It's clear that you are the real deal—not only handsome but intelligent and big-hearted too. And you already know how much I look up to and respect you, Mark. Congratulations! Cheers to tying the knot tomorrow!"

"Thank you, Izzy," Mark says. "But speaking of our big day, I think it's actually already begun." He looks at his phone to check the time. "It's almost one in the morning. I think we'd better call it a night, so we can get at least a few hours of sleep. My mom is serving Filipe and I brunch at ten, only nine hours from now."

"Oh, I forgot all about that," Filipe says. "We'd better get a move on."

The next day, Isabella and Catalina enjoy a lazy morning lolling about at home. The house begins to bustle with activity as everyone takes turns showering and getting ready.

"My, don't you two look stunning?" Toni says. He's seated in his recliner watching the news, dressed in his suit, tie already loosened, when Isabella and Catalina come downstairs. Isabella is wearing a simple sleeveless linen dress the colour of honey that shows off her tan and accentuates her prominent collarbone and slim figure. Catalina's low-cut cherry-red silk wrap dress hugs her shapely curves.

"Thank you, Papa. You look handsome yourself. Where's Maman?"

"Right behind you," Sylvie says, appearing at the top of the stairs in a classy navy suit-dress with pointy-toed cream slingbacks and a matching clutch.

"Since we don't need to leave for another half hour, why don't we take a few photos out back before we go?" Isabella asks.

The street outside the Anderson home is lined with cars when Toni pulls up, despite it being a small, intimate wedding with only twenty-five people on the guest list. Toni finds a spot one street over. The weather is perfect, calm and sunny with a slight breeze that cuts pleasantly through the thick humidity.

The driveway is tastefully lined with the flowerpots they'd helped Amelie assemble the morning before. The double front doors are ajar, and stepping into the front entrance, the foyer with cathedral ceilings makes a grand impression. The marble floors lead to an open concept living, dining, and kitchen area, the granite counters gleaming in the early afternoon sun, then through to the patio doors.

Outside, white folding chairs are arranged along either side of a long aisle of cut grass, with more vases of flowers placed every few feet on both sides. At the front, there is a podium where Mark and Filipe stand off to one side. Sylvie, Toni, and Catalina take a seat while Isabella walks to the front to join Mark and Filipe.

"You both could be on the front of *GQ* magazine," Isabella says, giving them brief hugs. "Are you as relaxed as you look?"

"I've got massive butterflies, but I'm glad you can't tell," Mark says.

"Not me," Filipe says. "I've never been surer or more ready for anything in my life."

The harpist begins to play, and the justice of the peace takes her place behind the podium. A hush falls over the small gathering as the grooms take their places, Isabella beside Mark, with both rings in hand. The ceremony has been tailored to Mark and Filipe's unique requests. They've both written their own vows and they've done away with the usual readings and hymns, keeping the entire service to just over half an hour. After they exchange their rings and kiss one another, Amelie and Filipe's mother Eva appear beside their sons.

"I just want to thank everyone for joining us today, to celebrate the union of my two favourite men in the world," Eva says.

It's easy to see where Filipe got his athletic build

and handsome good looks, his mother looking stunning in a gorgeous mahogany organza gown that brings out her pecan-brown eyes. When she finishes her speech welcoming Mark into her family, two servers dressed in tuxedos appear with trays of crystal flutes and circulate amongst the guests. When everyone has a glass, Amelie takes her turn to welcome Filipe.

"Now everyone, please join us in a toast, to the newly-weds," Amelie says.

The afternoon flows into evening, with a gorgeous catered meal followed by music and dancing. Shortly after midnight, Sylvie is ready to go, and, as the designated driver, she rounds up the rest of the crew.

The week goes by in a flurry of activity and soon it is the day before Isabella and Catalina return to Panama. Everyone is gathered outside on the deck when Isabella scrolls through her phone to see a new text from Eduardo.

"Oh my God," Isabella exclaims. Hand on heart, she reads the amazing news out loud. "*Buenas*, Izzy. I know you're still in Canada, but I just wanted to let you know right away that your painting sold for two thousand dollars."

"What?" Sylvie says. "I can't believe it!"

"Here, read it for yourself, Maman," Isabella says, passing her mother her phone.

"It does say two thousand dollars!" Sylvie says to the group, her eyes wide.

"I always knew my Izzy had a special talent," Toni says, beaming with pride.

"Well, I'm in shock," Isabella says, her hands shaking so much she drops her phone. "It wasn't long ago that Catalina and I wondered what exciting directions our lives might take. Now, here I am, having sold my art for a price I never could have imagined in my wildest dreams."

"This is such fantastic news," Catalina says. "I'm so proud of you. I was feeling sad to go back home. I've been having such a great time here. But now I'm excited to get back, to thank Tío in person, and to celebrate with you."

Chapter Twelve

Isabella can hardly contain herself. The cheque Eduardo wrote seems to be radiating from inside her purse; she can almost feel the heat against her hip. In her mind's eye, she sees the script handwriting, "two thousand dollars," in black ink. She walks up the sidewalk to the bank entrance. The armed security officer looks lazily through her purse before allowing her to enter. She joins the queue, waiting patiently for her turn.

"*Próximo cliente*," the teller on the far right calls out, not bothering to look up from her computer screen as Isabella approaches.

"*Hola, me gustaría hacer un depósito, por favor*," Isabella says, her Spanish flowing easily.

When the transaction is complete, Isabella walks back outside. It's started to rain, thick droplets that do little to relieve the heat of the day. Isabella pulls out her collapsible navy umbrella and walks briskly toward the bus shelter. She's waiting for the bus when she's overcome with the desire to connect with God and decides to make a pit stop at the church on the corner near her and Catalina's apartment.

Under the massive awning of the church, a homeless man is asleep under a folded cardboard tent, his pant leg flat from the knee down. Isabella steps around him, feeling uneasy. She opens the heavy wooden door, then shakes her soaked umbrella and sets it by the entrance. She makes her way to a pew near the back where she sits down on a smooth bench. There are a few other parishioners in the sanctuary, but not many. A woman in a dull grey smock dress is dusting the ornate stained glass windows that run along the walls.

Isabella closes her eyes and prays. She thanks God for the abundance and for the time in Winnipeg with her parents, Mark, and Filipe. She is about to express gratitude for Catalina when she stops. Her heart constricts. She wonders, not for the first time, if God disapproves of her relationship, if she needs to ask forgiveness for her sins. Tears form in the corners of her eyes and she weeps quietly, her chest feeling as though an anvil has been dropped on it. After a few moments in silence, she feels calmer, her tears like a cleansing ritual. She picks up the Bible on the pew beside her and flips to Matthew, then rereads one of her favourite passages for the hundredth time: "Therefore everyone who hears these words of mine and puts them into practice is like a wise man who built his house on the rock. The rain came down, the streams rose, and the winds blew and beat against the house; yet it did not fall, because it had its foundation on the rock."

Isabella closes the Bible. She sees a bright light in her

imagination and hears a voice telling her that she too is a child of God. She feels enveloped in an invisible embrace that sends shivers down her spine. The bright light turns into an old-fashioned quill pen, and she sees in her mind letters forming in the air in golden handwriting, spelling the word "compassion." She fishes a Kleenex from her purse and dabs at her eyes. She feels more at peace as she rises. She's confident she has built her life on the solid foundation of her belief in God. She remembers the times she felt tested. When Darius raped her. When her father was diagnosed with cancer. These things, she knows, are the rains and the winds of life. And yet, she's still standing.

Back outside, the rain has slackened, just a few tiny drips here and there. The homeless man is awake. He looks at her with a tired, defeated expression on his wrinkled face. Isabella thinks of the word "compassion" and digs in her purse for her wallet. She wouldn't normally give money, concerned that it would only be used to feed an addiction, but she feels compelled to share at least a small token from the sale of her art. She takes a five-dollar bill and places it in the rusty tin can by his feet, a smile on her face.

"*Buenas*," Isabella says, looking him in the eye.

"*Gracias*," he says, as he reaches out his hand and Isabella shakes it warmly.

Isabella sits down on the step beside him and attempts a brief exchange, but the man shuffles himself further under his cardboard structure and turns his back to her.

On the bus ride home, Isabella can't stop thinking about the homeless man. She wonders what misfortune brought him to his fate, whether he has a mental illness or an addiction or is simply down on his luck, perhaps unable to work due to his handicap? She's glad she made the decision to share a bit of her new-found abundance with him, knowing that five dollars isn't much but will at least buy him a decent meal or two if he spends it wisely.

"Izzy, you're soaked to the skin," Catalina fusses as soon as Isabella enters their cramped, dark apartment. "Leave your wet clothes by the door, *mi amor*. I'll hang them up while you go take a nice hot shower."

"Thank you," Isabella says. "That does sounds amazing."

When Isabella gets out of the shower, she discovers Catalina has brought in her terry robe and left it on the hook on the back of the door. She towels off, then pulls her robe on, tying the sash around her small waist. When she comes out of the steamy bathroom, she sees Catalina sitting on the daybed with two mugs of tea in front of her.

"Um, that smells like my favourite blend of camomile and honey, thank you," Isabella says, taking a seat beside Catalina. "How was your day?"

"It was fine," Catalina says. "I managed to miss the thunderstorm, getting home from grocery shopping just before it started. I stocked up, so we've got plenty of choices for the workweek ahead. It's going to be hard to get back into it, after such a lovely week away."

"Yes, I have to admit, I'm not really looking forward to it," Isabella says. "Work has become rather routine, and with Julio walking around surrounded by a cloud of doom all the time, not to mention knowing he told Alex about us, it's so uncomfortable."

"No kidding," Catalina says. "That guy is such a jerk. And he's not even good with the students. I don't know why Ms. Gomez puts up with him."

"I just wish I could rely on a steady income from painting," Isabella says. "I'd happily give up teaching if I knew I could continue to sell my work for the kind of money *The Rogue Scorpion* brought in. I wish I could trust in myself, but I'm scared to take a leap of faith. Speaking of taking a leap, I wonder if we should start looking for a bigger, brighter apartment? With two of us contributing to the rent, I think we can afford it."

"I would love that," Catalina says. "Let's look through the classifieds and set up some viewings for next weekend."

When dinner is finished and the dishes are put away, their lunches packed for work, Isabella gets out her sketchbook journal and starts a rough likeness of the homeless man, while his image is still fresh in her mind.

At work the next day, Isabella and Catalina discover Julio was let go while they were away, the rumour circulating that he was inappropriate with one of his young female students, who had to the courage to report him.

"What, are you a psychic?" Isabella asks Catalina. "You

just said yesterday that Ms. Gomez should fire him, and boom, now we find out she did exactly that."

"I know, right?" Catalina says. "Although I never imagined him to be that creepy, to have a thing for minors. That's just plain disgusting. And he had the nerve to judge us."

Isabella has a flash in her mind, of the word "compassion."

"I can't help but feel a little sorry for him," Isabella says. "I mean, what must have happened to him in his life? I always felt something was broken inside him, how he walked around disgruntled and depressed most of the time. Maybe he grew up with a father or uncle who sexually abused him, and that's why he was so hard on us? You never know someone else's story."

"Izzy, you're such a softie," Catalina says. "Always thinking the best of everyone. And I love that about you. But in this case, I think you're way off. Julio deserves everything he got and probably more."

"You might be right," Isabella says. "But remember what it says in the Bible about judging others?"

"You mean the many parts that say God will judge you as you have judged others?" Catalina says.

"Yeah," Isabella says. "So many people have judged us just for loving each other in a way that doesn't make sense to them, or feels wrong in their minds."

"I suppose you're right," Catalina says. "The line between right and wrong, good and evil, isn't always as clear as we might like to think. But just because I don't want anything to do with people like Julio doesn't mean I'm judging them. I'm being discerning." She stops to look at her phone. "Oh, look at the time. We've only got a few minutes to prepare before our first group of students arrives. I hope you have a positive and uplifting day, and share your upbeat outlook and sunny disposition with all of your students."

"Thank you, you too," Isabella says. She heads over to her workstation and gets the materials ready, determined to forget about Julio and focus on her students.

That evening after work, Isabella is scrolling lazily through social media when a notification pops up from Brian.

Hi Izzy, I hope you are well and still loving life in Panama. Things here in Duncan are pretty much same old, same old. I'm feeling like I need to switch things up a little, and I can't seem to stop thinking about Panama and how much I enjoyed the vibe there. I was thinking that maybe I might take some time off work in December and make the trip down over the Xmas holidays, but I thought I'd check in with you before I booked anything. I'd hate to miss you if you're planning to go away over the holidays yourself.

By the way, I ran into Alex the other day. He looked positively awful. I thought he might be drunk or high or something, he looked so spaced out. It looked like he hadn't taken a shower for a while and maybe slept in his clothes, it was that bad. I did see that his last book received some pretty nasty reviews. I don't know if you 2 are still in touch, but I couldn't help but remember what a jerk he was to you. Anyway, let me know what you think of my plans.

"I just received a message from a guy I used to know when I lived on Vancouver Island," Isabella says to Catalina. "He wants to come and visit over the Christmas holidays. What do you think?"

"To be honest, I haven't thought that far ahead," Catalina says. "I'm still thinking about my family drama, wondering how to repair things with my mother and Kamila before the holidays. And ever since we talked about work feeling like a drain, I've started daydreaming about going back to school."

"Sounds like I should pour us both a drink that has more punch than tea," Isabella says, getting up and going into the kitchen. She cracks open a bottle of Pinot Grigio and pours them both large goblets, then rejoins Catalina on the couch. "Brian said he saw Alex looking pretty down and out. I feel kinda sorry for him. He's got a good heart, deep down."

"You've got to be kidding me!" Catalina exclaims. "After what that asshole did to you?"

"Now, Catalina, there's no need to get all worked up again," Isabella says in a steady, soft voice. "I'm not saying what he did was okay. I'm just saying that he isn't all bad. I always felt he was a bit of a lost soul, and I guess I thought I could help him find his way if I just loved him enough. As it turned out, he was too hard to love, even for me."

"That's right," Catalina says, taking her voice level down a notch, making the effort to curb her emotional reaction a little. "I bet his own mother has a hard time with it. I think it's time for you to stop trying to save all the losers and lost souls and focus on yourself and on us. Put that energy into your painting and perhaps your dreams will become a reality."

"You're probably right," Isabella says. "But in that spirit, let's drop the talk of Alex and focus on you and your desire to go back to school. What is your heart calling you to do?"

"Well, that's the thing. I'm not as clear in my passions as you," Catalina says. She takes a sip. "I love tennis, but I'm not about to become a tennis pro at my age. You know how much I enjoy music and art, but I don't see a career for me in either of those arenas either. What do you think?"

"I think you've always trusted your heart and followed your intuition, so if you take some time to be still and listen, the answers will be revealed to you," Isabella says. "I've often been in awe of how confident and assertive you are, and I'm sure those skills will make whatever you choose a success."

"Thank you, and you're right," Catalina smiles. "There's no need to rush into making any decisions. I'll know when I know. For now, let's talk strategy on how we're going to repair my broken family."

Catalina and Isabella stay up for hours past their usual bedtime, completely absorbed in discussion. They explore possibilities, and while they don't come up with any sure-fire solutions, they both agree the first step is for Catalina to be the one to find the courage to reach out. Catalina sends a text to her mother, asking if she'll meet up with her at the mall, hoping that shopping will be neutral enough to get things under way. Ciara texts back right away, suggesting they meet up the following Saturday.

———

Catalina has sent her mother a text to meet her at Paul Bakery for coffee and croissants. When she arrives at the restaurant, she sees her mother already seated at the table. Ciara looks older than Catalina remembers, even though it's been just over a month since she saw her. Catalina takes a seat across from her, at a loss for words, an awkward silence stretching on after they say hello.

"You look well," Ciara says after a few strained moments. "What did you think of Canada? What were Isabella's parents like?"

"Thank you, *Mamá*," Catalina says. "I am well, and I had a great time in Canada. I got along really well with Mr. and Mrs. Ricci, but it only seemed to make our rift feel wider. I miss you. I love you. I'm hoping we can repair our relationship, or at least agree to disagree."

"I've missed you too," Ciara says. She reaches both her hands across the table and takes Catalina's in hers. "I've been praying. I went to confession. Our priest told me that even though it is clear from the Bible that homosexuality is a sin, we are all sinners, and it is not for us to judge one another. Still, I hate to think of God judging my Catalina, of you dooming your soul to hell. I just feel so overwhelmed."

Catalina is silent for a moment, her mother's painful words hard to hear.

"I appreciate you being honest about your feelings," Catalina says. "But the priest is right; we're all sinners. None of us knows what will happen to us when we die, but we do get to choose how we live. I'm not willing to be someone I'm not, even for your approval, but I want you in my life."

Just then the waitress approaches and asks them for their order, oblivious to the private moment she is interrupting. They place their orders, and when they are alone again, Ciara picks up where they left off.

"I think it would be best if we spend time together like this, just the two of us, and hold off on family get-togethers, at least for a while."

"You know what, you're right," Catalina says. "We've always done better without the group dynamics of our crazy family. I'm willing to do that, at least for now. Maybe with time, it will get easier?"

"At least it's a start," Ciara says. "But if you wouldn't mind, I'd really like to move on and talk about other things, okay? You know how uncomfortable I am talking about feelings, especially hurtful ones."

"Yeah, I know," Catalina agrees. "Let's talk about what we have on our shopping lists."

The two of them discuss the latest fashion over coffee, then head out on a mission to find a new pair of jeans for Catalina and a pair of shoes for Ciara. The conflict remains unresolved, but somehow forgotten, at least for a few hours.

Isabella practises yoga in the park while Catalina is at the mall with her mother. She's lying on her mat in *savasana*, in a state between consciousness and dreaming, when she experiences a mystical moment of clarity. As Isabella rolls up her mat, her mind is already spinning with ideas, and she can hardly wait to get home and talk about them with Catalina.

Over lunch, Catalina tells Isabella all about her visit with her mother and shows off her new dark denim jeans, much to Isabella's delight. Isabella waits until Catalina has finished telling her about her conversation with her mother before she brings up the ideas she formulated during yoga.

"While I was practising yoga today, I had the coolest vision," Isabella says. "I saw the word 'compassion' in golden letters again, but this time I sensed that I need to demonstrate compassion toward myself, just like you've been telling me."

"Thank God, you're coming around!" Catalina laughs. "But I do love that you have these crazy visions. Tell me more."

"Well, after I saw the word 'compassion,' I not only knew it was time to focus on my dream of becoming a successful artist, but I also had the inspiration for a whole series! I'm going to start with the homeless man I saw at the church, then Darius, Alex, and Julio. I'm going to call it *Lost Souls*. What do you think?"

"I think it sounds amazing, and it will absolutely be a success because it came to you in a vision. It's got to be an intuitive part of your purpose."

"Thank you for being such a rock star partner, supporting me in everything I do," Isabella says. "And as much as I can hardly wait to get to my easel, I think we should resume our search for a new apartment and try to set up a couple of viewings."

After researching online, Catalina and Isabella select three apartments that look like possibilities and set up appointments to view them.

"Well, that one was a dud," Isabella says. The landlord has just completed their tour of a two-bedroom in a brand-new apartment tower near the ocean. "I thought it would be so sweet to switch it up to something modern, but that place had absolutely no character at all."

"I have to agree," Catalina says. "It felt like a glorified cardboard box, all white walls and beige floors. And it was almost as small as the one we're in." She scratches the apartment off her list and reads the address for the next apartment out loud.

The second space turns out to be a better fit for them in terms of style and the open concept design, but the location is so far out from the city centre that it would make getting around by bus nearly impossible, plus there's no parking space for Catalina's car. Catalina crosses it off her list too.

"Let's hope this last one has it all, or we'll be back to the drawing board," Isabella says. "I'd forgotten how unpleasant house hunting can be."

"I know, it sucks, but at least we both agree we want a space that is open, with cozy character," Catalina says. They hop back into the car. "Did you punch in the address for the next place?" Catalina asks, putting the key in the ignition.

"Yep, it's all ready," Isabella says, pressing start on her phone map app.

Soon Catalina is turning onto the correct street. She gets an uncomfortable feeling in the pit of her stomach as she parks the car.

"I'm sorry, but this place is giving me the creeps," Catalina says, pointing to the goosebumps on her arm.

"If you don't feel good about it already, we might as well save our time," Isabella says. She sends a text to cancel the viewing and Catalina drives them back home.

"Well, I guess that was a total bust, but honestly, I'd rather stay put than move into either place we saw today. And that last neighbourhood didn't feel right at all," Catalina says.

"Yeah, there's no need no rush into anything," Isabella says. "I always say, 'When in doubt, do nothing.'"

"Oh, that's good advice," Catalina chuckles.

Over morning coffee the next day, Catalina shares a dream she had with Isabella.

"It felt so real, like it was really happening," Catalina says. "And when I woke up, not only did I remember every detail, but it also felt like a message because I was so happy. I dreamt I was an art broker."

"I think you should reach out to Tío and pick his brain."

"I think so too," Catalina says. "Maybe he'll turn out to be a guardian angel for both of us."

Catalina meets up with Eduardo a few days later at a casual restaurant near his gallery. He's only too delighted to have a protege, none of his children having any interest in art, and offers to take her under his wing. He tells her that she definitely has a good eye and the right kind of outgoing, assertive personality, but she'll need a fine arts degree from either the University of Panama or GANEXA University of Arts, depending on what she chooses to study. They get into a deep discussion about the different styles and history of art, both losing track of the time.

"Tío, can you believe it? We've been talking for almost three hours now," Catalina says, glancing over at her phone when the screen lights up with a text from Isabella.

"Yes, and the fact that you are so passionate is a good indicator that you're on the right path," Eduardo says. "Would you like me to take you for a tour of both campuses next week? I have a few contacts at both institutions."

"That is so generous of you, and yes, I would love that!" Catalina beams. "I know school will be expensive, but I think it's totally worth it to invest in myself and my future."

"I agree wholeheartedly, and I support you," Eduardo says, rising from his chair.

———

After discussing her meeting with Isabella, Catalina ends up choosing to attend the University of Panama to pursue an art history degree and enrols for the upcoming semester that begins in January. Her decision leads her and Isabella to search for a new apartment close to the university. Catalina makes an agreement with Ms. Gomez to stay on at the ESL centre part-time, confident she can manage the heavy load of full-time school and part-time work with Isabella's support.

At the end of the month, Catalina discovers a new listing for an apartment that ticks the most important boxes on their list. The rent is within their budget, and it's close to the metro and bus stations, almost smack in the middle between the university and ESL centre. It's a refurbished two-bedroom unit in an older building, with character to spare, and available for them to move in on October first. They both feel certain that their lives are moving in positive directions and that together, they will overcome whatever obstacles come their way.

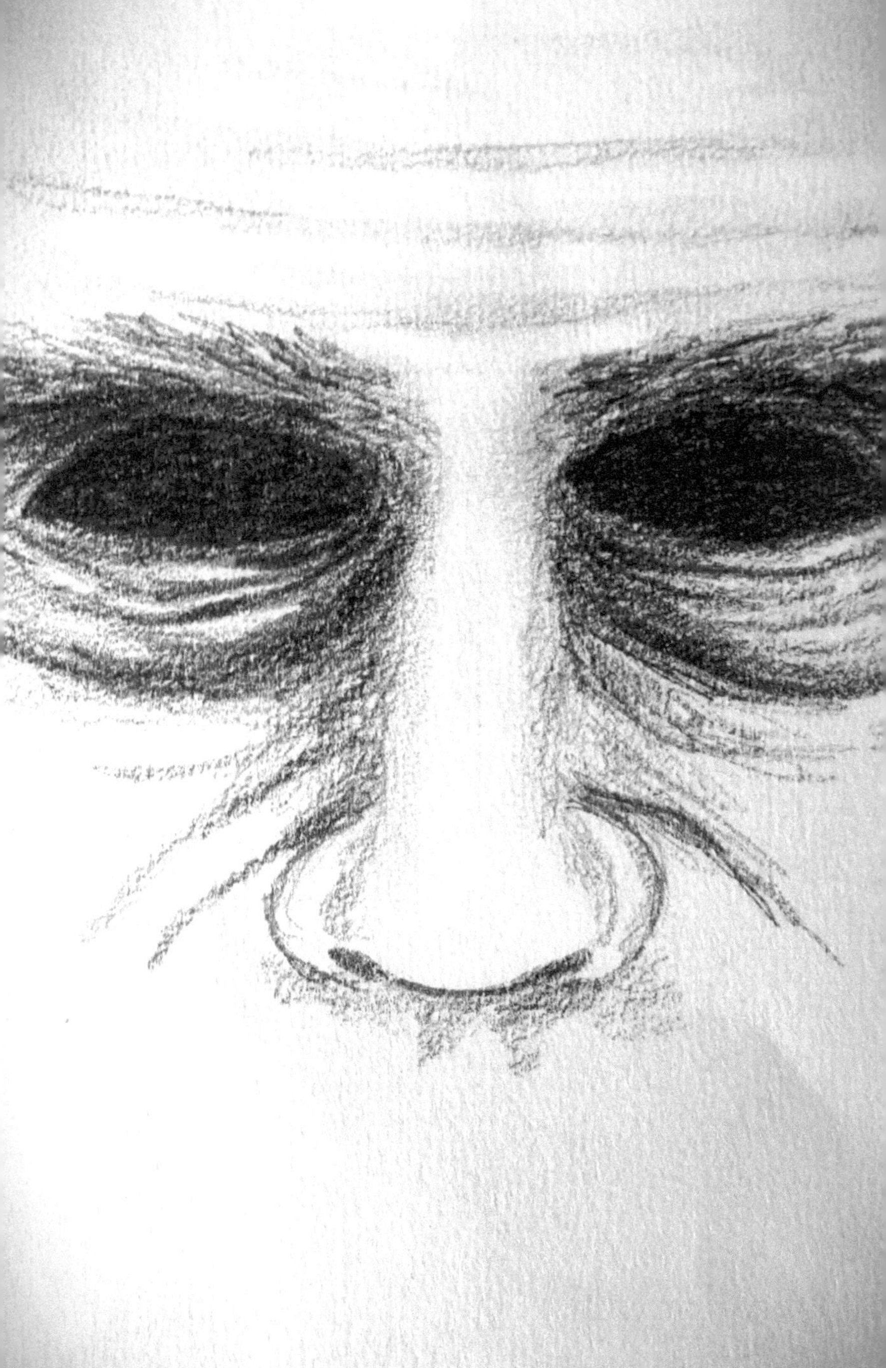

Chapter Thirteen

The first of October falls on a Monday, but the landlord of their new building reaches out to Catalina a few days before to inform her that the old tenant has moved out and the apartment is ready for them to move in early.

Their new apartment is on a busy side street, the building only four storeys, with eight units on each floor. They're on the top floor, which is amazing for the views from the master bedroom, kitchen window, and hall balcony, but not so great for hauling in furniture with no elevator.

Lucky for them, Catalina convinces Lorenzo and Geovani to help out again, as well as her cousin Nic.

It's surprising how much they're able to pack into Geovani's old faded white Isuzu pickup truck. Between the five of them, they manage to move everything in, finishing shortly after the sun sets. Catalina orders pizza and Isabella stocks the freshly cleaned fridge full of beer.

"It feels so bare," Catalina says, popping open a can of

Balboa while plopping onto the new grey leather couch, a gift from Eduardo. She looks around at the stacks of boxes amid their mismatched furnishings. "I must admit though, I'm going to enjoy getting this place spruced up and feeling like a home. Having an extra room will be so useful."

"I agree," Isabella says. "We'll have space for guests, and when no one is visiting, the spare room will make a nice, quiet space for you to study."

"Study?" Nic says, swiping at the stray lock of hair that's escaped his man-bun. "Are you taking a course?"

"Well, not yet, but I've registered for the next semester of uni. It starts up just after Christmas."

"Going back to school at your age?" Geovani teases. He winks, his slight lips pulled into a grin.

"Well, better late than never," Catalina says. "And besides, I never knew I wanted to be an art broker until now."

"An art broker?" Lorenzo asks as he lowers himself onto a checkered side chair to join his sister with a cold beer. "Tío will be thrilled when he finds out that someone in the family is interested in a career in art."

"Yes, he is. I already told him," Catalina says. "And of course, he's exhibiting Isabella's paintings too."

"Is this your latest creation?" Nic says, pointing to the large twenty-four-by-thirty-six-inch canvas with a cloth folded over it and propped up on an easel near the window.

"Yes, it's the first in a series I have in mind," Isabella says.

"Can I take a look?" Nic asks, already making his way over.

"Um, actually, I've only just gotten started . . ." Isabella begins to say, following right behind him, not quite ready to reveal her muse. But Nic is already removing the cloth.

"This has serious potential," Nic says. He steps back a bit and scratches his goatee, the other hand on his slim hip. "Trust me, growing up surrounded by art, I know what's good and what isn't, even though my father insists it's all subjective. You've really captured the essence of this character. Is he inspired by a real person, or from your imagination?"

"A real person," Isabella says. She's a little annoyed with Nic's uninvited critique, but she chooses not to get worked up about it. "I saw him outside the church near our old apartment."

"You go to church? Are you Catholic?" Geovani asks, suddenly interested in the conversation.

"Um, sort of, I guess," Isabella says. "At least, I was raised in the Catholic faith. But ever since I left home, I've been on a spiritual journey. I discovered Buddhism when I lived in Thailand, and some of the beliefs resonated with me, but I still felt like I was missing something. I've read some very interesting books on the subject. Eckhart Tolle's ideas feel like truth for me, although his writing is academic and abstract, not an easy read by any means. I still believe in the teachings of Jesus, though. He was definitely the real deal."

"Wow, that's got to be the most unusual story I've ever heard," Geovani says, his inquisitive nature overriding his tendency to be withdrawn. "I'd like to hear more."

"Ugh, please say no, Izzy," Lorenzo says, clapping

his huge hands over his ears in exaggeration. "If there's one thing that can spoil a conversation, it's a discussion about religion."

"Or politics," Nic adds with a laugh.

"Why don't you tell us more about your childhood, growing up in Canada, then?" Lorenzo suggests. "I have to admit, everything I know about Canada I learned in one history class, and I think there was, like, one paragraph. Something about Eskimos, hockey, and beavers."

"Oh my," Isabella laughs. "You do have some gaps. I'm more than happy to fill you in."

Over the next several hours, the unlikely fivesome get into deep conversations. By the time the men are ready to go, there has been a shift and, without saying it, Isabella knows she's broken through a barrier. It feels good to be witnessed and received, at least by these three members of Catalina's family. She feels like she's stepping more and more into the flow of life and her authentic self each day, *paso a paso y despacio.*

Isabella works on her painting of the homeless man in every minute of her spare time and ends up finishing by the end of October. When she shows it to Eduardo, she tells him about her inspiration for the rest of the *Lost Souls* series, and Eduardo is delighted by her ambition. He suggests they set a goal for Isabella to have her first exhibition in the spring.

"If you can keep up this intense pace, you should be

able to complete all four paintings you have in mind for this series," Eduardo says. "I work with a few other artists that I think would show well with your style, but I'd like to introduce you to them first. What do you think?"

"I'd love that," Isabella says. "I work at the ESL centre every weekday, but I'm free most weekends and evenings. If you let me know the date and time that works for everyone, if there is a conflict with work, I can clear my schedule with my manager."

The positive interactions between Lorenzo, Geovani, Nic, and Isabella have Catalina emboldened to try again to repair her relationship with her sister, but Kamila won't reply to her messages. During her weekly shopping date with her mother, they are browsing through a sale bin of handbags when Catalina decides to open up about her feelings with her mother.

"I know Kamila is strong-willed, and I respect that," Catalina says. "But I honestly don't know what I've done to upset her so much. She's the one who was rude and judgmental toward both Isabella and me."

"There's always two sides to every story," Ciara says. "I know you think that Kamila is stuck-up, but that tough exterior of hers is only a mask she wears to hide her sensitivity. Your sister has built so many walls around her heart; it is a fortress."

"Except when it comes to Papá," Catalina says. "In his eyes, she can do no wrong and she knows it."

"That's certainly true," Ciara says. "But sometimes it's a burden to be the favourite too."

"I never thought of that," Catalina says. She looks pensive. "But it doesn't help me solve this situation. Despite our differences, I love her, and I miss having my sister in my life."

"Sometimes in life we need to be patient," Ciara says.

"I know, I know, but I'm finding that so hard, especially with the holidays just around the corner. Not to mention Kamila's graduation from uni in the spring. With all this friction between us, it's bound to have an impact on our celebrations."

"You're right about that," Ciara says. "But there are some things in life we just have to accept, and I feel this is one of them. Kamila will come around when and if she's ready."

"*Vale Mamá*, I hear you," Catalina says. "I'll do my best to let it go and trust that all will be well. I'm grateful that at least you and I are in a good space again. Oh, and speaking of Kamila's graduation, I almost forgot to tell you; I've decided to pursue a fine arts degree at the University of Panama."

"What?" Ciara says. "That's amazing news! I never imagined you in the art field, but people change directions sometimes. Congratulations! I'm so proud of you."

"*Gracias*." Catalina takes her mother's slight hand in hers. "Tío is taking me under his wing."

"So much news to take in," Ciara stops to hold out two handbags. "But now, for the big question, am I going to buy this gorgeous black-and-white shoulder bag or the cherry-red clutch?"

"Why choose?" Catalina says with a laugh. "This sale is too good to pass up. If you're in doubt, my advice is to buy both."

On the day of Isabella's twenty-eighth birthday, the first thing she sees when she turns on her phone in the morning is a message from Mark.

Happy Birthday, beautiful! Are you and Catalina available for a FaceTime tonight?

Sure thing, Isabella texts back. *We'll ring you when we get back from work.*

When she opens her email, there is a birthday message from her parents, as well as a flood of messages on Facebook and Instagram.

"I feel so fortunate to have so many wonderful people in my life," Isabella says to Catalina, who is on her phone as well, beside her in bed.

"I agree, and I feel lucky too," Catalina says. "I've been trying my best to focus on the good relationships I have, instead of obsessing over the ones that feel distant."

"That's a good attitude," Isabella says. She stretches and gets out of bed, setting her phone on the dresser. "And I also think you should be proud of yourself for the progress you have made. You might not be as close with your mother as you felt before, but at least you two are seeing one another regularly. It's a good start."

"That's true," Catalina says, still cozy under their new duvet. "But I can't help but feel a little jealous of how quickly and completely both your parents came around."

"They were pretty amazing," Isabella says. "And speaking of them, I was wondering how you feel about inviting them to come down for a visit over the holidays? I know it would be a little cramped, but—"

Isabella doesn't have time to finish her sentence before Catalina interrupts, having come around to her side of the bed. She places her finger on Isabella's lips while pulling her in for an embrace.

"Shh, *mi amor*, there's no question and no need to ask. Your parents are always welcome in our home, any time, and I think it's a lovely idea."

"Thank you," Isabella says. She leans in to kiss Catalina. "Let's discuss it during our weekly FaceTime chat on Sunday."

After work, Catalina and Isabella stop in at their regular restaurant, treating themselves to takeout. Catalina has a bottle of Isabella's favourite white wine cooling in the fridge. They are just tidying up their dishes when Isabella's laptop rings.

"Happy birthday!" Mark and Filipe crow in unison as soon as Isabella answers. She takes a seat on the new couch, the computer set up on the coffee table.

"Thank you," Isabella says. "Catalina has been spoiling me with special little things all day. I feel so full of gratitude, and talking to you two is the icing on the cake."

"Where is Catalina?" Mark asks.

"Oh, she's just packing up our leftovers," Isabella says. Catalina shouts out "*hola*" from the kitchen.

"Filipe and I both have some banked vacation time we need to figure out what to do with, and I couldn't help thinking about how you asked us to come down to Panama," Mark says after Catalina comes over to join them.

"Really?" Isabella says, her hand to her heart. "That would be so amazing! When are you thinking?"

"I don't know. The sooner the better, I guess," Filipe says.

"Well, Izzy's parents are coming down for the Christmas holidays, but other than that, our calendar is wide open," Catalina says. "Although with me just starting school and still working part-time, I'll have more time to hang out if you come during the spring reading break."

"Oh, right, Izzy did mention that. I forgot to say congratulations," Mark says. "And trust me, you're right to anticipate being super busy. I still remember vividly how intense it was, juggling school with work and everything else."

"Sounds like spring break it is then," Isabella says. "Let us know once you have your tickets booked."

They share stories with one another, enjoying their connection for almost an hour. By the time they are ready to hang up and call it a night, both Catalina and Isabella are ready for some downtime. Catalina curls up on the couch in her satin robe with a book while Isabella retrieves her sketchbook journal.

Isabella flips through to one of the first entries, not long after she arrived in Thailand. She looks at her abstract drawings, so full of painful emotions, and remembers Darius, the snake charmer from Toronto, who pretended to be so friendly, only to drug and rape her. The memories are still painful but have softened a little with the passage of time. Her book almost full, she flips to one of the last fresh pages at the end and begins to draw the outline for her second painting in her *Lost Souls* series. As she is drawing, she feels a sharp pang of anger and her chest constricts, but then the word "compassion" comes into her mind again. It's difficult for her to feel anything close to compassion for Darius, but she encourages herself to imagine what kind of inner turmoil he must have been suffering from to behave with such brutal disrespect for another human being. She draws a close-up of his face, with creases in his brow and a hollow look in his eyes.

On the weekend, Catalina surprises Isabella with dinner reservations at an interesting-looking restaurant with a great rating that they've never been to. They get dressed up and decide to grab a taxi so that Catalina can enjoy celebrating without worrying about having to drive.

They arrive right on time for their reservation, and the taxi pulls into the parking lot just as a valet dressed in a crisp white suit jacket walks over to greet them.

"*Bienvenidos*," the valet says as soon as they exit the car. He gestures his hand toward the short flight of stairs at the end of a narrow wood-plank deck. Thick gold rope is strung between silver poles to cordon off the space, and the row of square windows that line the wall of the restaurant look like portholes, giving the effect of entering a yacht. Isabella lifts the hem of her floor-length linen dress, both women wearing the dresses they wore for Mark's wedding, their only formal clothes.

"This is so original," Isabella says, her eyes bright. "Oh, and look, Catalina, the door has an authentic ship's steering wheel as the handle. Who did you say recommended this place?"

"No one. I found it when I googled restaurants with a four-star rating or higher," Catalina says. "When I saw the online photos, it definitely intrigued me. Apparently, seafood is their speciality."

"Good thing I gave up on being a vegan when I moved down here," Isabella says as the handsome host, dressed in a pristine jacket similar to the valet's, opens the door.

Inside, the ambience is inviting, with the nautical theme continued. Their host leads them past a long, well-stocked bar lined with plush white leather stools and glassware gleaming in rows lit up by soft yellow pot lights, to their reserved table in a corner at the back. He pulls out the chair for Isabella as Catalina slides onto the bench seat.

"This is just so stunning," Isabella says. "I really feel spoiled."

"Then my plan is successful," Catalina says. She reaches across the table and takes Isabella's hand in hers, giving it an affectionate squeeze.

They are browsing the extensive menu when their server appears with a silver jug of ice water. He asks in Spanish if they would like a drink to start and Catalina orders a bottle of Prosecco. Once their crystal flutes have been filled, Catalina raises her glass and clinks Isabella's in a toast.

"To the love of my life, in celebration of the day God chose to bring you into this world, and in gratitude that the journey brought you here, to Panama, and to my heart."

A group of four men are sitting adjacent to them and ogling both women openly. Isabella catches it out of the corner of her eye but chooses to ignore it. She continues her conversation with Catalina, leaning in close and lowering her voice.

"Looks like these two next to us may need to get a room," one man says, loud enough for everyone seated nearby to hear, a scowl on his face.

"No need to be disheartened, Rico," one of his companions replies. "Maybe you can convince them both to come home with you, two for the price of one?"

The rude comment is followed by a loud burst of laughter from all the men at the table. Isabella is quietly mortified, but Catalina isn't about to be disrespected by anyone.

"In your wildest dreams would either one of us choose to go home with you," Catalina says, her face red as a ripe tomato. "I was just sitting here thinking how unfortunate for your mother that she birthed into the world a man as ugly and ignorant as you, but I was respectfully keeping my observations to myself. Perhaps you should consider doing the same?"

The jovial mood at the men's table suddenly shifts as Catalina rises from her seat and approaches them, her hand raised and ready to slap Rico across the face, when their server returns. Catalina lowers her hand.

"Please, sir, I invite you and your companions to take your drinks and move to another table on the other side of the restaurant, or leave, as you wish," he says quietly, but firmly in rapid Spanish. "As I've informed you before, we do not tolerate harassment of any kind here."

Rico starts to protest, but his buddies calm him down, and the foursome get up from their seats, then leave in a cloud of drama without paying their bill. Catalina blushes and returns to her seat, her clenched jaw pulling her neck muscles tighter.

"I'm so sorry," Isabella apologizes. "We never meant to cause a scene."

"It's not your fault," the server says. "Those four have been involved in more than one incident before. If they have the nerve to come back again, I won't be offering them a table. I don't condone disrespectful behaviour."

"Well, I must say, that is so refreshing to hear, and thank you," Catalina says. "What did you say your name was?"

"I'm Rudy."

"A pleasure to meet you, Rudy. The world needs more people like you, willing to stand up for what is right," Catalina says.

"I'm only doing my job. Are you ready to order?" Rudy asks.

"We need a few more minutes," Isabella says. "Do you have any recommendations?"

"Our chef can transform the simplest ingredients into something spectacular," Rudy says. "But if you want my opinion, the squid in white wine sauce is exquisite and the *ceviche* is the best in the city."

"Now that's lofty praise," Isabella laughs.

Despite the rocky beginning, Isabella and Catalina end up having a delightful birthday celebration, and by the time they are ready to leave several hours later, the incident is long forgotten.

During their FaceTime chat with Toni and Sylvie the following Sunday, everyone talks animatedly about their upcoming Christmas plans.

"I bit the bullet and bought tickets departing Winnipeg on December 23, with a connection through the US," Toni says.

"Oh, that's such great news," Catalina says. "Hold on while I grab my phone and put it in my calendar. What time are you scheduled to arrive?"

"Let me see now," Toni says, taking his reading glasses out of his shirt pocket to read the itinerary he printed off. "Our arrival time is 19:45."

"We'll be sure to double-check on the day to make sure your flight is on time," Isabella says. "Now, to really get you excited, how about I take you for a tour of the apartment, including our guest room?"

Isabella plucks the computer off the coffee table and goes for a stroll through the open concept living area and then into the spare room, where the double bed is made up and ready for their arrival, towels already washed and folded on the dresser.

"I'm so glad that you'll be here in time to celebrate Christmas Eve with us," Isabella says, returning to her spot on the couch beside Catalina.

"Yes, we are too," Sylvie agrees. "Is there a church near you where we can attend midnight Mass?"

"There's a Catholic church on practically every second street here," Isabella says with exaggeration. "Catalina and I don't attend regularly, but we have gone to a few services now and again, and we'd be delighted to take you."

"Your daughter seems to be becoming more spiritual every day," Catalina says. "She was extolling the virtues of Jesus to my brothers when they helped us move in, and I think she might have convinced my cousin Nic, who hasn't been in a church in almost a year, to give it another chance. Mind you, she was quick to tell him he didn't need to go to church to have a spiritual connection with God, but then went on to say he might find the sermons and belonging to the church community a positive influence in his life. He's so confused about everything, from God, to the state of the world, to what to do with his own life."

"That certainly sounds like our Izzy," Toni says. "Always the encouraging, positive, and optimistic one."

"Sometimes too much so," Sylvie and Catalina say at

exactly the same time. All four of them break out laughing, and they end the call with the promise to see one another again the following week.

With plans with her parents made, Isabella texts Brian that they already have guests staying over the holidays, but if he decides to come down, they'll be around and she would love to see him again. She's feeling excited about how things are unfolding and super jazzed about creating her *Lost Souls* series. In every spare moment, she is either sketching ideas in her journal or working on her second painting, of Darius. Reliving those painful memories continues to be an emotional experience for her, but somehow painting him has created a space for her to release some of the toxic energy still stagnant inside her. She finds comfort in her yoga practice, in long, teary conversations with Catalina, and during her frequent heart-to-heart conversations with God.

Without making a conscious decision, Isabella starts to drop into the church nearest to them several times a week. She discovers that making prayer in the church sanctuary a regular practice feels like coming home, to the refuge of her childhood, only more so because of how her inward journey has expanded. Her spiritual longing has led her back to the beginning, to the example set by Jesus, only now it's something deeper and more personal than it ever was before. She thinks about Santiago and Siddhartha and how their examples called her to strike out on a new and uncharted path toward fulfilment, so many years ago, when she went on her first adventure to Thailand. Her heart fills with a knowing; her soul is now at one with the world too.

———

The last Sunday of November, Nic sends Isabella a text, wondering if she would mind him tagging along with her to a church service. When Isabella tells Catalina, she decides she might as well join them too, instead of staying at home alone.

A half hour before the service begins, Nic shows up at their apartment looking the most conservative Isabella's ever seen him, having ditched his designer jeans for a proper pair of trousers and even donning a tie.

"It looks like miracles are happening already," Catalina teases. "But seriously, you look very handsome, *mi primo.*"

"I feel so happy," Isabella says, her face aglow as she steps outside their building and into the sun. "I think things are moving in positive directions for all three of us, and I can hardly wait to discover what life has in store."

Chapter Fourteen

It's December 23 and Isabella is so wound up with excitement about her parents' pending arrival, she can barely sit still. She's washed the bed linens in the spare room and made up the bed, fluffing the pillows. At the florist nearby, she picked up a poinsettia and placed the decorative pot on the desk. Catalina drove them to the discount grocery store nearest them the day before and stocked up on all of Toni's and Sylvie's favourite foods. She's even baked a batch of her mother's no-fail shortbread, the sweet scent of icing sugar and vanilla still lingering in the air.

The flight isn't due to arrive until quarter to eight, but at five Isabella is rechecking her phone to make sure it is still on time, pacing the floor impatiently as she waits for the Copa Airlines website to load, the internet in their apartment cutting in and out.

"*Mi amor*, you're going to wear a path into the floor if you don't stop with your nervous pacing," Catalina says, looking up from her spot on the couch where she's reclined, watching television. "You'd think it was royalty coming, not your parents who love you and accept you exactly as you are."

"I know, I know, you're right," Isabella says, still pacing. "It's just that it's the first time in my entire life that my parents have come to stay with me in my own place, and I so want them to feel proud of me." She comes over to sit beside Catalina on the couch, gently lifting her feet and placing them in her lap.

"I can appreciate that," Catalina says. "But you've done everything humanly possible to make our home as perfect and inviting as can be. Your parents are going to feel so spoiled, welcomed, and loved."

"Do you really think so?" Isabella asks, already back on her feet and heading into the kitchen, having spotted a lone crumb on the sparkling countertop.

"I know so," Catalina says with a sigh. "But clearly nothing I say is going to help you relax, so I'll stop trying. Let me know if there's anything else you want me to do."

"Thank you," Isabella says as she runs the dishcloth under hot water and squeezes it, then wipes down the entire counter again.

It's only a half-hour drive to the airport from their apartment, and it will take at least that long for Toni and Sylvie to get through customs and retrieve their luggage, but by seven o'clock Isabella is anxiously rushing Catalina to get a move on. Catalina has decided to go with the flow and not let Isabella's scattered energy bother her. She gathers up her keys and slides her feet into her shoes without complaint. On the drive to the airport, Isabella chatters on and on while Catalina just listens, a smile of detached bemusement on her face.

After finding a parking spot in the crowded lot outside the terminal, Isabella takes Catalina's hand, and they make their way to the pick-up zone outside the arrivals area. It's decked out for Christmas with decorations, wreaths, and trees in every spare nook. People are packed in and lined up along the hall on either side of a partitioned area. An automatic door opens and closes with each stream of new arrivals. Isabella smiles as reunited families embrace one another, the atmosphere of the holidays merry and bright.

Over an hour after seeing on the screen that the flight has arrived, Isabella spots her mother and father pulling their carry-on bags, eyes scanning the crowd, looking like lost sheep.

"Maman! Papa! Over here!" Isabella shouts out, waving her arms back and forth like windshield wipers and smiling ear to ear.

Toni and Sylvie quicken their steps and soon the four of them are sandwiched together in a joyful group hug, all talking at once.

"*Bienvenidos a Panamá,*" Catalina says, taking the handle of Sylvie's bag from her and leading the way through the crowd to the exit.

"How was your flight? Did you have any problems at customs with the Spanish-speaking officers? Was the airline food half-decent?" Isabella peppers them with one question after another before they have a chance to answer the first.

"The flight was lovely," Sylvie says. "There was a buzz of festive excitement in the air as soon as we boarded the plane, and the dinner was just scrumptious. We had wine with our meal, and they served a digestif with traditional Christmas pudding for dessert."

"We even watched a Christmas movie," Toni laughs.

"Oh, and it was priceless how all the flight attendants were wearing Christmas-themed accents, like ornament earrings, reindeer antler headbands, and tacky knit sweaters."

"How wonderful that you had such a great experience," Isabella says as they leave the building and step into the thick heat and humidity.

"I'm going to be a sticky mess before we even get to the car," Sylvie tut-tuts, following Catalina while rifling through her purse for a handkerchief to wipe her brow. "If it's this hot at night, I can only imagine how stifling it will feel in the heat of day."

"Don't worry, Maman. We have several fans and big windows that let in the natural breeze, and our apartment stays comfortable enough," Isabella says.

"Here we are then," Catalina says, clicking the button on her keys to open the hatch and lifting Sylvie's carry-on. Toni hefts the large suitcase he and Sylvie are sharing.

"Papa, your legs are far too long to scrunch up in the back," Isabella says as Toni goes to climb in behind the driver's seat. "You're sitting up front with Catalina and I'll hop in the back with Maman."

Catalina returns with the paid parking slip and climbs in behind the wheel. She navigates through the tight lot, past the exit booth, and into the traffic circle, before turning onto the main highway. On the drive through the city, Toni and Sylvie gawk out the window at all the Christmas displays that line the road.

"I think I detect the salty smell of the ocean through the crack in the window," Toni says.

"Yes, Papa, if you look to the left, you can make out the shoreline," Isabella says.

Soon Catalina is pulling onto their street and the four of them are making their way up the four flights of stairs. Toni is a little out of breath by the time they reach the top.

"Whew, I didn't realize how out of shape I am," Toni says with a whistle and a huge gasp of breath. He gives his now-rounded stomach a pat.

"Maybe by the time your two-week holiday is over, you'll be all trim again, walking up and down four flights of stairs every day," Isabella says, holding the door of the apartment open while Toni steps over the threshold.

"Don't count on it," Toni laughs as he inhales the scent of freshly baked cookies that is still permeating the air. "You know I can't resist all the Christmas treats."

Sylvie tut-tuts again, but she's too tired to put up much of an argument. She looks around the apartment and smiles.

"You girls have outdone yourselves," Sylvie says, with a note of approval. "Your apartment looks spotless, and you've decorated it so beautifully for the holidays."

"Thank you," Isabella says, smiling.

"You must be exhausted from your travels," Catalina says. "Do you want to head straight to bed or would you like a drink and a snack before crawling in?"

"I would love to take a shower, if you don't mind," Sylvie says. "But a little bite to eat does sound nice." She makes her way toward the guest room. "Oh my, the thoughtful touches just keep adding up. Look, Toni! Izzy remembered how much I love poinsettias!"

"They are certainly making a point of spoiling us," Toni agrees, walking over to take a look himself. "But that cozy bed is what's caught my eye. I'm going to close my eyes for a bit while you shower."

———

A half hour later, Toni and Sylvie join Isabella and Catalina in the living room to share stories from Christmases past over drinks and a small selection of snacks. They aren't long into it when Toni starts to yawn after every second word and Sylvie's head bobs.

"I guess it's time for us to say good night," Toni says, getting up and stretching his arms over his head with an exaggerated sigh. He goes over and pulls Isabella to him for a hug and kisses her on her forehead. "*Dormi bene, mia preziosa ragazza.*"

After Toni and Sylvie retire to their room, Isabella and Catalina tidy up and then head off to bed themselves. When Catalina returns from brushing her teeth, Isabella is already snoring slightly, asleep on top of the covers, the busy day having finally caught up to her.

"Good night, *mi amor*," Catalina murmurs quietly, kissing Isabella's cheek before turning out the light.

***

Isabella gets up bright and early again, tiptoeing from the room to let Catalina sleep some more. She puts on a pot of coffee, and while it is brewing, she starts chopping up mushrooms, onions, and garlic for the omelette she has planned as part of a big breakfast, including crisp bacon and mimosas made with champagne and freshly squeezed orange juice.

Toni is the first to emerge, shuffling over in his favourite plaid slippers, which are beginning to look a little threadbare along the seams.

"Good morning, Papa. How did you sleep?" Isabella says, giving her hands a quick wash at the sink before hugging her father and planting a peck on his cheek.

"Like a baby," Toni says. "I think I was asleep before my head hit the pillow."

"Like father, like daughter," Isabella laughs. "And it looks like Catalina and Maman are two peas in a pod too, enjoying sleeping in."

"Yes, although I heard your mother up more than once in the night. At one point she even had the lamp on, her nose in a book," Toni says. "But I was too worn out from travelling to pay much attention and fell back asleep right away."

Isabella pours Toni a large mug of coffee and stops to take a sip of her own.

"Looks like you're busy at it already," Toni says, noticing all the vegetables chopped up in a bowl and the carton of eggs on the counter. "Would you like a hand?"

"No thank you, it's all good. I'm sure we won't be eating for another hour at least," Isabella says. "You're on vacation, so just relax. I would have slipped out to the newsstand on the corner to grab a paper for you, but they're all in Spanish here."

"I'd much rather have a conversation with you," Toni says. "Why don't you update me on the progress with your art and your work at the English language school?"

Father and daughter slip into an easy flow of conversation while Isabella finishes prepping for breakfast. After tidying up the dishes, she joins her father on the couch. They decide to look for a Christmas movie on Netflix. They are scrolling through the seemingly unlimited options, unable to decide which one they want to watch, when Catalina slips by them to use the washroom and then joins them. Moments later, Sylvie appears, and the movie is all but forgotten as everyone engages in more small talk. Catalina helps Isabella finish the preparations for brunch, and everyone gathers around the small kitchen table.

"May I lead us in a prayer of thanks for this food?" Isabella asks, extending her arms out to join hands with her father and mother on either side of her.

"That would be lovely," Sylvie says, with a smile that lights up her eyes.

"Dear God, our beloved and generous Creator, thank you for bringing Maman and Papa safely to Catalina and

I, here in Panama, and for keeping them both in good health. Thank you for this meal and for all the earthly gifts you have provided. Most especially, we give thanks today for the birth of Jesus Christ, whose light shines the way for us and whose example shows us how to live with grace, humility, love, and acceptance. Amen."

There is a chorus of amens and a clinking of glasses before everyone digs in to enjoy the hearty breakfast.

After the meal is finished and all the dishes are put away, Sylvie is anxious to go for a walk about to explore the neighbourhood. Everyone heads out into the bright, clear December day to stroll the streets and enjoy the sunshine. Two hours of walking is enough for Toni, and they return home to spend the rest of the day relaxing in the apartment with games of cards and drinks at happy hour.

"There's still an hour until we're expected at your parents' house," Toni says, looking at his watch and seeing that it's just after seven.

"I can't decide if I'm more excited or nervous," Sylvie says. "I'm grateful your parents invited all of us for Christmas dinner, but I know there are still a lot of hurt feelings between you and your sister, and I admit, I'm a little anxious there might be some family drama."

"Try not to worry, *Señora* Sylvie," Catalina says. "Even though there are some unresolved issues, my family will be on their best behaviour. Christmas is a time when everyone agrees, without saying it, to put everything unpleasant behind us, at least for one day, and to focus on the meaning of the holidays."

"That's good to hear," Toni says. "I wonder if we might leave a bit early, so we can take a short tour of the Christmas lights on the way over?"

"That's a great idea, Papa," Isabella says. "It will only take me a few minutes to change and I can be ready to go. What do you think, Maman?"

"That does sound lovely," Sylvie says. "I hadn't planned to change though. I thought you said dinner would be casual?" She stands up and attempts to smooth out the wrinkles in her navy linen trousers.

"It is casual," Catalina says. "But everyone always changes into their best clothes for church, so you might want to consider wearing a dress or a skirt and blouse since we'll be going straight to midnight Mass at the church closest to my parents' house."

"Did you bring the gorgeous emerald-green suit-dress you usually wear, Maman?" Isabella asks. "I've always loved how beautiful you look wearing that with your pearls."

"I did pack it," Sylvie says, "But I worried it would be too formal down here."

"It will be perfect," Izzy says. "And Papa, I think you should change into your suit too."

———

Not long after, everyone is changed and ready to go, lined up at the door looking sharp in their Sunday best. The four of them head outside and cram into Catalina's compact car.

Catalina takes the scenic route along Balboa Avenue to show off all the most spectacular Christmas lights and nativity scenes on display. Palm trees have twinkly lights wrapped around their long, slender trunks. Stars, wreaths, and angels hang from the street lights. All the shops and restaurants that line the road are decked out with lights and decorations too.

"My goodness, look at the time. It's already five to eight," Sylvie pipes up from the back seat after glancing down at her watch. "I hope we're not going to be late?"

"Five to already?" Catalina says. "Where did the time go? But don't worry, *Señora* Sylvie. We're not far away now. We should be there almost on time."

"I do hate to be tardy our first visit," Sylvie frets.

"Don't worry so much," Isabella says, patting her mother's hand. "The attitude here is *mañana*. I'm absolutely positive that no one in Catalina's family will even notice what time it is when we arrive. They'll be too busy observing the two of you to see which one of you I take after the most."

"Or more likely, they'll be too far into enjoying a few Christmas cocktails," laughs Catalina. "We're only one street away now."

"This is a very interesting-looking neighbourhood, Catalina," Toni says. "I remember you telling me when you visited us that the houses here are all painted brightly, but I never imagined it would be this colourful. It's really very charming and feels so inviting."

"Thank you, *Señor* Toni," Catalina says. "My parents' house is the orchid-purple stucco house just over to the left."

Catalina pulls into the narrow alley behind her parents' house and parks behind Geovani's truck. Colourful twinkly lights are draped all along the broken-down wooden fence, and an ornate bronze angel is affixed to the gate handle.

"My, doesn't it look festive," Toni says, opening the gate for the women to pass through first.

"Wait until you see the beautiful nativity scene they've set up on the lawn," Sylvie says, the first to enter the yard. The usual clutter has been tidied away and replaced with a huge nativity scene including a straw manger and carved wooden figures of Mary, Joseph, the baby Jesus swaddled in his cradle, and an assortment of animals. Christmas music and laughter drift out of the open windows that line the wall of the house, and as they draw nearer, the aromas of coriander, oregano, onions, and garlic permeate the air.

"Yum, yum, I just love the smell of *Mamá's* Christmas Eve tamales," Catalina says as they come up the sidewalk toward the back door.

"Tamales?" Toni says. "That has to be a unique Panamanian tradition. I've never had tamales before, let alone at Christmas."

"Yes, I think it is," Catalina says. "And trust me, *Señor* Toni, once you taste *Mamá's* secret blend of banana leaves stuffed with corn dough, pulled pork, vegetables, and raisins, you'll be instantly addicted." She stops to open the screen, then calls out, "*Feliz Navidad mi familia!*"

"*Entren, entren,*" Ciara calls out from the kitchen, already scurrying over to the door to greet her guests. Luis, Lorenzo, and Geovani are right behind her, while Kamila remains conspicuously seated on the sofa in the living room.

"*Buenas noches, Madre,*" Catalina says, passing her mother a paper bag stuffed with gifts for under the tree while kissing her on her high cheekbone. "This is Izzy's father, El *Señor* Toni, and her mother, La *Señora* Sylvie. Toni, Sylvie, I'm pleased to introduce to you my mother, Ciara, and my father, Luis."

Toni takes the lead, lifting Ciara's extended hand for a kiss, then pulling her tiny frame next to him for a big bear hug. He hugs Luis, similar in height and size, with a few claps on his back. Everyone starts talking over one another in a crazy mix of Spanish and English as Ciara passes the bag of gifts to Geovani. He sets them under the enormous tree that is centre stage in the small living room, draped top to bottom in a mishmash of garland and ornaments. A warm breeze enters through an open window and a ceiling fan purrs overhead, rustling the tinsel on the tree.

Ciara encourages everyone to take a seat, Lorenzo and Geovani squished in beside Kamila on the couch, while Catalina directs Toni and Sylvie to chairs reserved for special guests.

"Where are the girls?" Catalina asks Geovani, looking around the room but seeing no sign of his children.

"Ah, I'm sorry to say that it's Marisa's turn to have them for Christmas Eve," Geovani replies, a sad look in his eyes.

"That is too bad. I would have loved to see my three gorgeous nieces and introduce them to Isabella. Children always bring such a special feel to the holidays. I'm sorry, *mi hermano*, that you have to take turns, but I guess we all just have to wait for next year," Catalina says.

Ciara and Luis both disappear into the kitchen and an awkward silence descends, no one sure what to say. Kamila is clearly still holding on to her grudge, not even looking her sister in the eye, her arms folded over her chest.

Luis returns moments later with a tray of his famous *ron ponche*, a Panamanian rum-spiked eggnog. Ciara follows behind with plates and bowls filled with predinner snacks and appetizers, including the traditional tamales Catalina spoke of on the way in.

After a few drinks the atmosphere begins to shift a little, a mix of Spanish, English, and even a few bits of Italian and French thrown in.

"I'm curious about that gorgeous nativity scene out back," Toni says. "Is it new? Do you know who carved all the sculptures?"

"*Papá* built the entire project with his own two hands, starting with the manger just after he and *Mamá* were married," Catalina says, getting up and taking Toni by the hand to lead him out the back door for a closer look. Sylvie and Isabella follow close behind.

"It's incredible, the workmanship and detail that your father has crafted into each piece," Toni says with appreciation. "Did Izzy tell you I like to tinker around with woodworking too?"

"No, she didn't mention it," Catalina says. "I suppose we all still have so much to learn about one another."

"Yes, we do, but I'm just so happy that you and my Izzy have found one another," Toni says as he pulls Catalina to him and holds her close. "I never imagined in my wildest dreams that I would be welcoming a woman as my daughter's chosen life partner, but it's so clear how much the two of you love and respect one another. It's really opened my eyes and given me an understanding that I was missing out on before."

Just then, Kamila walks outside and secretly witnesses the tender scene, having been sent by Ciara to round everyone up for dinner. She stops in her tracks and stands still, watching from the dark doorway as if in a trance. She stays silent for a few moments before calling out.

"*Madre* says it's time to come in," Kamila says, her face softening into a slight smile that only Isabella notices.

Everyone gathers around the long rectangular teak table, laden with a massive carved turkey, bowls of zesty minced vegetables, a roast ham, and potato salad. Luis opens a bottle of Chablis and pours everyone a glass.

"*Salud!*" Luis says, raising his glass with a nod of his head.

"*Y buen provecho,*" Ciara adds.

Glasses clink and everyone starts filling their plates.

"May I lead us all in prayer?" Isabella asks.

There is a pause, followed by a few murmurs of surprise, but then Luis says he would be honoured to pass the tradition to her this year. He reaches his arms to either side, holding out his hands to Kamila and Catalina, who are seated across the table from each other and next to him at the head.

"Dear Creator," Isabella begins. "Thank you for gathering us all together on this most special of occasions, to celebrate the birth of Jesus, who taught all humanity to live in faith, showing loving kindness to one another. *Jesús es la luz que nos guía,*" she continues in Spanish, then switches to Italian. "*Che ci ha insegnato che siamo tutti uno, tutti figli di Dio.*" In French she adds, "*Qui pardonne nos peches et nous accepte dans toutes nos imperfections.* We thank you for this food and all the gifts we are so fortunate to receive. Amen."

A hush falls over the table and there are few with a dry eye.

"*Gracias, mi amor,*" Catalina says.

"*Si, pero es hora de comer,*" Luis says, lifting his fork.

After a long, leisurely meal filled with side conversations, jokes, and stories from the past, Ciara is the first to get up and start bustling about the kitchen. Everyone else pitches in to tidy up and put all the leftovers into containers. Catalina is drying the last of the dishes when Kamila comes over and whispers in her ear.

"Do you mind coming outside with me, so we can have a conversation in private before Mass?"

"Um, I, yeah, sure, I guess," Catalina whispers back, butterflies already taking flight in her stomach, her senses heightened as the hurt feelings from their last conversation surface.

"I need to tell you how sorry I am," Kamila blurts out as soon as they are outside and out of earshot. "I've behaved so badly toward you and Isabella, without knowing anything about her, or about love that isn't traditional. I realized tonight, when I saw how completely Mr. Ricci accepts you, how blind and ignorant I've been, and I feel terrible. I hope you can forgive me?"

"I, I don't know what to say," Catalina says, stumbling over her words as her heart inches up into her throat, feeling a strange combination of relief mixed with trepidation.

"Don't say anything," Kamila says. She reaches for her sister's hand and places it in her own. There is a surge of energy exchanged in the gesture, and Catalina thinks she can hear angels whispering in the breeze.

Kamila pulls her sister to her and lays her head against her chest. The tears Catalina has been holding back release in a sob of gratitude as they stand there is silence, words somehow unnecessary. Everything Catalina has been praying for since the falling-out seems held in reverence inside their embrace. Time seems to stop, but in reality, it is only minutes later when Catalina pulls away and looks Kamila in the eye while rustling her sister's beautiful mass of curls affectionately.

"I forgive you, completely," Catalina says with a smile.

"Can you forgive me for all the horrible things I said? And, more importantly, can you truly accept me, and Isabella too?"

"I believe I can, and I know I want to," Kamila says. She smiles back, and it's like all the heaviness has evaporated into thin air. They can both sense that their hearts are already beginning to heal.

"C'mon then, we better get back inside before Mama starts to fuss that we'll be late for church," Catalina says, taking her sister by the hand.

When they re-enter the house, Ciara is at the door. She looks from one daughter to the other and knows, without asking, that all is well.

Christmas morning, Isabella is the first one up again. It's just past nine, and after not returning home until well into the early hours of the morning, not to mention the eggnog and wine she consumed, her head feels like a taut rubber band, ready to snap. She swallows back two Tylenol, then sighs, thankful that she has the entire day to recover and possibly the opportunity to nap later if she desires.

Isabella chooses to shake things up a little and delay making coffee. Instead, she refills her glass with water to rehydrate, then goes over by the hall window and retrieves her yoga mat. She unrolls it and spreads it out, the sunlight filtering in. She crosses her legs and sits in a *mudra* pose, then closes her eyes and focuses on her breath, in and out, in and out.

Thoughts of the previous evening bubble up in her head. She smiles, remembering how happy Catalina looked when she shared Kamila's apology with her on the way to church, how being at peace with her sister, finally, felt like the most beautiful gift of all. Isabella forces herself to resist the temptation to think and relaxes into stillness. Less than a minute later, a line from *A New Earth* comes to her mind: "The greatest difficulty is the mental resistance to things that arise, and the underlying assumption that they should not."

She sits with this wisdom and smiles again. She wonders, without self-judgment, only curiosity, if she will ever be able to feel at peace with all things. She thinks about how impossible it felt to accept other people's ideas and judgments about her and Catalina, and how she struggled to be okay with it, despite knowing that other people's stories are not her concern. Her smile broadens. With a tear of joy in her eye, she accepts herself as she is, with all her imperfections, knowing she has time to learn, that she's only getting started on her path. She tiptoes into her bedroom and quietly retrieves her sketchbook journal, then plunks down on the couch to draw.

Isabella feels like her pencil is being moved by divine intervention. She watches as though a bystander as the blank page transforms into a scene that depicts herself embodied as a sunflower. Her arms are branches that reach for the sun in the sky above. Her feet are roots, supported by the solid, moist earth.

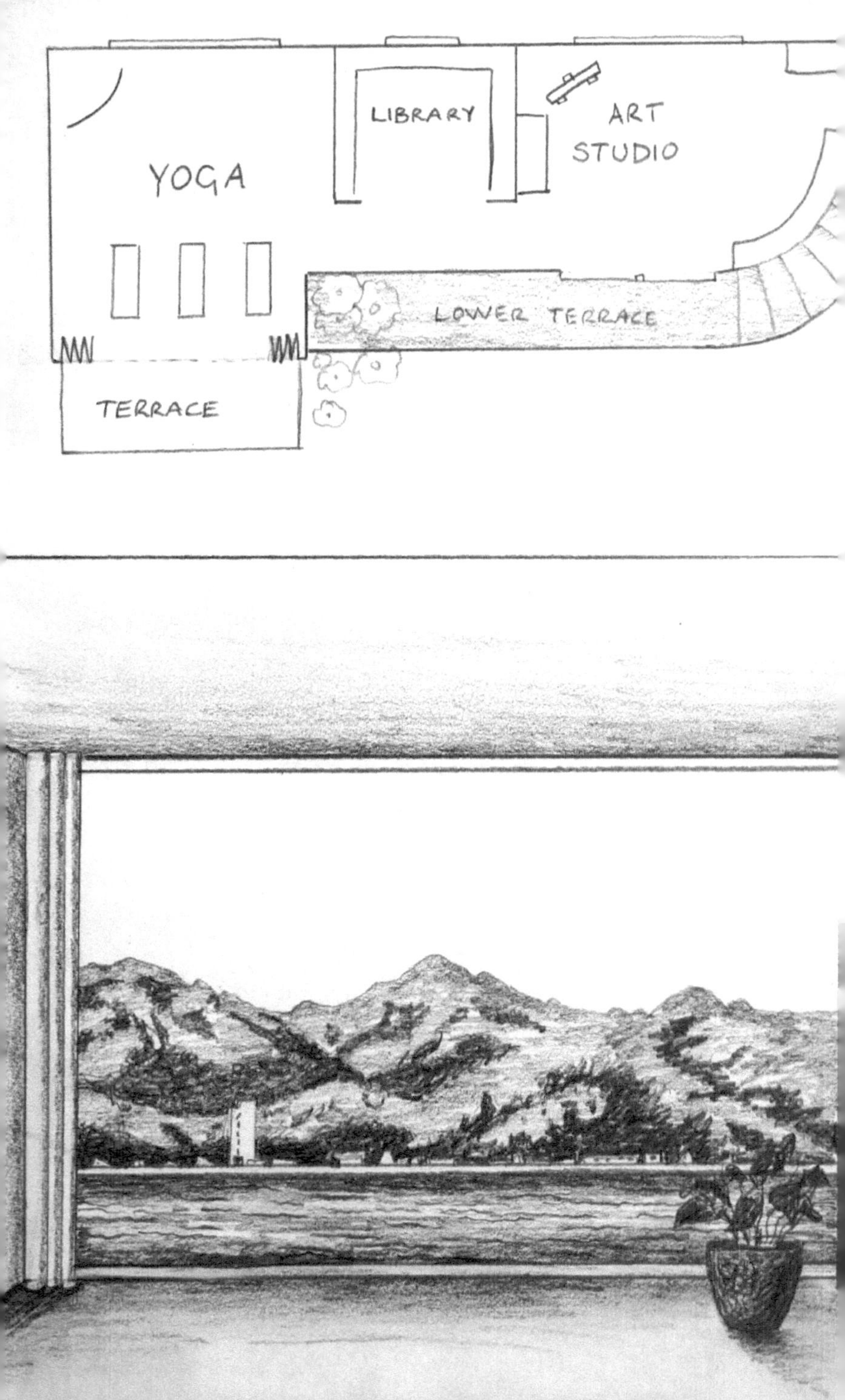

YOGA
LIBRARY
ART
STUDIO
LOWER TERRACE
TERRACE

Chapter Fifteen

Isabella is so engaged in life, it feels like Sylvie and Toni have barely vacated the guest room when Mark and Filipe are scheduled to arrive for a two-week visit at the start of the university spring break. Isabella and Catalina have washed and changed the sheets and taken down all the Christmas decorations after celebrating Three Kings Day, the Panamanian tradition where everyone burns their trees and the children leave out their shoes at bedtime to be filled with gifts from the three kings. For the occasion, Isabella convinced Catalina to ignore the fact that they are full-grown adults so that they could leave out their shoes too. She bought Catalina a pair of birthstone earrings and Catalina gifted her with a gold cross necklace.

The day that Mark and Filipe arrive in Panama, the airport is deserted, the decorations long gone, a totally different vibe from when Toni and Sylvie arrived. There are only a few other people in the waiting area, and Mark and Filipe are through customs, have collected their luggage, and are walking toward Isabella and Catalina less than forty minutes after their plane lands.

"This hot weather is like a kiss on my sun-starved skin," Mark says as soon as he steps out from the air-conditioned airport terminal.

"I'm with you, all the way," Filipe agrees. "It was minus fifteen when we left Winnipeg. What did you say the temperature is here, Izzy?"

"I checked my weather app while we were waiting, and it showed thirty-one," Isabella answers. "I was hoping we might get a little rain to freshen things up, but no such luck. They're predicting hot and dry for the next seven days. It's too bad your first time here is near the end of a particularly scorching dry season, but I'm sure that compared to the bleak and freezing weather back home, it's heaven."

"You're not kidding," Mark says. "I don't know what I was thinking, packing a rain jacket and umbrella, but I guess my mother's training to always be prepared has stuck with me."

Back at the apartment, Mark and Filipe get settled into the guest room and make themselves right at home. Over the first few days, they take in city tours, including the canal, Casco Viejo, and Panama Viejo, as well as several lively dance clubs. Four days into the holiday, Isabella surprises them with the news that she rented a two-bedroom, two-bathroom apartment in the

Coronado Bay condominium tower, right on the beach, for two nights.

⸻

They've barely unpacked and put away their things, Isabella insisting that Mark and Filipe take the master bedroom with the king bed, when both men are itching to go down to the beach.

"Filipe, you've got to come check out this incredible view from the balcony!" Mark calls out, the first to change into his swim trunks, his sunscreen and towel packed in a cloth bag.

"I know, right? I was observing it from the floor-to-ceiling windows of our suite," Filipe says as he steps over the ledge to join his husband on the small balcony. It barely has enough room for a well-used one-burner barbeque and two outdoor chairs that have seen better days. "I can't get over how pristine the beach is, and I've never seen such unusual-looking sand before. The black sections sparkle like diamonds in the sun."

"I can hardly wait to walk on it; it looks so silky soft," Mark says. He turns around and checks out Filipe. "Oh wow! Does my man ever rock a speedo!"

"What, this old thing?" Filipe says with mock humility, knowing full well the effect of his tight, skimpy black faux-leather swimsuit. He leans in for a kiss. "I'm glad you're enjoying the view, but I'm seriously stoked to splash about in the ocean with you."

"All right you two lovebirds," Isabella says with a laugh

as she walks over to join them. "Let's quit talking about it and get down there."

———

The sun is sparkling, the rays of light dancing on the ocean waves. Catalina leads the group to her and Isabella's favourite spot near the black rock formation, just a little to the right of the gate of the condominium building. She opens the golf umbrella she found in the kitchen closet of the condo and spreads out two towels on the sand, already quite hot to the touch. She takes off her cover-up and rolls it up, then tucks it into her beach bag.

"This is absolutely spectacular," Mark says, following suit and taking off his T-shirt. He looks up and down the beach. "There's, like, maybe ten other people out here at prime time on the weekend, and the vibe is so chill. I'm just loving it."

"That's why we love it here too," Catalina says. "Remember the first time we were here, *mi amor*?"

"Do I?" Isabella laughs as she sits down to join them. "How could I forget? That's the weekend we fell in love. In fact, if I recall correctly, it all started after I got such a badass sunburn, and you offered to—"

"Whoa, enough info," Mark laughs, clapping his hands over his ears.

"Oh please," Isabella laughs along with him. "What I was going to say, before you cut me off, was that I suffered quite a serious burn because the cool breeze coming off the ocean was so deceiving. Trust me, you'll want to lather on the sunscreen and make use of the shade of the umbrella."

"Not me," Filipe says. "I never burn."

"Okay, but don't say we didn't warn you," Catalina says. "I'm darker than you and I can get a bit red if I'm not careful. We're so close to the equator here. The sun is way more intense than anything you guys get up north."

"Okay, all right already, I'm converted," Filipe laughs. "Pass me the sunscreen."

Several hours slip by, all four of them relaxed in one another's company, enjoying the tranquil energy of the sun mixed in with frequent forays into the warm salt water of the ocean. Filipe and Mark are both strong swimmers and they have fun bodysurfing in the gentle waves. Not long after noon, Isabella's stomach growls, their cue to pack up and go get a bite to eat. They decide to make a stop on their walk back at a super-mini for a few groceries, to assemble a picnic lunch at the condo.

Isabella and Catalina are so engaged in conversation, they miss the turn and end up going in the wrong direction. As they attempt to get their bearings, they literally stumble onto a posh-looking street neither of them has been on before.

"I never expected to find mansions like these," Filipe says, his eyes wide as they pass a massive home, the view from the street slightly obscured by a high security fence, but the grandeur and sheer size of the property still visible from the road.

"Yeah, no," Isabella says. "It's not like Canada at all, where rich people live in one community and poor in another. There can be a crumbling, abandoned shack beside a mansion beside an empty lot overgrown with weeds."

"Hey, you guys, check out this pathway with the cool graffiti along the wall," Catalina says. "It looks like it might lead down to a beach." She points to the right where a brick wall painted bright white depicts several scenes in a row.

"Cool!" Mark says, moving forward to join Catalina. "What the heck does '*aprecia tu planeta*' mean?"

"It's very similar to the English version: appreciate your planet," Catalina says.

"Oh, there's a beautiful painting of the sun further down," Isabella says, taking Catalina by the hand and picking up her pace.

The foursome makes their way along the pathway, looking at all the colourful images in turn. Before they know it, they are standing at the top of a set of cement stairs leading down to a sandy beach.

"Oh my God, this is the best view I've seen in Coronado yet," Catalina says, shading her eyes with her hand despite her sunglasses and hat, the sun high and blinding as it reflects off the ocean. "You can see the entire range of Chame mountains from here!"

"This is absolutely gorgeous," Filipe says, already descending the steep stairs. "How lucky are the owners of all these homes to not only have these spectacular views but beach access too? I can only imagine what they must go for."

"Way out of our league, I'm afraid," Mark says. "But I see several condominium towers a little further down, in the distance. I wonder, do you know anything about them, Catalina?"

"I'm not 100 percent sure," Catalina says. "I think they might actually be a part of a community called Serena? Or perhaps Gorgona? I've never seen them from this perspective, so I can't be certain."

"It might be fun to contact a realtor tomorrow and go have a look around," Filipe says. "What do you think?" He slips off his flip-flops and carries them as he moves closer to the silky wet sand to walk along the ocean edge.

"I think I love what a dreamer you are," Mark says.

"Yes, Filipe and Isabella are two peas in a pod," Catalina says. "It's a good thing they have us to keep them grounded. But if you guys want to have a look about, I know an expat who lives out here who is a realtor, and I'm happy to reach out."

After a few more minutes of talking and walking along the beach where the sand and the ocean converge, they head back to the street, resuming their search for a super-mini market. Along the way, Isabella spies a small, undeveloped lot with a sign, "*Se vende.*" On an impulse, she takes a photo of the contact information, curious to find out what an empty lot in the area might cost.

The rest of the day is filled with more lazing in the sun, then dinner and dancing at Picasso's into the wee hours of the night.

The next morning, Isabella is the first one up, as usual. She tiptoes from the bedroom after retrieving her sketchbook journal and pencil from the nightstand drawer and her robe from the hook on the back of the door. She walks barefoot into the kitchen and puts on a pot of coffee, then heads out onto the balcony after pouring herself a big, steaming mug.

The sun is still rising in the east, the sky pure blue, not a cloud in sight. *It's going to be another scorcher*, she thinks to herself, grateful for the protection of the overhang. She curls up on one of the well-worn chairs and opens her sketchbook, only one blank page left.

She writes the date in the bottom right-hand corner, then starts to draw a blueprint for her and Catalina's dream home. She creates a floor plan for a two-storey, the second floor with a yoga room, art studio, and library. On the main level, she sketches gigantic floor-to-ceiling windows along the wall that faces the ocean, capturing the incredible mountain view she witnessed the previous day. As the images form on the page, she thinks about the lot for sale. She's always loved the fun, busy vibe of the city and found Coronado to be sleepy and a little boring, yet somehow, she feels a shift inside, her spirit drawn to the tranquil energy and the beauty of the ocean.

When she finishes her rough sketch, it is still early, and no one else is up. She takes a sip of her coffee, now lukewarm, then flips back near the beginning of her journal, to the image she drew of herself sitting on a street corner, her knees to her chest, feeling deflated after a day of rejections from art galleries back when she still lived in Winnipeg and worked as a server at the tavern. She smiles as she considers how far she's come since then, with the sale of *The Rogue Scorpion* painting in the fall and her *Lost Souls* series progressing. She never imagined back then all the changes that were yet to come.

Her depiction of herself as an anime-inspired warrior is still difficult for her to look at. Isabella shudders as she remembers how degrading it felt to be taken advantage of, to be raped by a stranger pretending to be a friend. *I was so naive back then*, she thinks to herself. In the same moment, she knows she can still be way too trusting, but accepts herself as she is. The memories are painful, even though she has moved on. Catalina's love has had the power to transform her feelings of shame into acceptance, yet the heavy feeling seems to always be lurking, just below the surface of her consciousness.

When she looks at the image of Alex with two faces, Isabella's hand instinctively goes to the place on her cheek where he hit her, the thin scar still a slight pink ridge. It's almost hard to believe that not that long ago, she was willing to accept what little he had to offer. She knows that on some level, she didn't believe she deserved better. She wonders if maybe she just wasn't aware that the kind of love she shares with Catalina existed. But then she thinks of the example set by her parents and knows that isn't the truth, that the trauma of being raped when she was in Thailand was the root of her low self-esteem.

Isabella turns the pages. She looks at the drawing she

made of the beach in Coronado, back when it was only a figment of her imagination, but which turned out to be a premonition. The images of Casco are on the opposite page. She marvels at how her ability to listen to her intuition took off after making the impulsive decision to come to Panama. She remembers looking out the window and feeling the energy of the place as soon as she arrived, like an invitation.

The image of Catalina reclined on her towel on the beach still has the power to take her breath away. Isabella's hand travels from her cheek to her chest. Hand on heart, she recalls how strange it felt to fall in love with a woman. She smiles to herself, then stops her reverie for a moment to say a prayer of gratitude to God for sending her so many life-affirming surprises, but most of all, for bringing her the love of her life, her soulmate and best friend.

Isabella flips the pages to the Biblical-looking drawing she made of her and Catalina, stuck in purgatory. It is one of her favourites. She is reminded of the challenges she had when her parents, and Catalina's family, struggled to accept their relationship. Once so painful, now a distant memory, Isabella is present to the wisdom she is learning about being patient and trusting the process of life.

In stark contrast, the drawing of the scorpion with Alex's face, clinging to the folds of her drapes at her old apartment, still has the power to make her heartbeat quicken. She hasn't seen a single scorpion since, yet she remains absolutely terrified of them. She remembers Brian telling her about seeing Alex, that he looked unkempt, like he was falling apart. She thinks about how that used to tug at her heartstrings and realizes that she no longer cares one way or the other what happens to him. She doesn't wish him any harm, but she feels detached in a way that feels healthier, her focus on her own well-being.

The image of the homeless man on the church steps, which has transformed into the first painting in the *Lost Souls* series, always brings up feelings of compassion for her. The contrast of his misfortune only seems to highlight her own blessings. She feels connected with her spiritual self, full of gratitude, and present to her ever-deepening relationship with God.

She gazes at the image she drew of herself, embodied as a sunflower, her arms as branches reaching for the sky and her feet like roots, grounded in the earth. The joy captured on the page resonates fully for her, of the happy space she was in, and still is. She knows this too shall pass, as all things—good and bad—do. And yet, the blueprint for her dream home with Catalina kindles her imagination. She wonders if the future will bring about a move, if she will achieve the career success she dreams of, and what will unfold for Catalina as she embarks on her new path as an art broker.

Isabella accepts the part of herself that is a dreamer while at the same time embracing her faith in God and her purpose, knowing she doesn't have to figure it all out. She smiles to herself as she ponders what surprises and possibilities might lie ahead, knowing she only has to listen to the whispering of her heart to find her way.

Just as she closes her journal and gets up from her

chair, Mark opens the door and steps out onto the balcony to join her.

"Good morning, Miss Early Bird," Mark says, his eyes drawn to the journal in her hand. "Have you sketched out your inspiration for your next painting?"

"As a matter of fact, I was inspired, but not for my next painting," Isabella confides. "Our walk about yesterday has my imagination in overdrive, thinking about a future where Catalina and I have the money and resources to make a move out here."

"That's intense, not to mention ambitious, but so like you," Mark says. "I must admit, my dear friend, I've always admired how you are able to stay so positive and optimistic despite the challenges you've faced."

"Thank you," Isabella says. "That means a lot. And, as Catalina pointed out yesterday, Filipe is much the same way. I'm so happy we've found our soulmates. Even if Catalina and I haven't quite got as firm of a foundation as you two, we're getting there."

"Are you kidding?" Mark says, his eyebrows raised in surprise. "You're clearly a talented, gifted artist, and you're finally getting the recognition you deserve. Trust me on this one. You're going to be so successful that it's going to blow your socks off. And the dream you have, of building a home out here, as well as all your heart desires . . . I believe your dreams are all going to come true."

"Now who's being the idealist?" Isabella jokes. Her stomach growls, breaking the tender moment. "Sounds like it's time for some breakfast. What do you say? Do you want to help me put together some fried eggs and bacon?"

"Sounds delicious," Mark says. "And if the smell of bacon can't wake up our two sleepyheads, nothing can."

The rest of the two-day getaway seems to fly by, and soon they are packing up and driving back to the city.

There, they fall into an easy flow, comfortable and in agreement about how they want to fill their days. Mark and Filipe explore the city while Catalina and Isabella go to work, and Catalina is engaged in school studies during the last week of their visit. In no time at all, it's time for Mark and Filipe to return to Canada, but not before an allegiance has been made, all four of them certain of the solid foundation of their friendship.

Later that spring, Isabella finishes her final painting in the *Lost Souls* series, just one week before Catalina's first semester at university ends. She reaches out to Eduardo, and he agrees to organize the reveal and promotion as a part of a larger exhibition at his art gallery, as planned.

The *Lost Souls* series features four large canvas oil paintings. Isabella and Eduardo choose to display them all in the same style of simple ebony wooden frames, side by side in a row against an off-white wall that creates a stunning impression.

The work of the other artists who will join the exhibition complements Isabella's style perfectly. Oscar Marillo and Maria Berrio, both originally from Columbia, are presenting some of their work, along with Maria Raquel Cochez and Gerardo Canova from Panama.

Oscar is the closest to Isabella in age, and his *Untitled* pieces from 2012 and 2013 in pastel hues of blue, yellow, and grey beautifully convey his inventive portrayal of the universality of the human experience. Maria has chosen to showcase two larger-than-life collages made from patterned Japanese paper and watercolour that depict strong yet vulnerable and multi-layered women. Maria Raquel's abstracts and Gerardo's female portraits in *Goddess of Dreams* and *Stillness Devotee* complete the exhibition.

When Eduardo announces the premiere will open on the fortuitous Cinco de Mayo, Isabella wastes no time in calling up her parents on FaceTime.

"Maman, Papa, can you believe this is really happening?" Isabella says, her cheeks pink and her eyes sparkling. She turns to look at Catalina, seated on the living room couch beside her. "And my crazy-smart partner also has amazing news to share."

"Izzy, please, my news is nothing compared to what you've accomplished, and besides—"

"She got her first exam back yesterday—98 per cent for a solid A+ in the course!" Isabella interjects without waiting.

"My, my, your news is exciting, and we're so happy for both of you," Toni says.

"Thank you, Papa," Isabella says, bubbling over with so much joy that she can't stop rambling. "But what I want to know is, when are you flying down to join us for the celebrations?"

"You know how much your mother and I would love to come, but I'm afraid we really can't afford it right now—" Toni starts to say.

This time it's Sylvie who cuts him off.

"Now, dear, you mustn't keep your news from them," Sylvie begins. "I know you don't want to burst their bubbles, but if anything were to happen and you hadn't told them . . ." She stops before finishing her sentence, choking back her emotions with a sob.

"What news?" Isabella says, her intuition suddenly in overdrive. "Papa?"

"*Mi ragazza bella*, I'm so sorry," Toni says, his shoulders slumped forward. "I was going to call you with the news, but then you reached out, so happy with the announcement of your exhibition, and, well, I just hate to have to tell you. I started feeling unwell soon after we got back from Panama. At first, I was just tired and had some bone aches, but when I started having painful urination and swelling in my legs, I finally caved and went to my doctor for a checkup. He did some tests, and the long and short of it is that the prostate cancer is back."

"Oh my God," Isabella says, her hand to her throat. Tears well in her eyes. "That is horrible news. I'm so sorry, Papa. But I'm sure once you get started on your treatment and back on a healthy eating plan, you will be better. Maybe you can't make it for the exhibition premiere, but—"

"No, Izzy," Sylvie says. She takes a tissue and dabs at

the corner of her eye. "Last time your father caught the cancer early, in stage 2. This time, it's already in stage 4. His oncologist, you remember Dr. Cohen I'm sure, said it's not curable. It's too far along."

"What? You can't be serious, this can't be true, I, I . . ." Isabella flounders.

"Don't worry, Izzy. Dr. Cohen says there are treatments to extend my life and also reduce my symptoms. It's all good," Toni says, his own eyes now full of tears, not fooling anyone with his brave words.

"Oh, Papa, I have to come and be with you," Isabella says, her voice quivering. Catalina squeezes her hand. "I'm going to reach out to Eduardo and ask him to delay the exhibition, indefinitely."

"Absolutely not. I forbid you to delay," Toni says. "You can wait and fly out to be with us after your exhibition."

"But, Papa, it's only an exhibition. You mean more to me than anything in the world. Please, I need to be there with you."

"I understand, and I want you here with me too, *mi bella*," Toni says. "You must dig deep and find your faith and courage. I'm going to hang in as long as I can, and I need you to believe that. You and Catalina can come after the exhibition, when she is on her summer school break."

"That is the sensible thing to do," Sylvie says. "How long does the exhibit run for?"

"A whole month," Isabella says. "Until June fifth. That just feels too far away. I won't be able to focus and enjoy myself with Papa suffering."

"Yes, you will, because you're going to promise me,"

Toni says. "I've been dreaming about this moment my whole life. You will wear your beautiful gown and take tons of photos and have the time of your life, with your lovely Catalina by your side."

Isabella sits in silence for a few moments, the atmosphere heavy.

"Okay, Papa. I will promise, if that's truly what you want," Isabella says, her voice soft, her face set with resolve.

"It is," Toni says. "Now, let's stop all the doom and gloom and talk about happier things."

They stay on the line for a while longer, but it is difficult for all of them to focus on anything else.

After hanging up, Isabella sits in stunned silence. Catalina holds her in her arms. Several agonizing minutes pass before Isabella clears her throat and begins to speak.

"This is unbearable," Isabella says. "And so ironic that it is only now, when I'm about to achieve the most incredible success, more than I've ever dreamed of, that I truly realize my relationships are the most important thing in the world to me. Not recognition, money, or fame, not a dream home. None of it means anything, really, without my papa I just can't imagine, I'm not ready . . ."

There are no words to properly describe how she feels. Isabella sobs and leans her head in to rest on Catalina's shoulder. Catalina holds her close and runs her hand across her back in a soothing motion.

"Shh, shh, there, there, *mi amor*," Catalina whispers. She strokes Isabella's long, wavy hair. "Close your eyes and go deep inside, where God lives in you. Look to your faith and trust in life. Your love for your father is eternal, as all love is. Everything is going to be all right, you'll see."

———

That night, Isabella can't sleep. She tosses and turns, the sheets in a knot around her legs. Eventually she gives up and gets out of bed. She paces the apartment, then ends up choosing to go outside for a walk in the fresh air to the park nearest to their apartment.

As she walks along in the dark, lost in a confusion of thoughts and emotions, a huge thunderstorm erupts out of nowhere. The rain pours down in a deluge, soaking her to the skin. She runs to seek shelter under a canopy tree. The rain pours down all around her in a sheet, like a curtain-veil, completely separating her from the rest of the world. She feels so alone. She sits cross-legged on the soft earth, her hands in a *mudra*. She closes her eyes. She forces herself to quiet the troubled thoughts that are marching through her mind like an army of worker ants. In silence, she begins to pray, the words pouring out of her in a stream as forceful as the rain all around her.

Dearest God, Creator of all things, it's me, Isabella. I come to you in prayer, seeking your guidance, needing your loving strength more than I ever have before. I don't know how to do this. I want to trust the process of life, and yet, I don't know how to let my father go. I'm not ready. My father is the mirror in which the reflection of myself is the closest to perfection. He sees me with total unconditional love and acceptance. His love has been the rock of my foundation, and I'm afraid without it, I will crumble. Where will I turn to without his fatherly presence to comfort and guide me?

Even as I think these words, with you as my witness, I know the answer. I know that you are my father and my mother too. With your spirit in my heart, I'm never alone. You are with me, for eternity. You are with him too, and he will always be with me in spirit. It doesn't mean it won't be hard. It will likely be the hardest thing I've yet had to endure. But I know I can do this. I've got everything I need, including my beautiful Catalina. The people who love me will help me. We'll all support one another. I made a promise to my father, and I plan on keeping it.

Thank you, dearest God, for giving me this awareness. For filling my earthly vessel with the strength, courage, and wisdom to live my life in faith. I don't have all the answers. I don't know what lies ahead for my father, or for me. But I trust that life will unfold according to your divine plan, with a purposeful design, beyond my comprehension.

Amen.

When she finishes her prayer, Isabella feels the presence of God envelop her from around and from within. She feels held in a tender embrace, so pure that her heart almost feels as though it might burst with the intensity. She feels the same energy course through her that she feels when she is making love with Catalina, the same light she feels when she is fully immersed in nature, in the presence of a waterfall or a butterfly, in awareness of the miracle of all creation.

The rain stops as suddenly as it began. Isabella opens her eyes and blinks, as though awakening from a dream.

She stands and shakes the droplets of rain from her hair, then squares her shoulders. She feels God's strength coursing through her veins, each part of her—mind, body, soul—filled with courage and resolve. She's ready.

About the Author

Lynda Faye Schmidt is a storyteller who writes from the heart. Her novels are emotionally impacting and character-driven. A huge part of her writing journey has been her daily journaling practice, and she has also written a guided journal.

Before becoming a writer, Lynda earned a Bachelor of Education. She taught in a variety of settings, sharing her love of reading, writing and creating with children.

After her move to the Middle East in 2015, Lynda kicked off her writing career with her blog, *Musings of an Emotional Creature.* She was also a contributor for *DQ Living* magazine.

Lynda has published two novels based on real life as a series, *The Healing* and *The Holding.* She launched her guided journal, *The Holding & The Healing Companion Journal* on October 23, 2022. Lynda's third novel, *The Rogue Scorpion*, was released on April 23, 2023.

Lynda is a Canadian expat. She lives in Panama with her husband, David and her furry companion, Lola. She believes solid routines are the foundation for her wellness and spends her days writing, practicing yoga, exercising in her home gym, spending time in nature and connecting with the people she loves.

For more information, log onto her website at www.lyndafayeschmidt.com.

With Gratitude

Thank you to my husband and partner in life, David Schmidt, who loves and supports me unconditionally, always. Our love is the foundation of everything.

I'm fortunate to have deep, meaningful relationships and connections that bring me so much joy. I cherish the gift of friends who feel like family and family who feel like friends. The list is too long to include here, but they know who they are.

Thank you to everyone who was part of the team of talented professionals that manifested the manuscript for *The Rogue Scorpion* into reality.

I'm indebted to Ria Cornall for collaborating with me and creating the beautiful artwork for the cover and each chapter. After writing two novels whose main character wrote in journals as a reflective and healing tool, I wanted Isabella, as an artist, to have her sketchbook journal, and I couldn't have done this without Ria.

My publisher, Anne O'Connell, of OC Publishing, is a rockstar of strength and integrity. She brought together the designers and editors after her own careful and deliberate edits. I always look forward to the process of refining and smoothing out the rough edges, with Anne as my advisor and dear friend.

Thank you to Sarah MacFarlane, for her precision copy editing skills. I'm indebted to David Edelstein for the inspirational cover design that incorporated the Scorpio constellation, as well as his work on the interior design, e-book conversion, and proofreading. I would have been lost without Mary and Fabio, who graciously agreed to edit the Panamanian Spanish sections.

I'm grateful to advanced readers for providing valuable feedback and thoughtful reviews. Thank you, Karen Dean, Lyndi Allison, Ramona Coulombe, and Carol Kujala.

www.ingramcontent.com/pod-product-compliance
Lightning Source LLC
Chambersburg PA
CBHW032147190726
48290CB00005BB/1444